The Beginning of the End

1 THE ARMAGEDDON TRILOGY

The Beginning
of the End

J.E. BECKER

Tate Publishing & Enterprises

The Beginning Of The End: The Armageddon Trilogy
Copyright © 2008 by J.E. Becker. All rights reserved.

This title is also available as a Tate Out Loud product. Visit www.tatepublishing.com for more information.

No part of this publication may be reproduced, stored in a retrieval system or transmitted in any way by any means, electronic, mechanical, photocopy, recording or otherwise without the prior permission of the author except as provided by USA copyright law.

All Scripture quotations are taken from the *Holy Bible, King James Version*, Cambridge, 1769. Used by permission. All rights reserved.

The Tanakh © 1985 by the Jewish Publication Society

The opinions expressed by the author are not necessarily those of Tate Publishing, LLC.

Published by Tate Publishing & Enterprises, LLC
127 E. Trade Center Terrace | Mustang, Oklahoma 73064 USA
1.888.361.9473 | www.tatepublishing.com

Tate Publishing is committed to excellence in the publishing industry. The company reflects the philosophy established by the founders, based on Psalm 68:11,

"The Lord gave the word and great was the company of those who published it."

Book design copyright © 2008 by Tate Publishing, LLC. All rights reserved.
Cover and interior design by Kandi Evans

Published in the United States of America
ISBN: 978-1-60604-285-4
1. Fiction:Religious:Apocalyptical
2. Fiction:General:Suspense
10.03.25

Dedication

This book is dedicated to my late husband, Harvey L. Becker, who gave me up every morning from 5:00 to 7:00 a.m. to put this story into words.

Acknowledgements

I would like to acknowledge Bonnie Grant, who made me believe this book could be published, as well as the rest of my critique group at Christian Writers Guild: Robert Graves, Cynthia Simmons, and Brenda Ward, who made me do it right. I also acknowledge Evelyn Kissler London, who edited one chapter. I want to thank my readers Jonathon Zuilkowski, Bruce Alden, Denise Hanson, and my Granddaughter Rachel Dettmann, who assured me it was a good read. I also want to thank Meghan Barnes, editor at Tate Publishing, whose work made me look good.

Introduction

Normally a novel does not require an introduction; however, since many of the terms in this book may be foreign to some readers, I offer this brief explanation for reference.

Al Mahdi–The Islamic messiah, believed in by both Sunni and Shiite Muslims, who will come out of concealment just before judgment day and create a great kingdom of justice and peace. He will be a descendent of the Prophet through his daughter Fatima's son, Hussain, come in the forty-second generation, be an Assyrian, a Hashamite, a prince, and have a broad forehead and a pointed nose, according to the writings of Muslim prophets.

Ashkenazi Jews–East European Jews, the elite who formed the nation Israel in the beginning.

Beit HaMikdash–House of the Holy Place (temple or tabernacle of God).

Chabad–A Hebrew Acronym for chochma (wisdom), bina (understanding), and da'as (knowledge), which became the name of a Hasidic sect of Judaism.

Halacha–The body of Jewish Law.

Hizbullah–Iranian-originated, Lebanon-based terrorist organization dedicated to destroying Israel.

Hudna–An agreement in the Sharia law of the Islamists that allows Muslims to make a covenant with infidels for a period of time less than ten years (which must be broken before ten years) for the purpose of regaining strength for the battle and a concession. We would call the one entering such an agreement with them a "sucker."

Intifadas–Two separate Palestinian uprisings against Israel with terrorist acts and suicide bombers.

Islamic Jihad for a Free Palestine–A terrorist division of Hizbullah.

Knesset–The Israeli ruling body; one hundred twenty ministers of the Knesset (MKs) are made up from over thirty different political parties.

Kadima Party–The new moderate party formed by Sharon when he left the Likud Party.

Labor Party–The Socialist Worker Party that wants good for all Israelis. Willing to give land for peace.

Likud Party–Right-wing party, pro-settlement, looking to retain all lands won from the Arabs.

Lubavitch–City of brotherly love, the city in Belarus where Chabad began. Hence it is another name for the movement founded by Rabbi Shneur (1745–1812), who also wrote the seminal Hasidic work, Tanya, as well as the Shulchan Arunc Ha'Rav—a code of Jewish Law.

Meretz Party–Liberal party against all settlements, anti Shaas, peace at any cost.

Mezuza–A small scroll placed in a holder on the door post that contained the Scripture from Deuteronomy "Hear, Oh Israel, the Lord thy G-d is one Lord" (6:4).

Moschiach–The Lubavitch Hebrew name for Messiah that differs in spelling from other sects using Maschiach.

Mufti–Islamic overseer of the mosques in Jerusalem.

National Religious Party–Religiously Zionist and pro settlements.

Rebbe–The name for rabbi in the Chabad sect.

Shaas Party–Right-wing party of Sephardic Jews, heavily committed to Halacha (Jewish Law).

Sharia Law–The ruling laws of Islam.

Sephardic Jews–Jews of North African and Middle Eastern descent.

Tanakh–The Hebrew Bible translated into English.

Torah–The first five books of the Bible.

Waqf–The Muslim administrative body responsible for the Haram al-Sharif (Arab's name for the Temple Mount) in Jerusalem is often referred to as the Waqf.

Yeshiva–A Hebrew school that teaches the Torah (the Law) and the Talmud, the Jewish Oral Law, which contains tradition and the 613 "must dos" for Orthodox Jews to keep the law.

Zakat–One of the five sacred pillars of Islam, which requires Muslims to give two-point-five percent of their incomes to charity. By this collection terrorists buy the favor of the people.

Characters

Chabad Lubavitch Jews

Rachel Lieberman–Recent graduate from Harvard, employed by the Israeli Embassy in Washington, D.C.

Simon Lieberman–Father of Rachel Lieberman—a real estate and development magnate of the D.C. area.

Dan and Sheila Lieberman–Brother and sister-in-law to Rachel.

US Government

John Anderson–Current president of the US, in his first term.

Senator J. Quinton Rice–Member of a secret organization of financiers promoting global power.

Jonathan Chase–Head of CIA.

Russell Hamilton–Secretary of state.

Dr. Harris–Head of NASA.

Alec Johnston–Secretary of treasury.

Dan Jordan–Armed forces Joint Chief of Staff.

Charles Stone–Secretary of defense.

Jack Trent–National security advisor.

Israelis in America

Ja'cov Levy–Israeli ambassador to the US.

Avraham Lechtman–Assistant to the Israeli ambassador.

Israelis from Israel

MKs–Ministers of the Knesset, Israel's governing body.

Haik Ra'amon–Prime minister of Israel (Labor party).

Jessie Solomon–Shaas party MK, father of David Solomon, also head of a Jerusalem Yeshiva.

Esther Solomon–Jesse Solomon's wife.

Rabbi Rosenfeld–Liaison between Israel and the Vatican; liaison between the rabbis and temple construction crews.

Yudleman and Kutter–Labor Party delegates (MKs).

Avi Housan–Religious Party delegate (MK).

Plaunt and Ben'dar–Meretz Party delegates (MKs).

Yitshak Sharian–Mayor of Jerusalem.

IDF-Israeli Defense Force

General Shaul Shofat–IDF's Chief of Staff.

General Uri Saguy–Head of Israeli intelligence.

Captain David Solomon–IDF field security officer in intelligence, often used to secure important missions.

Katz, Matza, Landau, Hillman, Feldman, Bendor—Men assigned to David as his security team.

Johnny Leventhal—Also in IDF intelligence along with David, often competing.

Israeli Priests

Askanazi Chief Rabbi—Yigeal Shapiro.
Sephardic Chief Rabbi—Yahuda Hacohen.

Palestine

Nabil Dakkah—Head of the Palestinian government.

Jordan

King Alahahm Hassih—Ruler of Jordan.

Iraq

Ghazi Faysul Hussayni—Hashamite prince newly elected to be king of Babylon in a constitutional monarchy and a cousin of the king of Jordan.

Lebanon

Julius Leucus Adoni´ (pronounced with the accent on the long *i*)–Lebonese banker with negotiating skills.

Vatican

Peter II–Pope, formerly a cardinal from Milan.

Tony Cirillo–Personal secretary to the pope—Italian.

Jerome McFarland–Personal secretary to the pope—American, from Texas.

John McCutchen–Irish cardinal, the Vatican's secretary of state.

Loni Mondella–Prefect of the papal household.

Hizbullah

Sa'id El Alqauwi–Planner for Islamic Jihad for a Free Palestine, a division of Hizbullah.

Albar Nassum - Head of terrorist attack in Washington.

Divine Characters

Catholics–Virgin Mary, mother of Jesus.

Lamb of Godders–Yeshua, the Lamb of God, the sacrificed Jesus.

Jews–Moschiach (Messiah) and the Prophet, as defined by Moses.

Adoni´ (Ashtor)–Ancient name of god among the heathen—present god of fortresses—whose munitions are stored in heaven; represented in sign by the dragon in the sky.

Prologue

Sitting at his desk, Sa'id el Alqauwi, a prominent planner for the Islamic Jihad for a Free Palestine, frowned. He shuffled the papers in front of him again.

Time grows short, he thought. *Will we get what we need soon enough to set everything up?*

A short knock on the door interrupted his thoughts. Albar Nassum stuck his head inside.

"We got it!"

"Good," said the older man, relieved. "Which hotel?" He needed this information to complete his plans for *Operation Washington*.

Albar strode into the room, threw his hands up in the air, fingers spread, and declared, "Ta da! The Israeli Delegation will stay at the West-Westin Hotel, on the second floor, in the east hall." Then he pounded his fist into his right hand and said, "Boom!"

"Well now," said Sa'id, smiling at his lieutenant's antics, "you can't get more specific than that, can you? Our contact in Washington came through in spades. With this final bit of information, our man can hire on at the West-Westin."

At last we will hit them again. The first suicide bomb attack in the United States capital since 9/11. With money from Iran, a US-based agent providing the explosives, and us supplying the gunmen and the suicide bomber, we are all set. So much for the latest attempt at the Israeli Peace Process…

—

Senator Rice picked up his private phone in his office on the second ring. He had been alerted earlier in the day to expect it. He leaned back in his chair, smiling and nodding as he listened to the voice on the phone. He answered when appropriate, but mostly he just listened.

"Senator Rice, you *do* understand that the peace in the Middle East is paramount to our plans. It *must* succeed this time. We are counting on you to convey our wishes to the president."

"I understand," replied the senator. "I'm sure the president's goals are in line with ours. We will do all that we can."

"I'm sure you will," answered the voice, displaying confidence.

After hanging up, Senator Rice felt a surge of satisfaction. He was part of a great effort to transform society. He made a small link in the chain that stretched around the world, but they were depending on *him*. He *would* not fail them.

Chapter 1

Rachel Lieberman trembled with excitement—five more minutes. She was leaving early today. All day long she savored the coming evening. How would it be? What would be her role? At the stroke of four, she was up and out her office door at the Israeli Embassy.

The first of the delegations, the Israelis, would arrive tonight, and *she* would meet them. The Palestinians and the Religious Delegation were due in tomorrow. Day after tomorrow the Middle East Peace Conference would convene and begin deciding the final fate of Jerusalem. Just think of it! She shivered again as she nearly skipped down the hall.

The Peace Accord held at Camp David in 2000 failed on this very issue—that along with Arafat's obstinate nature. After all that had happened since then, the 2006 war with Hizbullah and all that followed, it was hoped that by including the religious delegations a solution to the problem would work out. Then, too, new leaders led the two opposing sides, so maybe they had a chance. Rachel hoped so, because she was going to have a part in the historic event—albeit a small part—but a part nonetheless.

Having worked at the embassy only three months, Papa's connections probably had something to do with her involvement, but so what. Being close to the political affairs of Israel was something she had dreamed of all through college. But this wasn't just any affair; this conference was tantamount to the peace of the Middle East, the settling of the Palestinian problem once and for all. After the two nuclear exchanges and the economic losses, all but a few jihadists wanted a settlement, at least for now.

She reached the elevators and pressed the down button. The elevator on the right opened almost immediately, and she stepped through the doors. An Israeli clerk standing in the back looked up. His eyes brightened as they swept over the slim, five foot seven, dark-haired beauty. Rachel, lost in her own thoughts, missed his admiring glances. She stepped out at parking level B and hurried toward her car.

Rachel was twenty-two. She graduated the previous summer from Harvard at the top of her class in political science. Her passion was politics—Israeli politics. Seeing her people, the Jews, settled in a world of peace, however, served as only part of her drive. She passionately looked for her Moschiach. Rachel, like her father, Simon Lieberman, belonged to the Chabad Lubavitch Hasidim, one of the smaller sects among the Orthodox Jews. Both she and her father hoped that the settling of the Jerusalem problem would finally bring peace and reveal the long-awaited Jewish Messiah.

She had been taught by the Lubavitch Rebbes that the Moschiach would start the age of *the end of days* (the end of prophesied time as given by the Hebrew Bible). Besides bringing redemption to Israel and the world, he would also bring in the glorious kingdom so long prophesied. Had not the great sage, Rebbe Schneerson, said it was time? In fact, some of his followers believed him to be the Moschiach, but the stroke that killed him in 1994 dashed that hope; although some die-hards stubbornly clung to the notion, expecting him to be resurrected to fulfill the prophecy. But Rachel doubted that. She envisioned a younger, more vibrant man. Nevertheless, it *was* time, according to Habad's secret oral tradition, which predicted that the Moschiach would come after the seventh Rebbe. Schneerson had been the seventh since the founding of the sect nearly two hundred years ago. Rachel believed this with her whole being.

The phone rang just as she opened the door to her apartment. *Oh no,* she thought, *I don't need this.* The traffic had already made her late. She picked up her cordless and walked into her bedroom.

"Rachel, we're ready," her father's enthusiastic voice burst into her ear.

"That's great, Papa," she said as she tucked the phone under her chin and drew a plastic covered garment from her closet.

"I tell you it took some doing on such short notice. What with all the equipment to rent and the extra phone jacks to install. On top of everything else, the last tenant left a truckload of trash to clear out. Then I had to furnish it," finished Simon, flushed with excitement. He was in his early fifties, three inches taller than Rachel, but he had the same gray/blue eyes and dark straight hair, now streaked with gray. Besides being a devout Jew, he was a shrewd business man, having a large real estate development company that owned shopping centers, office parks, and warehouses scattered in the outskirts of the D.C. area.

"What time does their flight arrive?"

"Tonight at 7:05. I'm meeting Ambassador Levy and his oily new assistant at 6:00," she continued as she drew a pair of shoes from the bottom of her closet.

"Oily?" he asked.

"Yeah, he's so slick, charm seems to ooze from his pores like perspiration. Makes me sick." She gathered her lingerie from the bureau drawer, along with her stockings.

Her father laughed. "Oh, Rachel, when are you going to start being civil toward men."

"Humph, when I finally meet one worth being civil to."

Simon sighed. It was his fault that she was so selective. He had filled her full of religious notions from the time she was a child. So much so that her standards were extreme—way above his.

"But getting back to what we were talking about, how are you going to get such a large delegation back from the base."

She paused, trying to give him her full attention, but it was hard since she had collected her clothes and was now ready to shower.

"We drive two armored vans to Andrews Air Force Base. The State Department will send us one. I understand the Israeli advance team also will be there with one. Then we take them to their hotel and have dinner." She paused. "Oh, Papa, I am so excited. But they probably only included me because you are donating the offices for the Israeli Delegation. After all, I've just been at the embassy a short time."

"No doubt about *that*," her father replied. "When Ya'cov called asking for a favor, I told him, 'A favor for a favor,' because I knew how much you wanted to participate."

She frowned. *I am right after all. Oh well, at least I am going.* Then she sighed as she reached for a towel in the linen closet.

"Actually I'm just as excited," Simon continued. "Just think, Rachel, history will be made this week. You could possibly get to practice your Hebrew or your Arabic."

"Oh, Papa, I'm sure they all speak English. Besides, they won't allow me in the actual conference room anyway." She bit her lip in frustration. She hated to rush him off the phone because she knew he shared her feelings, but time was getting short.

"I know, but suppose they let something slip in the car thinking you don't understand."

"Maybe, I don't know," her voice trailed off. She was tapping her toe impatiently. "But let me go now. I have to get ready."

After hanging up the phone, Rachel undressed and stepped into the shower. She had a feeling that tonight was the beginning of everything. She wanted to look her best. Last week she had shopped for the "just right" suit, a light gray wool/silk blend with smart tailored lines. The skirt was short enough to show off her slender legs, fashionably short but decent. She laughed as she thought of her college English professor, who always compared the length of an essay to a woman's skirt—saying it should be long enough to cover the subject but short enough to be interesting. Rachel's purpose was to make a statement. First impressions are important if one wants to be taken seriously. Besides, dressing well bolstered her confidence. After all she was going to meet the prime minister of Israel *in person*.

Drying herself, she quickly dressed, leaving her blouse until after she applied her makeup. Finished, she tucked a simple white, silk monogrammed blouse into her skirt. Then she brushed her straight, nearly black hair until it shone. It fell to her shoulders softly as it curved slightly around her classic oval face. As she put on her earrings, she noted in the mirror that the bluish tint to the suit picked up the color of her eyes. *Not too shabby*, she thought. Then she grabbed her jacket and slipped into her pumps, which added at least two more inches to her height.

In college the guys had pursued Rachel relentlessly until they discovered her icy response to physical contact. After several hassles to preserve her virginity, she hadn't bothered to date at all, setting herself apart and remaining aloof.

None of her contemporaries knew of her religious leanings. She had learned long ago not to reveal them among the Gentiles. Even so, her name gave her away; how could Lieberman be anything but Jewish? By the time she reached college she let on that she was just a secular Jew—an intellectual—not interested in religion at all.

Neither did she advertise her strict Torah-based convictions concerning dating, none of which fit into the moral code of the twenty-first century. She simply put them into practice.

Choosing to stick to the books, Rachel became an expert on

Israeli affairs through research and careful attention to political happenings. It paid off by earning her a position at the embassy, even though those positions were usually filled by Israelis. It was a small start, she knew that. But at least it got her foot in the door. Now, with the conference, she would finally be close to some real political activity. It was a chance to prove to herself her efforts and sacrifices had been worth it. She picked up her keys and small clutch purse and headed for the door.

Chapter 2

Captain David Solomon unbuckled his seatbelt and stretched to his full five foot eleven height, his hands reaching toward the ceiling of the plane. His sandy, slightly wavy hair dropped over his brow nearly hiding his opal-like green eyes as he bent over to look at his watch. Just another hour to go and they should reach Andrews Air Force Base, somewhere just north of D.C. It had been a *long* day as they flew west almost keeping up with the sun. *Nothing like a fast plane to destroy the concept of time,* he thought as he looked up the aisles of the section reserved for the official delegates. The mostly empty back of the plane held his men and the secretaries.

He and his men had been assigned to temporary duty as security for the Israeli officials. Normally David was regular Army Intelligence, but he was chosen for this assignment because of his past association with the Mossad and because he had some experience in dealing with terrorism during the two Intifadas, not to mention his intelligence work during the war with Hizbullah.

Ordinarily a conference such as this would be held in Camp David, the presidential retreat in the mountains of western Maryland. The retreat had its own security force of navy and marine personnel, who made it safe for any visiting foreign dignitaries. But with the larger delegations, the inclusion of the pope and other Christian leaders of the Old City's churches, Camp David's rustic cabins would have proved inadequate. Instead, the State Department commandeered a floor of a large hotel near where the conference would convene to house some of the delegations.

On the way back from the restroom, David looked in on his men. Several dozed with seats laid back. He spoke to Bader and Landau on the first row and returned to the elite section.

He glanced up the aisle at the delegation he was sworn to protect. The Prime Minister, Haik Ra'amon, talked with Rabbi David Rosenfeld, who had been a delegate to the negotiations with the Vatican. (He came as a liaison to the religious delegation headed by the pope.) Two Labor MKs, Yudelman and Kutter, sat directly behind the prime minister and the rabbi. The Meretz Party delegates, Plaut and Ben-dor, sat behind them.

Most of the delegates were handpicked by the Labor Party now back in power. The Likud Party had failed to maintain a stable coalition government due to the demands of the religious parties and the stalling of the peace process. Sharon's collapse and the rise of Hamas in Palestinian politics also played a part. Then when Olmert's short interim government came to power and failed to destroy Hizbullah, the people demanded a change. Labor corrected the weakened military influence by making an army officer head of defense. This caused the delegation to be more balanced politically than it would have been if Labor had retained its former strength, or if Kadima had continued. As it was, Labor barely regained power. The people blamed Kadima for its bad choices, especially after the economy went down because of the nuclear destruction of Tel Aviv. They were ready for Labor, the peace party.

Most of the delegates were Ministers (MKs) of the Knesset, Israel's ruling body. Besides the rabbi, another exception was Yitshak Sharian, the mayor of Jerusalem, who had been invited because he knew the municipal problems intimately. He sat in front of David. Beside him was Avi Housan, the one delegate from the National

Religious Party, a concession made to the uproar from the religious community. The rest of the delegates in the center row were Yisrael Ba'aliya and the Gil party delegates, who were considered middle-of-the-road politically.

David frowned as he settled back into his seat. He wished a delegate from the Shas had made the team, like his father who was himself a Shas MK. Still he was grateful that Meretz had only two delegates. They were liable to give back all the territory Israel had won in the earlier wars, just for the sake of peace itself. He knew they were there to ensure that the peace process continued, but David firmly believed in using Israel's advantage to gain something. The peace had become possible because Hamas had finally relinquished their intention of annihilating the Jewish nation of Israel, at least in words. They had to because of the consequences of the latest war. Their Palestinian people needed to recover. They were the hardest hit. The constant attacks had worn down the Israelis as well.

David, 28, had been brought up in the strict influence of the Torah. But in his early twenties, after he confirmed his army career, he broke away from some of the traditions. The rigors of military life left little time to practice a strict religion, especially in regard to food. In fact, most Orthodox Jews did not serve in the regular army at all. A few belonged to special units that also included religious studies. But David, encouraged by his father to think for himself, developed his own studies. The prophetic scriptures fascinated him, and he looked forward to this conference as a turning point in history—possibly a prophetic event.

In his late teens he had participated in many archaeological digs, including the infamous temple tunnel that later caused a riot. He fervently believed that the original Ark of the Covenant would be found and the temple site returned to the Jews, for then and only then could the Arabs and the Jews both practice their faiths in peace.

The excitement of anticipation overcame his fatigue. He was sure the Old City would figure heavily in the negotiations. That was why the Christians were included. They had demanded a say after the Camp David accords failed. Would this conference with the Arabs on the settlement of Jerusalem grant them at least a portion of the holy mount? That was dreaming of course. Nevertheless, David thought the coming compromise would have to be as much religious as it was political, because of the religious upsurge that had engulfed the country after the short nuclear exchange. Men were looking to their maker. They had to be pacified for the peace to be permanent. He was only an observer, he reminded himself, but at least he could hope.

Chapter 3

Prime Minister Haik Ra'amon pushed the button for the stewardess. The perky blonde answered his call.

"Yes, sir, what can I get you?"

"I'd like a glass of water, please," he said, noticing she had lost some of her perk.

"I will be right back with it," she said as she brushed her limp hair behind her ear.

"I guess we are all getting tired of this flight," he half muttered under his breath after she left. She returned momentarily with the drink.

"Thank you very much," said Haik, flashing her his famous boyish grin.

Haik Ra'amon was only 45, a young man to be in such an important position. A fit, two hundred pound six footer, he was kept in shape more by nervous energy than physical activity. His dark hair curled slightly, and his dark brown eyes were shaded with heavy eyebrows. He had an average nose, slightly aquiline, and although clean shaven in contrast to some of the others, a five o'clock shadow indicated a heavy beard. All in all he had a pleasant face that sparkled when he smiled. His distinctive European look pointed to an Ashkenazi descent.

He had risen fast in politics, probably because he stood with the people and they seemed to know it. His father had been a blue collar worker, thus Haik had been determined to raise the lowly worker's living standard. He was barely in his thirties when he was elected a minister of the Knesset (MK). Starting in the Labor Young Guard full of dovish philosophies (peace at any cost) and for then "heretical" socio-economic ideas, he eventually became a leader. Then he used the decaying Histadrut, a once powerful labor organization (later led by Peretz), as one of his early steps to the prime minister's office. Coming against what he called "elitist, cynical apparatchiks" he ran against them and won the secretary-general's post of the organization. His financial overhaul of its ponderous and redundant bureaucracy earned him a healthy respect.

He languished through the lean years, barely hanging on to his seat in the Knesset, when Labor lost ground to the Likud Party, who was intent on building settlements. That managed to spark a Palestinian Intifada. Then the war with Hizbullah changed everything.

Although the IDF managed to force Hizbullah back from the border in South Lebanon, later an accident at the border had brought Syria into the picture. Bashar Assad had been looking for an excuse to attack Israel to boost his clout with other Arab nations. Ehud's Kadima Party decided to end the problem once and for all by sending a nuclear attack against Damascus, the headquarters of the many terrorist organizations afflicting them. Not only that, but the city was the depot for importing arms from oil rich Iran. They completely obliterated Damascus.

Iran, who had an alliance with Syria, immediately retaliated. Using the small warhead developed by North Korea, they wiped out Tel Aviv and only a limited surrounding area. Israel had feared any nuclear bomb would mean their demise; however, due to the use of the new limited warhead fitted to a rocket, the rest of the country escaped.

This brought the US into the picture, who followed with a heavy bombardment of Terhran but spared the Iranian people a nuclear assault.

The world, sobered by the exchanges, raged at the countries involved, particularly the US and Israel. Terrorists, whose ranks were much depleted with their Damascus leaders destroyed, were ready to talk peace with Israel, and the two-state solution was back on the table. Discouraged by the country's economic downturn (Tel Aviv had been the New York City of Israel) and weary of war, the people had voted the "peace speaking Labor Party" back to power and began rebuilding their economy. Ra'amon had been the voice leading them.

Of course he made enemies on his rise to the top—of former friends even. One of whom was known to say, "he appears as an appealing boy and so persuasive. Actually he is so slick. he could sell ice to the Eskimos. Haik manipulates and is a relentless underminer who sticks with it until he gets his way; but at the same time he is foolish and immature with an enormous thirst for power—dangerous traits." The opportunity came, and he ran in the new election as Labor's stellar leader.

After finishing his drink, Haik put his seat back and closed his eyes. *Might as well relax,* he thought. *It will be a long evening before bed. That is if I can relax. I'm probably too keyed up to rest. I want to do well for Israel. I want to make my mark in history. Maybe have a name like David Ben-Gurian.*

Chapter 4

When Rachel drove into the parking lot at the embassy, both Ambassador Levy and Avraham Lechtman were waiting. She got out of her car with a worried look on her face.

"I'm not late am I?" she asked.

"No," replied the ambassador, "we had to pick up the other van from State before five thirty, so we came straight here."

"You're looking awfully sharp tonight, Rachel darling," Avraham drawled. "Setting your sights on the prime minister? He's a widower, you know. His wife and daughter were killed in an automobile accident last year." A polished and experienced womanizer, the ambassador's young assistant had been making overtures to Rachel, but her repeated rebuff had embittered him toward her.

"Of course not. And no, I didn't know he was widowed," Rachel said coolly. *Do men always think women are stalking them?* she asked herself with indignation. *Why do I let him get to me?* "Did you expect me to have dinner with the delegation in rags?" she continued, her words dripping with sarcasm.

"No, I never expect to see *you* in rags. Actually, I would prefer to see you in nothing at all," he whispered, leering at her.

Rachel didn't bother to answer she glowered instead, color flushing her face. *He is disgusting.*

"Children, children, let's be civil," said the older Levy, who was too far away to hear Avreham's last statement or he would have strongly rebuked the young man. "We must present a united front. How can we make peace with the Arabs if we can't get along ourselves?" Then he laughed, relaxing the mounting tension.

"It's time we started for the base. Rachel, in view of the circumstances, you better come with me. I don't think I want to chance you two in the same vehicle."

The plane was down by the time they reached Andrews. The delegation departed the plane into a special security room reserved for visiting dignitaries. David and his men went first. David smiled as he recognized a familiar face.

"Shalom, ole buddy," greeted Johnny Leventhal, grasping David's hand and pushing him back in a playful manner.

"Shalom, Johnny. Everything set up?"

"Yee-ap. Everything...at the hotel, the conference, and the office."

David nodded as he placed his hand on the back of his neck and rubbed. David and Johnny were co-officers and rivals for advancement. They had been competing ever since they finished their *sadir* (required service) together then both entered the intelligence branch.

A strong contrast to David's light hair and complexion, Johnny had mounds of black curly hair and a heavy close-cut black beard that just rimmed his chin. Tall and square shouldered with a handsome figure, he was as laid back and easy going as David was conscientious and responsible, which was probably the reason David was in charge of the mission instead of Johnny. Johnny led the advance team that had arrived a few days before to make all the preliminary arrangements.

"I have assigned my men to secure the hotel tonight. I know you and your men are tired," offered Johnny. "Been there, done that."

David sighed. "Good, I appreciate it. Time enough to go over everything with you tomorrow."

By this time all the other delegates had filed into the room. Ambassador Levy greeted the prime minister. "It's good to see you again, Haik. Did you have a smooth flight?"

"Long," Ra'amon said, shaking his hand. Then the Ambassador began making introductions.

"You know Avreham, of course." The two shook hands.

Rachel stood by, waiting to be noticed. She had recognized Ra'amon as soon as he stepped into the room. From that moment on her eyes never left him. Finally, Ambassador Levy turned to her.

"This is Rachel Lieberman, one of our aids. Her father is the one loaning us some office space."

"A pleasure. I'm never too tired to admire an attractive face," he said, charming Rachel with his winning smile. "Tell your father how much we appreciate it."

"It's an honor to meet you, sir," Rachel said, somewhat awed but smiling. "But you will meet my father tomorrow. You can thank him yourself in person." She tingled with excitement as he shook her hand. The prime minister turned and introduced the rest of his delegation. Rachel watched him, fascinated by his smooth mannerisms. She had seen pictures of Ra'amon, but she had not imagined him to be so personable.

David, quietly observing and keenly aware of the dark-haired beauty, thought to himself, *This trip could be interesting in more ways than one.* He had known only fleeting relationships with the opposite sex, many quite attractive, but he had found them all to be shallow. Besides that, he was somewhat old fashioned, looking for chastity, but he looked for intelligence as well. He wondered what lay behind those lovely eyes.

Chapter 5

The group loaded into the three vans and drove to the hotel, where they were allowed a short break to refresh themselves before the eight o'clock meal. Rachel took advantage of the time to refresh herself as well. She missed the others. Ambassador Levy had already directed the delegates to an elegant private dining room where a long table was already set. Ambassador Levy seated himself next to the prime minister. Avraham sat next to one of the labor MKs on the other side of the table. The other ministers clustered around them on both sides. Much to her chagrin this put Rachel farther down the table next to the rabbi and across the table from Johnny, David, his men, one of the secretaries, and beside the others.

What does my carefully chosen outfit and efforts to impress matter now, she despaired. *I'm surrounded with inconsequentials. Who needs to impress the military anyway?* Withdrawing and setting herself to endure the rest of the evening, Rachel portrayed a formidable aloofness.

Long after the waiters had brought the food and everyone was eating, David leaned toward the opposite side of the table in an attempt to breach her defenses. He asked, "Are you from Jerusalem?"

"No, I'm from Washington," she said, noticing the unusual kaleidoscope of his blue-green eyes as he stared at her.

"I mean originally," he said as he slowly broke into a grin.

"I was born here. I am an American. I just work at the embassy," she answered with a cool, almost dead tone.

"Isn't that a bit unusual?" David asked.

Rachel was amused at his confusion and took advantage of the situation. She was well practiced at cutting off those she disdained. That seemed the only way to deal with men who pursued her with annoying frequency. It enabled her to keep her distance. She raised one eyebrow and replied without even a hint of a smile.

"Being an American? No, there are several million of us."

Johnny laughed. "You just blew it, old buddy," he said.

"No." David laughed too, a little flushed because now everyone knew she was playing with his words. Seemingly undaunted, he continued, "I mean *being* an American *and* working in the embassy. I thought you had to be an Israeli to do that."

"Normally yes, but they hired me because of my passion for Eretz Is-ra-el," she said with flare, softening just a bit. *That isn't strictly true,* she thought. *It's because I have close connections with the ambassador through the synagogue, but he doesn't have to know that.* Suddenly she realized what she was doing. She was ashamed of herself for answering him like a lawyer trying to trip up a vulnerable witness. He wasn't being fresh but trying to be friendly, a countryman from the land, and she was being just plain rude. *Is it the wine affecting me, or just my disappointment for being left out,* she wondered, trying to find an excuse for her behavior. *Or am I becoming hardened against all men?* The thought alarmed her.

"Israel is like my second home," she explained. "My father contributes heavily to the Jewish National Fund and is always donating to special projects. We've been over to visit many times," she finished with a sparkle of excitement and a friendliness she hoped showed in her eyes.

She could see that David noticed her quick change of attitude. *I have confused him.*

Johnny watched them react one with the other and frowned, as if berating himself for not engaging her before David.

"Ah," said the rabbi, interrupting the conversation. "And are you as passionate about the Torah as you are about the land?"

"Oh, yes," she said with fervor, releasing a pent up breath; then she explained further. "My papa taught me the Torah as a child. You see, my family belongs to the Chabad Lubavitch sect. We're very Torah orientated."

"But," he replied, "aren't they anti-Zionist?"

"Of course. After all, the Zionists are secular, but Papa and I believe the land is connected to the coming of the *Moschiach*. We don't adhere to the dress code either," she said then laughed. "My papa thinks it's bad for business."

Johnny frowned in disgust at her obvious religious zeal. Had Rachel been watching him she would have caught his displeasure. Instead she focused on the rabbi.

"And what business is he in?" the rabbi asked.

"Real estate development. You know, warehouses, shopping centers, buildings, etcetera."

"I'm surprised he didn't find a place for you in his business. More opportunity for an enterprising young lady than the embassy."

"But I'm not *interested* in real estate," Rachel stated outright, displaying an unmistakable contempt. Then she revealed the reason for her passion. "You see, I studied political science in college so I could be where the action is—especially Jewish action. Real estate would be totally boring."

She glanced back at David to catch his reaction. He nodded his head and smiled. *He seems to approve.* Somehow that pleased her.

Then one of the Meretz MKs diverted the rabbi's attention, causing a lull in their conversation. At this point Rachel picked up on the conversation of the secretaries, who were chattering away in Hebrew. The one called Deidrienne frowned at her.

Women are the same the world over, she thought. *They don't want anyone else messing with their men. They don't know I understand them.*

She smiled back at Diedrienne. Like two rivals squaring off over a coveted prize, Rachel picked up the challenge. No harm in a little flirtation with the captain. After all, he would be gone in a week anyway. *Besides, he seems to be more than an attractive male.*

David missed Merrill taunting Deidrienne about his attention to Rachel, having been distracted by the rabbi's comments to the MK. He did, however, catch Rachel's knowing smile at the secretaries. It was obvious that she understood their words.

Later, after they finished dessert, Ambassador Levy arose and announced, "*Rabotai* (gentlemen)—and ladies," he quickly added. "We shall not keep you from your beds any longer. We will bring the vans in the morning at 9:30. That will give you some twelve hours to rest and to try to adjust to our time. Good night all, and we will see you in the morning."

With that everyone arose and slowly began to disperse. The Israeli delegation headed toward the elevators. The ambassador stopped to speak with several MKs as the embassy's trio worked their way toward the lobby exit.

"Well, Rachel dear, what did you think of the evening?" Avreham asked, catching her arm as she hurried ahead of him.

Ignoring the hand on her arm she sighed. "I was stuck down at the end of the table where nothing was happening. I guess I am a little disappointed. No one even mentioned the conference where I was sitting."

"It was only mentioned in passing at our end," interrupted the Ambassador as he caught up to them. "That's to be expected. Preliminary committees from both the Arabs and the Israelis have been working all along. Now the principal leaders are here to work out the final details. No one will be saying much outside the conference room."

Rachel nodded, satisfied that she really hadn't missed anything.

Chapter 6

"Move it up about ten degrees," instructed George Allen as he sighted through the lens of a large telescope.

"That's not where we stopped photographing last night," protested his able assistant, Sandy Coolridge.

"I know, but I have a feeling about this sector. Could be we'll get lucky."

"As in finding another comet as spectacular as Hale-Bop?" she said and laughed as she cranked the long tube up.

Climbing the stairs to the lens, George adjusted the camera focusing on deep space.

George and Sandy were amateur astronomers photographing on clear nights and developing their pictures with high anticipation. By photographing against known bodies they would be able to detect a foreign body moving across the background.

On the morning following the change of direction, Sandy frowned as she lifted the picture out of the developing solution.

"What's going on here?" she muttered as she tried to make sense of what she saw. "George?"

George looked over her shoulder, hoping for a find. "Strange. Might be something closer in, out of focus. Tonight let's try that same shot closer in, maybe inside the solar system, and see what we get."

Chapter 7

Sister Anna Maria hurried from the dining room where she had just finished setting the table for the pope, his secretary of state, and two personal secretaries. This morning, as usual, the nuns scurried to prepare breakfast. Later the Santissimo Padre (Holy Father) was due to leave for an important diplomatic mission in America. Tomorrow duties would relax, as the four of them were expected to be gone at least a week. Of course she and the other four sisters who looked after the eighteen-room papal apartment would still have household duties. But it would be less rigorous minus meals to prepare.

Sister Anna Maria had accompanied the pope and his personal valet, Georgio, back from the Castle Gandolfo (the pope's country villa) just a week ago to help the pope get ready for the trip to America. Georgio was in charge of his wardrobe and had ordered a new *cossak* from the House of Gammerelli, papal tailors for two hundred years. The pope must look his best for this important conference.

"They're coming," said the sister as she burst into the kitchen. "Bring out the oatmeal and coffee. The cream and the fruit are already on the sideboard."

Sister Alecia pushed open the swinging doors, carefully balancing the huge tray with steaming dishes of oatmeal. Sister Anna

Maria dropped four slices of salt-rising bread into the toaster, and the room filled with its pungent odor just as the four men came through the door.

"Ah, Sister Maria, it smells heavenly. A fresh-baked loaf no doubt," said Pope Peter II cheerfully, revealing his high spirits as he vigorously rubbed his hands together. Salt-rising bread was his favorite.

"Of course," she replied, smiling to herself as she left the room. *He sure is in a good mood today*, she thought. Then the nuns retreated completely from the dining room. The men used that time to go over schedules and business for the day and preferred not to be interrupted.

—

The fathers selected their juice or fruit from the sideboard and sat down at the table.

"John, will you bless the food this morning?" asked the pope, addressing the secretary of state. Afterward they all made the sign of the cross and began eating.

Irishman John McCutchen served as personal secretary to the three previous popes and was himself a contender for pope at the conclave last December. Although he was well liked by almost everybody, it came down to a question of whether he could be firm in tough situations. After all, the pope was the last word. He had to be strong. So the cardinals had elected the former secretary of state, the Italian, Angelo Solini from Milan, pope. He in turn chose John to become his secretary of state. It was a winning combination because both men knew the intricacies of the former pope's programs and were willing to continue his conservative objectives.

Angelo chose Peter as his papal name because of the Malachy prophecy that said Peter the Roman would be the last pope. The last before what, the prophecy didn't say. But Pope Peter sincerely hoped it meant the kingdom of God on the earth. The popes before him had fulfilled the prophecy to date; therefore it seemed only natural for him to complete it. Besides, he felt a fervent calling to unite the world in peace. Somehow he knew that was his destiny.

"Tomorrow we begin a great new era—the beginning of the end of problems in the Middle East," declared Pope Peter.

"May it truly be, Santissimo Padre," said Antonio Cirillo, the pope's Italian secretary.

Jerome McFarland, the English-speaking secretary (the first from America to ever serve a pope), frowned, his lack of optimism showing.

"Do you not think so, Jerry?" asked the Holy Father.

"The problem I see is Iran," he replied. "They surely haven't given up just because of the war. They will probably regroup Hizbullah and be back at it…Well, I don't see how it will work, especially since they don't have any say in this conference. And what about Syria? What will happen to what's left of it?" he said as he hiked one of his cowboy-boot-footed feet on top of his other knee. (Jerry was from Texas.)

"How could they?" asked the pope. "None of them have anything to do with Jerusalem as a city."

"But the Jordanians will be there," he protested.

"That is only because of the holy sites on the Temple Mount. We are there for a similar reason—the Christian holy sites. All three religions that have a claim to the Old City have to be represented."

"But the Palestinians represent Islam, don't they?"

"Originally the Israelis gave the elder King Hussein jurisdiction over the Temple Mount."

"That," he exclaimed emphatically, "may be a problem. Since the Palestinians took it away from the Jordanians and put it under their Waqf."

"No, my son," he replied as he gazed at Jerry with affection. "Don't you remember, Prince Hussayni had already announced that they would return it to the Palestinians at the economic conference. I think that's just a formality. It's the close trade relationship with Jordan that made the Palestinians ask for their presence at the meeting."

"Excuse me, Padre," interrupted Father McCutchen, "is there anything you need me to do? If not I have some last minute instructions for my aids and some odds and ends to take care of before we leave."

"Have you collected all the papers I asked for?"

"Yes, Holy Father, they are already packed."

"Very well. We will see you at departure."

As Father McCutchen left he nearly collided with Father Loni Mondello, who was coming in the door. They exchanged greetings and the secretary of state left.

"Good morning, Santissimo Padre," said Father Mondello with a cheery smile.

The pope nodded and smiled with a closed mouth, because his mouth was full of his last piece of toast.

"Everything is settled. I have arranged for your private boarding of the plane. Even though the passengers will be scrutinized fully, we will not set down the helicopter until the plane has left the gate. They will have a stairway near the runway."

"Why the extra precaution? Isn't airport security enough?"

"No, not this time, because part of Hizbulla still exists, and a few of the other Islamic fundamentalist groups oppose this conference adamantly. I will call the army post just before you leave, as usual."

Vatican City had a heliport at the rear of the property for the pope's convenience. Once notified, the Italian Air Force Base kept the pope's aircraft in view on its radar screen all during its connecting flight as a common procedure. The base was on alert to scramble fighter jets if any object should even begin to approach the aircraft.

"Ah, Loni, you always take such good care of me," said the pope with affection.

"I try to," murmured the father. Father Mondello was a pleasant man in his early sixties. As prefect of the pontifical household, he made all the arrangements for trips, audiences, and special papal events.

Secretary Cirillo asked Mondello, "What about security in Washington?"

"The State Department will provide it. Your security officer will call them with the flight number and time of arrival enroute. They too will meet the plane before it reaches the gate. You will then be escorted in unmarked cars with dark windows to special guest quarters of the State Department."

Pope Peter shook his head. "What a world we live in that such precautions should be necessary." Then he brightened as he added, "But maybe this conference will change everything. I must prepare myself in prayer."

With that remark the breakfast conference ended. The fathers went off to care for last minute details; Jerry's boots clopped on the smooth marble floor as he marched down the hallway. Pope Peter quietly shuffled into his personal chapel to pray.

Chapter 8

Nabil Dakkah, prime minister of the Palestinian Authority in Nablas, drove into Amman with his deputies and body guards. After meeting the rest of the Arab Delegation, they would all fly to the conference together in the former king's private plane. Others joined the Palestinians because the settlement and the peace affected the whole Arab world.

Nabil was a quiet man in his late forties. Not exactly tall at five foot ten, but he walked tall. His slightly graying hair mingled with the black in a salt and pepper effect—more pepper than salt. He did not wear the traditional Arab head dress, the *keffiyen*, so much associated with Arafat, but instead a simple green military beret. His green eyes almost matched the beret and looked all the greener for it.

After Arafat died the Palestinians elected a colleague of Arafat's, but he failed to get control of the terrorist groups completely. Hamas, running as a party, won the majority. But the political leaders in the parliament did not control the military branch, whose leaders had fled to Damascus. As a result near anarchy had reigned, especially in the Gaza strip. The governments of several leaders failed after the 2006 war before Dakkah came to power. Dakkah, though undeclared, was not a militant Islamist but more moderate than a declared moderate. After Dakkah's election he spoke to the terrorists who persisted in trying to disrupt the peace process in progress.

They were so close to a final peace. His compassionate heart was for the people. He had to unite them. When he came to office he gave a speech saying, "My brothers, this is an opportune day for all Palestinians. We have fought long and hard, suffered many losses, and now we need to unite with one goal. Have we come this far just to self destruct?" He paused for effect.

It was clear he blamed the remnants of Izzadin Kassam, the former militant branch of Hamas, for continuing problems. Except for these stragglers, the former terrorist organization had become a political party accepting the inevitability of Israel remaining a nation; the nuclear exchange had determined that.

"At this rate we will solve the Israeli's problems for them by killing each other off. My brothers, listen to me," he beckoned with his hands in a pleading manner. "We cannot go back and undo all that has been done. The past is forever lost—gone. All we can do is live in the now. We cannot close our eyes to today because it is not what we wish it were either. We have to face reality and accept the players of this game. Even after the war Israel remains a powerful nation. Can we change that with hit or miss strikes of terrorist groups? No, we cannot. Will our Arab neighbors fight another war? No, they are signing peace treaties. We have to face the truth—the now truth—or go on losing our young men for generations. When faced with this choice, it is not logical to go on hating and killing when we have an opportunity to rebuild.

"My brothers, Israel is tired of war. They too are having to rebuild. Now that Labor is back in power, they are willing to give us land and our own rule. If we do not accept this, we and only we are the ones who lose, not them. Come, let us heal our differences. Let us work for the good of our people. Let us show the Israelis we can produce a stable, law abiding community. Let us show that we too can prosper. Does not Allah desire to set up a good life for us all when the Mahdi comes. Let us declare a *hudna*. Who is to say, he may yet establish Arab supremacy over the Middle East through peace?

"My brothers, I believe we can still reach our goals this way. Put down your arms and your terrorist acts. Let us declare an economic war. Let us prosper as they do. These acts of terror only hurt our own people with the border closings and such."

He continued to preach this message to the community at every opportunity. Gradually the people listened and began to give him their support. He continued to rule the territories with a gentle but firm hand. He won the respect of the Israeli Government by repressing Arab extremists and keeping order at the check points between Israel and the territories. Islamic doctrine allowed for peace treaties to be made with the enemy when they lost ground, enabling them to rebuild their strength. Thus the leading imans allowed this period of secession from violence.

A vigorous economy returned to the area. Interaction with Jordan increased. Daily, trucks loaded with produce from the rich Jericho plain crossed the Allenby Bridge passing into Jordan, while trade from Jordan came to the territories. Israeli Kibbutzim, whose farms had encroached on Jordanian land before the settlement of the border, continued to farm it by paying leases to the Arab nation. They shared their farming secrets with the Palestinians. Co-ops developed between both peoples. Even the security fences were torn down. The greenhouses of the Gaza strip were rebuilt. A free market atmosphere turned the hearts of the people toward business and away from political unrest. Dakkah, being a strong leader and a good negotiator, was mainly responsible for their prosperity. Now they looked to him to negotiate East Jerusalem for them to be their capital city.

—

Having heard that the Palestinians had arrived, the former crown

Prince of Jordan, now King Ghahazi Faysul Hassayni of Iraq, was first to greet them.

Addressing Dakkah warmly, he said, "Nabil, my friend, how are you? This is a historic moment, no?"

"Yes, it is what we have all worked for—hoped for—prayed for," he said. "Are you going to the conference?"

"Yes, I am going along to represent the Arabs' interest as a whole. Come and have some refreshment before we all leave for the plane."

"Has our friend, Adoni´, from Lebanon arrived yet?"

"Yes, he flew in earlier this morning. He's waiting inside." Hassayni wasn't quite sure how he felt about that. He was hoping Dakkah wasn't too taken with the Lebanese. Somehow Adoni´ was too slick, too full of himself, something. That was one reason he wanted to re-establish his relationship with Dakkah before they met Adoni´.

Hassayni had been an heir to the throne in Jordan and Iraq through his great uncle, King Faysal II, who was assassinated in 1958. After the war with the US and the failure of the Iraqis to form a successful government, they had invited him to assume the position of king of Iraq. They adjusted the constitution to include a Monarch. It had worked out quite well because of his neutral attitude toward the different factions dividing the country. Iraq was prospering again. Having worked with Dakkah while still active in Jordan, he wanted to see him before he joined the others. He had aspirations of leading the New Middle East, but he was unhappy with the rise to prominence of the Lebanese banker.

Continuing to make small talk, he led the whole group down a hallway to a large drawing room with tall windows draped in maroon brocade and an oriental carpet with blended reds where a strong whiff of coffee teased their noses.

—

Standing beside Jordon's young King Alahahn Hassih near a window, Adoni´ looked up as Dakkah came into the room and headed straight toward them. The rest of the delegation approached a small table set with assorted fruits and cakes and a large silver coffee urn. King Hassayni trailed behind forgotten.

The young king reached for Dakkah's hand and shook it smiling. They had a strong relationship because of the trade across the border.

Dakkah said, "Your first big conference, Alahahn. Are you nervous?"

"Not really. I'm not the novice you suppose, nor is this my first trip to Washington. I lived in D.C. when I attended the School of Foreign Services at Georgetown University."

"That's right, I'd forgotten. So you are not so green after all." Actually, it was Dakkah who was the real greenhorn.

Alahahn added to cover any embarrassment, "But you have recruited a good man here." He nodded toward his companion.

"It is good to see you again, my friend," said J. Leucus Adoni´. "We will walk into history together, no?"

"I believe it. The future of our people is riding on this conference," replied Dakkah as he wrinkled up his brow.

"Don't worry, my friend, I think the chances are good. I have had my people researching, and they have uncovered some interesting things," declared Adoni´.

"Really, like what?"

"Oh, some of the other parties at work in this issue, for instance a powerful international business men's society. I have been trying to understand their motives. I believe we can use them to gain our objective."

"You mean exploit them before they can exploit us?" he said with a laugh.

"Something like that. They're one of the many power groups looking to institute a New World Order," he replied.

Adoní had a striking appearance. He was just six foot tall with an athletic build, weighing around 180 pounds. He had dark hair with glints of red in it. It probably would wave if it were permitted to grow longer, but it was clipped short in a serious business man's cut. His finely chiseled facial features made a regally handsome face. But it was his eyes that were impressive. They revealed great intelligence and reflected many moods. Being dark mahogany brown with a black ring around the iris, they could pierce a subordinate with a look or seduce him with softness, but they were most devastating in anger. That brought out the red in them, and then they seemed to blaze like fire. Of course few had witnessed their fire because Adoní was generally an even-tempered man.

Born February 5, 1962, of a Jewish mother and a Syrian father at the precise moment when seven planets were in conjunction in Aquarius, he was immediately dubbed a child of destiny by his father. Living in Mosul, Iraq at the time, Aviv Danak saw the significance. Was he not being born on the site of ancient greatness, Mosul, near the tel of Ninevah? He himself had an impressive lineage of descent. One of his forefathers, a former general under Alexander the Great, had been the first Seleucus, founder of the Seleucid Dynasty, which took over Syria after the great conqueror's death. Because of his proud heritage and superstitious nature, Danak predicted that his son was destined for greatness. So he gave him an appropriate name—Julius (for Julius Caesar) Leucus (short for Seleucus) Adoní (pronounced with a long "i" meaning "Lord" in his mother's Hebrew) Danak. Leucus had dropped the family name of Danak after the death of his parents. His father had instilled in him the significance of his birth, and he believed his own future greatness would emerge in time. Four names had been cumbersome in business, so he kept the name of destiny, shortening the first name to an initial.

In Adoní's youth, at the age of fourteen, he came to the atten-

THE BEGINNING OF THE END

tion of a high-ranking officer in the Ba'athist Party because of his uncommon good looks. The officer took him to become one of his *intimate friends*. Although his parents were upset, they knew better than to protest. The rumors spread among the people said that to refuse such a request in the face of absolute power meant death. The next six years Leucus was closely associated with the raw power of Saddam Hussein's regime. The officer had seen to the boy's education, probably better than he would have otherwise. Then he took a younger lover and released Adoni´ back to his parents. They immediately moved back to Syria. Shortly after, Adoni´'s father died and life became hard.

His mother's single brother came to their rescue and took young Adoni´ into his savings and loan business in Damascus. Being highly intelligent, Leucus learned quickly. He was soon making shrewd loans that increased the assets of the bank and at the same time charmed the prospective clients as he learned to negotiate to everyone's benefit. Because of his adeptness, his uncle had continually promoted him to more responsibility. Finally he put him in charge of all the branches in Lebanon.

Being the sole heir at his uncle's death, he became a multi-millionaire and turned his attentions toward political endeavors. He needed Lebanon to make peace with Israel so he could invest heavily in the Middle East-North African Development Bank and expand his financial empire. By getting into politics he hoped to help bring the peace along. Assad, former dictator of Syria, took notice of him and used him as an economic advisor. He offered his services to the prime minister of Lebanon, and to everyone's surprise and satisfaction he paved the way toward a final solution in the peace process. It was here he had met Nabil Dakkah as they negotiated with the refugees.

Chapter 9

The king stood listening, fascinated by the intrigue that would clearly be involved. King Hassih had been impressed by the amazing way Adoni´ had handled the Palestinian refugee problem. Everybody—the Lebanese, the Jordanians, and especially the refugees themselves—were satisfied with the settlement. After the, Syria/Iran/Israel nuclear exchange he had approached the Lebanese Government with a proposal. He proposed that the Palestinians, still languishing in the refugee camps, be dispersed to South Lebanon and Syria (beyond Damascus) to help rebuild the devastation caused by the war in exchange for land. He negotiated with Dakkah for the rest to rebuild the Palestinian territories in Gaza. (Hamas, having lost its leadership and funding from Damascus, was now defunct.) In fact, the refugees looked upon Adoni´ as a kind of savior who finally freed them from their camps and gave them land of their own. The Israeli government was desperate, and the Lebanese knew it. Hizbullah had been pouring millions of dollars of relief money into Lebanon from the collections of "Zakat" to woo their loyalty. It didn't work because the people were afraid of more reprisals against Hizbullah.

Adoni´ had shared his ideas for the conference with the king before Dakkah arrived. Though Israel had remained adamant in the past about dividing Jerusalem, lately they seemed to be wavering.

THE BEGINNING OF THE END

Jordan's young king thought Adoni´ just might have the solution to push them over the edge, especially with the changes in the Israeli Government. If anyone could do it, he could. He had never seen a smoother, more able negotiator.

Having finished their refreshments, the group boarded the king's personal helicopter for the trip to the Queen Alia International Airport.

Chapter 10

David arose early the next morning. Later he would check with Johnny on the security of the hotel, but first he needed a cup of coffee. As he started down the hall on the way to the coffee shop he ran his finger inside his collar and jerked his head, trying to loosen its constraining tightness.

"What's the matter, Captain?" asked one of the security men posted at the elevators, laughing. "Not used to wearing a tie?"

"No, and the irksome thing is choking me," replied David

The security team had been advised before they left Israel to wear business suits so they could blend in with the people around them. So except for their communicators, they looked like the normal hotel clientele. David was used to casual army uniforms that seldom required a tie.

After David finished his coffee he returned to the second floor where their delegation had the east wing of the hotel. The elevators stood at the junction of the main hall and the hall bisecting the rooms. The only other entrance to their wing was the stairwells, one at the far end of the building in the short hall round the corner, and another close to a service elevator in the front hall. Close circuit cameras surveyed all movement from both ends. The hotel had excellent security on the second floor because they often hosted visiting dignitaries. *It was easy to secure,* thought David. Nevertheless, they would not depend on that. They needed to stay alert at all times.

He tapped on Johnny's door and announced himself. Johnny's roommate let him in. Johnny's bed was empty.

"Johnny, you in there?" he called, looking toward the bathroom.

"Yo," was the reply.

"I saw only one man at the elevator in the hall. Are your off-duty men up?"

"I think so. I heard some showers going next door." Johnny came out of the bathroom wiping his face with a towel, his face shining and beardless except in designated areas. "Actually, only three men patrol the hall at night. The elevators cannot reach this floor after midnight because there are no security men to give access. They have to insert a card for the elevators to stop at this floor. And the stairwell doors require access cards as well." Johnny frowned.

"Okay," said David. "That's good. That spares men. Now I'd like to see a layout of the hotel so I can brief my men before breakfast. They are on their way here now." David was aware that Johnny felt slighted to have to be under his command. He knew he was also sensitive about his decisions, but he couldn't let that interfere with his doing his own job.

Johnny handed him his own layout of the hotel just before David's men streamed into the room—Matza, Bader, Landau, Katz, Hillman, and Feldman.

"Shalom, Captain, Johnny," his men called out almost in unison as they entered the room.

He frowned. "Shalom," repeated David, still preoccupied with the hotel plan. "Gather round. I want you to see how the hotel is laid out just in case we have any problems when we are all here. Johnny, how have you planned for the main hall? I see a potential problem here."

"How so?"

David answered, "The service elevator at the end of our main hall. Do the employees have cards to that elevator to access this floor?"

"Only our security guys have cards. They insert them for anyone authorized to reach the second floor after they check them out. The stairwell doors can be exited from the floor but not entered without a card," said Johnny.

"Ah," said David. This hotel's security is impressive. What about Palestinian access?"

"They can't get here from their wing. Each delegation has its own secure entrances."

David nodded his approval then asked, "How have you planned?"

"I have two men assigned to that elevator in the basement, one in the main hall downstairs and two in our main hall. I also have two more at the end of the hall at the other stairwell during the day," Johnny replied.

"Good. I hope you picked your basement guards carefully. You and your men will continue to secure our home base, at least during the day, since your men are already familiar with the hotel. This is our greatest vulnerability. I will split my men between the conference and the office, and we will rotate the night duty. Double shifts may be unavoidable. I can probably spare two to help you out. Two may be all we need at the office and two at the conference since the State Department will have security there as well.

"Feldman, I'm putting you in charge of the office complex. Landau, you are in charge at the conference. My job is to secure the courier of documents, so I will be in and out. The State Department will have their men there as well. Any questions?"

"Yeah," said Katz, the clown of the company. "Who gets to guard that gorgeous dame that sat across the table from us last night? *Ayzeh hatikha* (What a piece)."

"She needs guarding?" asked David, half knowing what to expect.

"From the look in your eye, when she spoke to you last night, I'd say she needs protection," said Katz, laughing.

"Yeah, Captain, I'd volunteer for that job myself," added Matza.

"Okay, guys, knock it off," said David with a wry smile. "We're here to protect the delegation, remember? Besides, she's an American."

With a light mood they descended to the special breakfast room designated for the conference delegates.

Chapter 11

The secret service agent down the hall from the Oval Office called ahead on his communicator and announced the code name for the senator on his way in.

"Acknowledged," said Peters, the agent at the president's door. A few moments later he smiled at the approaching man. "Good morning, Senator," he said as he opened the door. "The president is expecting you."

"Senator," nodded President John Anderson, waiting behind his desk. He arose to shake hands with J. Quentin Rice, the senator from New York. "I can guess why you are here. I've been expecting to hear from you all week."

"Really," replied the senator, trying to act surprised but failing.

"You're here to tell me what the *society* wants out of the Jerusalem conference," the president continued

The senator, besides his government role, also represented a group of men inside and outside the US who more or less controlled the world—at least economically. Rice was their spokesman to the president.

"You already know?"

"No, not exactly, but I can guess. They want a settlement that will leave Jerusalem in the control of neither the Arabs nor the Jews so that the Middle East will finally cease to be a thorn in the world's side. Maybe make it an international city under the control of the UN. Am I right?" *Actually he has come to straighten me out,* he thought, unable to deny the power that the group exerted on the highest office in the land. He sighed as he regained his seat. *If the American people only knew how little they had to do with electing their own leader, they would be totally disillusioned.* But without the money and power of the "establishment's society," neither party could elect a president. It rankled him that he was beholden to them. But that was how it was, so what else could he do but at least listen?

What he mouthed to the senator was the general view of the past two presidents, and he himself had stood against their policy because of pressure from American Jewry.

"Well, close," said the senator with a frown on his face. "You're right about wanting to get rid of the thorn in the side. But I doubt if we can persuade either party to make Jerusalem an international city. They are too nationalistic at the moment. Israel never has kowtowed to the United Nations unless they were forced to. Besides, they have some sort of holy attachment to the city. What the society would really like is to eliminate the religious tension in the area. That is one reason we have pushed for Vatican and the orthodox delegates to be involved. If we could get the three major religions of the Middle East to agree on something it would be a start. Eventually the society hopes they can merge all three religions into one. Then we can set up a standard for all to obey. I don't think total peace will be established until we can all agree on God."

"Oh, I don't see how that's possible now. What with Iran's president still screaming for Israel's demise and sending threats toward the West in spite of all that's happened. Seems like he will only be satisfied when Islam rules the world."

"I know. He is a real problem. He doesn't realize that he almost brought the world to the brink of an unthinkable war. That's why it is so crucial to get this peace in the Middle East settled."

"So what am I supposed to do to help?" asked the president. "You know I am only the neutral host to this conference."

"You and I are to encourage any tendency in that direction," he said. "A word here and a suggestion there will do a lot. It's such a tremendous step for them to finally sit down together on the issue of Jerusalem. Israel has balked for so long. They both have vital interests there."

The president gave tacit agreement to do what he could. They shook hands, and the senator left.

Chapter 12

The vans arrived at 9:30 as promised. Ambassador Levy exchanged greetings with the delegation then turned aside to speak to David, leaving the prime minister with Lechtman, his assistant.

"Where is Mr. Lieberman?" asked Prime Minister Ra'amon.

"He will meet us at the office," said Avraham. "Rachel, his daughter, will take us."

"Oh, yes, the lovely Miss Rachel. And here she is now."

Rachel got out of her car and came running over to them.

"Finally," she replied. "A fender-bender slowed traffic. Did you sleep well, Mr. Prime Minister?"

Rachel panted slightly from her rush. He noticed that she looked as fresh as a buttercup in her pale yellow shirtwaist dress with a matching jacket.

"I'm rearing to go," replied Haik Ra'amon, smiling and punching the air with his right fist. The sooner they got business out of the way, he hoped they could see a little of the US Capital. After all, this was all they had to do today once the secretaries were familiarized with the set up. This was his first trip to the US, and he was naturally interested in a little sight seeing.

Meanwhile Ambassador Levy asked David, "How do you want us to travel?"

"I think some of my men should ride in each vehicle."

"Yes, that would be wise. I don't anticipate any trouble, but you never know. Why don't you accompany Rachel since she will be in the lead?" said the ambassador.

"I can handle that," David said and smiled. "Johnny," he called.

"Yo," he said as he turned away from the rest of the security team.

"Take Feldman and ride in the third van for rear guard. Laundau, you take the middle, and Matza, you and Katz take the front van." Hillman and Bader had remained behind with Johnny's men guarding their floor.

"But what about you, Captain?" asked Feldman.

"I go in the lead car," said David. "Keep your eyes open and your communicators and weapons handy. This may be America, but our enemies stalk the world."

As they began to load the vehicles, Ambassador Levy walked over to where Rachel and Avraham were standing.

"Rachel," he said, "You take the lead. Captain Solomon will be riding with you."

She turned to go to her car.

"Damn," muttered Johnny under his breath. "There's a definite advantage to being in charge." He watched with envy as David got into Rachel's car.

"Oh, and Rachel," the Ambassador continued," we will probably need you to run back and forth between the conference and the office later. A van is too conspicuous for a courier. It's good that the office is close to the conference, but your Honda would blend in traffic better."

Johnny's jealousy of David hardened even more as he realized that David would ride with Rachel all week.

Katz watched David as he opened the door and climbed into the passenger's seat of Rachel's car just ahead of them. As they pulled out in caravan, Katz turned to Matza and slapped him on the knee.

"Will you look at that. The cat just climbed in with the mouse."

Avraham, who was driving, overheard the remark and said, "More like a shrew. Anyway I wouldn't worry about *that* mouse unless he likes them frozen."

"Not an easy mark, I take it," said Katz.

"You take it right," replied Avraham.

"Aw, come on, Katz. You know the captain is not a skirt chaser. I don't think he's even interested in women much. At least he's never had a serious girl friend as long as I have known him."

"What about Deidrienne?"

"She doesn't count. You know that. It's just that she runs after him all the time. Come to think of it, the captain doesn't even make coarse jokes about women," said Matza.

"That's because he's so religious, but that dame will make him look twice," Katz retorted.

Katz and Matza had become inseparable ever since they joined the army after their immigration from Russia. Both coming from the southern regions near the steppes, they already had a lot in common—all, that is, except their appearance. They were a virtual Mutt and Jeff, comic characters in the funny papers of the 1940s. Matza was short and squatty, and Katz tall and lanky. Matza had blond curly hair and blue eyes; Katz had dark hair, straight with a cowlick, and dark brown eyes that crinkled with mirth. Matza played the straight man to Katz's comic. Wherever they went, laughter followed. David was particularly fond of both. They in turn respected their captain, being fiercely loyal to him.

"You know," continued Katz suddenly serious, "I have a feeling about this one. Maybe one of these days we will celebrate a wedding."

"Maybe so, maybe so," replied Matza

"Huh!" snorted Avraham.

Rachel wove her way through traffic as a skilled Washingtonian. David remarked in awe of it, "We have traffic in Jerusalem, but it's never like this."

"This is nothing," replied Rachel. "You should see it at rush hour or just go near the mall or the capitol where all the tourists are. Is this your first trip out of the country?"

"No, I have been to Eastern Europe on assignments, but not to America."

"Were you security for other conferences there?" she asked with genuine interest.

"No, I had a special assignment with the Mossad."

"Ooooh, the mighty Mossad—and you can't talk about it, right?" Smiling she waved her hand with a flourish, as if making fun.

"That's right," he almost whispered. David couldn't figure her out. One minute she was cold, the next she was teasing. She seemed genuinely interested in Israel, but now she was joking about the Mossad. He changed the subject. "I'm really looking forward to this conference. It could bring a lasting peace to my country. I'm anxious to see the outcome."

"So am I," she answered with feeling, sober again. "My father twisted Ambassador Levy's arm to let me take part. I haven't been at the embassy too long."

"You mentioned that you were of the Lubavitch Hasidim last night. Aren't you the sect that thought Schneerson was the Messiah?"

"Only some of us," she replied with an earnest but more relaxed voice. "I, myself, always believed the Moschiach had to be a younger man, one in vigorous good health. I mean, after all, how could a ninety-four-year-old man bring the nations to peace?"

"Exactly," said David.

"Are you looking for the Moschiach too?" asked Rachel. "Most of the men I know are not. Even the young men at my synagogue don't seem to really believe in his coming." She glanced over to catch his reaction to her question.

"Yes, I believe it is time. You see, my father was head of a *yeshiva*, so I've been exposed to the Scriptures all of my life. But I don't practice kosher anymore," he said apologetically. "I got away from it after I left home. But I've always been interested in prophecy. In fact, I believe this conference may be of prophetic significance."

"I do too," replied Rachel.

Suddenly Rachel realized her heart was pounding with excitement. Finally, here was a man who thought like she did. *Amazing.* It was such a unique experience for her to even be enjoying a conversation with a *man*. Then she added with passion, "I just *know* the Moschiach is out there somewhere even now, waiting to step forth. I actually believe his time could be tied to the settlement of Jerusalem."

"You may be right. But I think the restoration of the temple may also be a factor. I used to dig with some of the archaeologists near the Temple Mount. They longed for the day when they could excavate under the mount itself, looking for the ancient furniture supposedly hidden there at the time of the Babylonian captivity, especially the Ark of the Covenant. They believe Solomon built a special room to hide the ark in times of trouble. Lots of legends about the ark exist since it disappeared by the second temple era."

"Did they find anything?"

"Nothing major, at least not when I was involved. I did hear a rumor that some sort of ark was found last year. But you can never tell about that. Rumors are always circulating about it. Besides, the rabbis from Ethiopia believe the original Ark of Moses' time is in a church in Axsum."

"How could that be?" asked Rachel, becoming more intrigued.

"The Ethiopians have a legend that Menelik, the supposed son of the Queen of Sheba and Solomon, carried it down to Ethiopia. But it's more likely that faithful priests whisked the ark away and took it to Egypt sometime during the reign of the wicked King Mannassah.

"Then they took it up the Nile to Elephantine Island at Aswan where the priestly colony built a temple and served it for several hundred years. Eventually they lost favor with the Egyptians and were forced to flee on up the river. An American journalist traced the path of the ark to Lake Tana where it spent approximately another six hundred years. Then in the fourth century AD when the king of Ethiopia converted to Christianity, the Christians took the ark away from the Jews in a great conflict and put it in a church."

"Is it still there?" asked Rachel, fascinated with the possibility.

"Well, the Ethiopian priests who have immigrated to Israel believe it. They say all of Ethiopia believes it."

"Will they give it back to the Jews, do you think?"

"Not according to what I've heard. It's their national treasure. Our Ethiopian priests think they will never part with it. It is the center of Ethiopia's Coptic Christianity because it supposedly contains the original Ten Commandments God gave to Moses. They even have a priest who gives up his whole life just to serve the ark. He's called 'The Guardian of the Ark'"

"How utterly fascinating," said Rachel as she pulled to the curb. The vans swung in behind her. "Well, here we are, and just when the conversation was getting really interesting. We will have to talk about this some more. I want to know all about it," she said, warming toward David.

I've met a true believer at last, thought Rachel as she climbed out of the car. *An attractive man at that.* Excitement stirred as joy mounted in her heart. She was not usually moved by male attractiveness, but she sensed that David was different.

Simon Lieberman came over to the car after they emerged.

Flushed with emotion Rachel said, "Papa, this is Captain Solomon, head of the security team."

"Simon Lieberman," he said, extending his hand. "I'm glad to meet you, Captain."

"Call me David," he returned easily.

Then they turned to the rest of the delegation with more introductions. Simon took the lead toward the building.

Chapter 13

"Come," said Simon, "I'll show you what I have prepared for you. Johnny says I picked a good building to secure."

The building was old, rather ordinary, not too tall (only five stories), but the interior had been modernized and was quite pleasant. I've put you on the top floor to make it easy to secure," said Simon as he reached the elevators.

After the party emerged on the fifth floor, Haik Ra'amon followed Simon down the hall to Suite 510. Inside he walked to a window in one of the offices as Simon pointed to the nearest building, which was across two large parking lots.

"As you can see, it would be difficult to access this end of the building from another building with surveillance or listening devices."

Haik nodded his approval. "Very well chosen," he said. "And nicely furnished, I might add."

It was a good looking set of offices in spite of the rush to prepare it. The former tenant's color scheme had been neutral shades of gray with touches of black. Simon had rented two magenta-on-maroon patterned divans and various end tables of chrome and glass. Sculptured metal lamps topped with black shades stood on the end tables in the reception room. Oversized flower prints framed in chrome and glass hung on the walls.

The office itself was similar in color scheme but offered little but necessities: a large table, computer desks with computers, phones, paper, and a fax machine. The small complex had two offices, one of which contained cots, sleeping quarters for security. Also included was a small conference room for delegation deliberations.

While still in Israel, security had planned the use of the offices. The secretaries would transcribe every word spoken in the conference. Audio tapes recording the speeches of the delegates would periodically be delivered to the office secretaries by David for transcribing

The purpose was twofold. The Israelis would use the transcriptions when making proposals and countering proposals. This assured accuracy and eliminated countless misunderstandings. Also, they were available to fax the government back in Israel if necessary.

The office served as a private meeting place as well. The state building had rooms for such matters, but the Israelis, being paranoid about security, preferred their own arrangements.

After surveying the set up, the prime minister voiced his approval.

"Simon, this is the complete answer to our needs. I have but one question. How far are we away from the conference?"

"It's only fifteen blocks from the State Department. A plus for your courier," he replied.

"Great—perfect," he said, satisfied that the details were taken care of. Now he could look forward to the conference and the history that he would make. "Perhaps we could take in a little sight seeing the rest of the day," he said to Ambassador Levy. "It looks like you have already worked out everything here."

"If you like," the ambassador replied.

―

David, also speaking to Ambassador Levy, asked, "Would it be possible to check out the conference area at the State Department?

Johnny is probably already familiar with it. But he won't be working the conference. I need to see it myself before tomorrow."

"State's security men can show you around tomorrow. It's all cut and dried," interjected Johnny.

"I don't know, but we can ask," said the ambassador, completely ignoring Johnny and heading for the phone in the reception room. After making arrangements he turned to David and said, "The receptionist said to come on over. She will have some of their security people show you around. Rachel, you take Captain Solomon over. I've got to see to some things this afternoon. Avraham and the other driver can take the delegation around Washington after they drop me off."

Rachel looked at David and said, "Let's go."

"Johnny, keep a lookout over the delegation as you go," David ordered, catching a look on Johnny's face he didn't understand, but before he could think what it meant, his attention was averted by Katz.

Smirking at David with a twinkle in his eyes, Katz asked, "Sure *you* don't need some help, Captain?"

David took Rachel by the arm and said, "I'm ready." Then he smiled back at Katz and lifted his eyebrows twice in rapid succession like Magnum PI, while Johnny looked on in absolute dismay.

Diedrienne rubbed her stomach as if trying to remove a queasy feeling. She too had watched the whole scene play out before her. She gripped her hands so tightly they turned white.

Chapter 14

When they got into the car, Rachel watched David loosen his tie.

"I hope you don't mind if I relax a moment. I'm not used to wearing suits and ties. I'm usually in army khakis. I feel like a fish out of water."

"Then why are you wearing them?" asked Rachel, now remembering that's why he looks different today. *Like a bouncer for a bar* she had thought earlier, because his athletic body looked out of place in a suit somehow.

"So we can blend in with the others of the conference and in the hotel."

"Oh, and I suppose the CIA or the FBI or whoever of our guys will do the same."

"Of course."

"How exciting. Imagine the intrigue. All you guys skulking around, peering into everyone's eyes, and speaking mysteriously into your communicators." She threw him a look with shoulders hunched, mimicking her words.

David laughed. "Well I don't know that it's as melodramatic as *that*. But it is serious business." His jaw tightened grimly and his eyes darkened. "We have suffered too many losses at the hands of the terrorists to take any chances. Even some of our own people are against this conference. The settlers in East Jerusalem protest more and more. Settlements were the policy of a former Likud administration, and now that Labor is back in power the settlements are afraid of this conference."

Frowning and serious again Rachel asked, "But they wouldn't come against their fellow Jews, would they?"

David tightened. "I don't know. They are getting desperate. The disengagement was a heart-wrenching episode for those who had invested so much in the Gaza settlements—all those greenhouses. Now it's those in East Jerusalem who are upset. I have often wondered what I would do if I had to confront them in my job. Not everyone in Israel wants this peace, you know. That's the reason we have such tight security both at the hotel and the office."

"Well, tomorrow is the big day," said Rachel, turning the conversation back to the conference.

"Oh, not much will happen tomorrow. It will be mostly speeches given by all the dignitaries stating their positions. The next day they will 'get down to brass tacks,' as you Americans say."

"I've been thinking about what you said going to the office. Where did you get your information? About the ark, I mean?"

"Different places—most archaeologists have some theory or other about it, and I have talked to a lot of them."

"Yes, but you talked of the possibility of it being taken to Ethiopia by priests. Where did you get that?"

"From one of the Ethiopian rabbis. He told me about an American journalist who talked to him when he was researching for a book. The American did an interesting investigation. I got the book and read it. He wrote it as investigative journalism rather than scientific research. It touched off a debate in the archaeological community. You see, as I said before, a lot of the Israeli rabbis believe the ark is buried under the Temple Mount. All kinds of legends exist. The book I mentioned is an American publication. Perhaps we could pick up one at a book store if you are interested."

"Am I," said Rachel enthusiastically. "Let's see, where is the nearest bookstore. Oh yes, there's a Barnes and Noble not far from your hotel. We could stop when I take you back." She slowed down and turned into the back parking lot at the State Department.

Since it was a rather cool day, Rachel opted to wait in the reception room rather than stay in the car while David met with the US team. They walked around to the front where security men met them at the door. David was expected and so was ushered down the hall.

Rachel made herself comfortable on a couch. She picked up a magazine, but she couldn't read. Her mind was too full of the recent conversations. David was certainly an attractive man, especially those soft eyes, but Rachel had dealt with too many good-looking faces to be impressed by that. She was more impressed by his interests and his obvious compassion for his people. How easy it had been to talk to him. *I hope I am going to see a lot of him this week,* she thought. She went back over every word that had been spoken between them.

Perhaps if she got that book she would understand his passion for the ark. She had never given that much thought before. The Lubavitch sect concentrated on joyful praise of their God and righteous living—"being good and doing good" to bring on the redemption era when their Messiah would set the world aright.

She knew of groups in the land that longed for the Temple Mount and tried to access it, causing a great uproar among the Arabs. But she had always thought they were just like Abraham, trying to bring God's promise to pass by human intervention. Some of the Hasidim believed the Moschiach himself would build the temple. It was all so confusing. An hour passed quickly as she thought on all these things.

David suddenly walked in and said smiling, "Let's go somewhere and get some lunch, okay?"

"Why not?" She returned the smile, delighted with the suggestion. "There's a nice little restaurant close to the bookstore, and we can look for that book too."

"You really are interested, aren't you?" commented David as they reached the car and he opened the door for her. Finally he had found a woman who was interested in more than clothes and trinkets. Deidrienne, for instance, cared nothing about the conference, only the chance to see America.

Rachel slipped into the front seat and switched on the ignition.

"Yes, I want to know all about everything that has to do with the *Moschiach*."

"Are you familiar with what the prophets say?"

She pulled into traffic. "About the *Moschiach* or his kingdom?"

"Both."

"Well, I only know what our rebbes have taught us. Papa taught me Torah. I haven't studied the prophets myself."

"You should. How else are you going to recognize the Messiah?" He paused a moment before he charged ahead with his own personal convictions. "I believe we have allowed our traditions to stifle us by following too closely to the rabbis."

"But they study all the time," she protested.

"And they can't agree," he came right back. "There can only be one truth, right?"

"I never really thought about that," she replied thoughtfully as she stopped for a red light.

"That's why every man should study the Scriptures for himself so he can evaluate what others teach. My father is a great believer in each person discovering the truth for himself, with foundational guidance, of course. That way you don't get led astray by strange teachings."

"But shouldn't the rebbes be right?"

"Not necessarily. We have rabbis in all different kinds of movements. For instance, Arafat appointed Rabbi Moshe Hirsh to be his advisor on Jewish affairs because he was active in promoting peace with the Arabs. Actually, he's a radical anti-Zionist who believes Jews shouldn't have anything to do with the government until the Messiah comes and sets up his kingdom. Some of that crowd even participated in Amadiajad's Anti-Holocaust Conference. On the other hand, Rabbi Meshi-Zehav excommunicated Hirsh from most of the synagogues in Jerusalem because of his political leanings. So you see, there are rabbis and there are rabbis," explained David. "Politics often generate doctrine and vice versa."

"I guess I've never been exposed to any other rebbes besides our own," said Rachel, realizing David knew more about these things than she did. "Have you studied the prophets for yourself then?" she asked.

"Oh yes, especially when I was involved with the digs. You can read Hebrew, can't you? I know you understand it."

"How do you know that?" she said, surprised.

"Because you understood the secretaries last night."

"You are very observant."

"It's my job, remember?"

"Of course. I should have realized. To answer your question, yes, I read Hebrew and Arabic and speak them both too. My papa insisted. He said if I really wanted to be involved with the politics of Israel, I needed to know the languages."

It was David's turn to be impressed. She was not only intelligent but extremely dedicated to prepare herself completely.

After they arrived at the bookstore and went in, David went straight to the clerk at the counter and asked, "Do you have *The Sign and the Seal,* by Graham Hancock?"

"I'll be glad to check," the clerk replied and turned to the microfiche viewer. "It's in religion. The books are placed by author alphabetically."

"Thank you," said David, and they went to find the religion section.

Rachel found the book and drew it from the shelf. "Not exactly a little book," she commented. "Over five hundred pages, and just look at the notes at the back."

"Sure you want to read it now that you have seen it?"

"Are you kidding? I was a political science major; big books don't scare me. Besides, what does it matter how big a book is if it is something you want to know?"

When they approached the counter, David removed his billfold and said, "This is my gift to you." Rachel protested, but David won out. After paying for the book with his credit card, he said, "Now, how about that lunch?"

"Do you like Thai cuisine?" Rachel asked as they pulled out into traffic.

"I don't know. Never had any."

"Actually it's a Siamese restaurant, but they specialize in Thai. Some of it's hot. Game?"

"Sure, why not."

―

Busara's was crowded even though it was after one o'clock. They were seated at one of the small round tables near the rear.

As soon as the waitress left, Rachel started in on David again with her questions. She was insatiable. David had opened up a new avenue for her thinking, so as always she pursued her subject of the moment to the limit of her resources. She wanted to find out all she could from David before the week was over. "You said I should study the prophets, but there are so many. Where should I start?"

"Start with *Yesha'yahu* (Isaiah) and read to the end. As you read, mark the passages or maybe make a list of the passages that you think have to do with the *Moschiach* or his kingdom. If you don't mark them in some way, you won't be able to find them again. After reading so far, you will find that different prophets will often speak about the same event. By putting them together, you begin to see what God has predicted about the *Moschiach*," explained David. "At least that's how I study."

"That almost sounds like taking notes for a college term paper."

"Well, I wouldn't know about that. I never went to college. My father, being who he was, kept me in school all my life. So when I went into the military to serve my two years, I liked it so much that I made a career out of it. The only studying I ever did was to get into intelligence."

"But you haven't stopped studying the Tanakh have you?" she asked with concern.

"Tanakh? I thought you read Hebrew."

"Oh, of course, you would read the Scriptures in Hebrew. I usually read the English version. That's what we use at the synagogue."

"To answer your question, no I haven't stopped studying, but it is easier to be objective about what I read outside the school atmosphere. Besides, being in the military keeps me abreast of what's happening politically. Like you, I want to be where the action is."

She smiled brightly. She noticed a soft look in his eye—an admiration. His response thrilled her. *They truly were kindred spirits.*

Taking note that something had passed between them and feeling awkward, she suddenly quipped teasingly, "After I get my notes together and formulate a thesis, shall I present it to you as my professor for a grade?"

David blinked at her sudden change.

"But seriously," she continued, the teasing eyes gone, "I don't know anyone I could discuss this with, except maybe my father. Although he's as anxious for the *Moschiach* to come as I am, we both learned all we know from the rebbes and their writings. So I don't think he knows much more about the prophecies than I do. That is not a very big subject at the synagogue."

Both lapsed into silence as they thought about it.

"*I know*," said David, brightening with inspiration, "You could send it to me in Israel. Then I could reply, and we could challenge each other to more study." *What a stroke of genius,* he thought. Now that he had finally met someone with a brain, he didn't want to lose contact. Especially since that brain was encased in such a lovely package. For the first time in ages he felt himself being physically aroused. David marveled at his reaction. *Could she be for me? With her frequent trips to Israel, our relationship does have a chance, doesn't it? That is if correspondence keeps it alive.*

Rachel accepted the proposal readily. Their food came, and they spent the rest of the luncheon in light conversation concerning its merits. Then Rachel dropped him at the hotel that was nearby.

Chapter 15

The historic conference was set to begin at 1:00 p.m. in the Loy Henderson Auditorium in the State Department building. Being more appropriate to their number than the larger Dean Acheson Auditorium next door, it also had an attached lounge that made it more comfortable for the delegates.

Soft light shone down the cream-colored walls, illuminating several choice photographs of Washington. Continuous mahogany tables were set in the shape of a rectangle. Chairs ringed the outside perimeter so that all the delegates could face one another. Recessed ceiling spots focused on the tables below made up for the subdued light from high windows on one wall, which came from an atrium. Large cushioned armchairs and microphones in front also marked each place at the table. A portable speaker's rostrum occupied the center of one of the shorter end tables near the door. Here the speeches would be delivered.

The head table, the one with the speaker's rostrum, was designated to the US delegation, the host of the conference. Here the president and the State department officials would sit, posturing a neutral stance. The table to the right belonged to the Israeli delegation, which faced the table to the left designated to the Palestinians. The remaining table, opposite the head table, was for the religious representatives. It was an intimate arrangement, set up to encourage communication.

State security men were stationed at every approach to the conference room. All security stations, as well as the conference room itself, were visibly monitored on closed circuit TV (without audio) from the State Department's security room. All phones open to the security teams were in that room, as well as the tape machines for recording the speakers also handled by the State Department.

David, Laundau, and two others took a cab to the State Department early that morning to a briefing of all the conference security teams. At 12:30 the delegations began to arrive. David stationed the two conference men at assigned points and went to the security room where he would periodically remove copies of the tapes for transport.

—

George Seabright, the assistant director at the Smithsonian's Central Bureau for Astronomical Telegrams, picked up the phone and said, "Hello."

"Yes, this is George Allen with Pacific Observatories. I'd like to report the sighting of a collision in our solar system," replied an excited voice.

"Within our solar system?" the director repeated in a serious voice. He knew the scientific community was aware of possible asteroid collisions with the earth, having found more and more evidence on the earth of what they assumed were ancient impacts. It had once been an assignment to hunt for "near-Earth objects" until it was canceled for lack of funds. "What and where?"

"Well, it must be two uncharted asteroids. I can't identify them because nothing is supposed to be there. We were looking for comets in sector 314 when we caught it. But we are only amateurs. You better get some expert to check it out."

Seabright didn't discount the source. Had not the Shoemaker/Levy comet been sighted by amateurs?

"We'll check it out," he said as he recorded the information.

After hanging up, the amateur comet and asteroid hunter called a colleague in Kitt Peak, Arizona, who had a thirty-six inch telescope.

"Jim, this is George Allen. I've got something for you."

"Okay, shoot, what have you got?"

"Well it looks like a good size asteroid collided with something."

"Are you serious?"

"I'm afraid so."

"Awe, George, how could the big scopes have missed something like that?"

"Maybe because it's approaching straight on. I don't know. We saw it by accident ourselves. We were shooting for deeper space when this showed up, blurring our image."

"How do you know it's big?"

"Have to be for us to even catch it."

"Did it disintegrate?"

"Don't know."

"We could be in trouble if some of the fragments head toward us. I'll check it out and call you back tomorrow."

The reported find having been put on the circuit, the Hubble space telescope took up the search. It didn't have to wait for night to probe the heavens. Ever since the collision of the Shoemaker-Levy 9 comet with Jupiter, the astronomical community had been highly aware of Earth's vulnerability to collisions. Now such a report was taken seriously. In fact, the House Committee on Science, Space, and Technology had prepared legislation to authorize NASA to catalog all asteroids and comets over a kilometer in diameter that cross the earth's orbit. But somehow it lost its preeminence to the search for other planetary systems deep in space.

At the report the full team was called in to evaluate the data at the Johnson Space Center in Houston. Several rows of computers filled the room, along with various other machines for tracking. The chairs at the consoles filled up as the operators responded to the summons.

"Oh my God," said the one at the controls when the telescope zeroed in on the sector reported. "Look at the size of that! It must be one of the larger asteroids. I wonder if it is Eros. It looks about that size."

"There's no way to tell since ninety percent of the asteroids out there are unidentified," remarked another as they gazed at the large screen at the front of the room. "Yeah, but how could one that large not be charted?"

The others gasped in shock as they noted its heading. "I think it's headed toward us," voiced one of the viewers after making some rough calculations.

The team went into action immediately, calculating speed and direction, estimating mass, and determining what impact it would have on the earth if any. "It's going to come close. Not only that, but the fragments from the other body are out there too. No telling where they might end up."

After checking and rechecking their data they called Dr. Harris, the director of NASA, to come to the center. Dr. Davies, the chief astronomer over the Hubble, gave the report to him.

"Sir, it looks like a large asteroid is going to cross Earth's orbit close in, but at an oblique angle. We don't think it will collide, but we could get ourselves another moon if the earth's gravitational field captures it. Also, it looks like a lot of space debris from the collision trails in its wake. The dust may block out the sun for a few days. Could set off earthquakes even. Though it's small compared to Earth, if it comes really close it could still affect us," reported Davies. Others added more detail.

THE BEGINNING OF THE END

Dr. Harris listened carefully, nodding gravely when they finished. Then he asked, "When?"

"Couldn't be more than a day or two judging from the position of the collision."

"I better inform the National Security Office—no, I think we need to go directly to the president. It's too close. This will cause a major panic, and he will need all the time we can give him." He turned to Herman Barnes, one of the engineers, and said, "Will you call the president for me?"

Barnes dialed the White House. The switchboard put him through to the president's personal secretary.

"Barnes of NASA calling. We need to speak to the president. It's of the utmost importance."

"I'm sorry, the president has gone to the Middle East Conference on Jerusalem. He's unavailable."

"Can't you get in touch with him there?" asked Davies.

"Technically, yes, but he specifically said he's not to be disturbed. This is a very important meeting," she said, wielding her secretarial power to protect her boss.

Davies turned to Dr. Harris and said, "She says he can't be reached. He's at the Middle East Conference."

Dr. Harris let out a string of swear words then added, "Give me that phone! Young lady, this is Dr. Harris, head of NASA. We have a national emergency. Hell, it's a world emergency. You get hold of the president *right now* and have him call me at the Johnson Space Center. Do you understand?"

"Yes, sir," she answered timidly. After looking up the number she called the State Department and reached the receptionist.

"This is the president's secretary. I need to get a message to the president."

"You know I can't interrupt the meeting in progress," replied the receptionist.

"Sorry, but I've been told there is some national emergency. Have him call Houston at this number." After dictating the number, she hung up.

The receptionist called the security room.

"Someone needs to call the president out of the meeting and have him call NASA. They say there's a national emergency."

"Okay, will do," replied the state's security officer. He called Peters, one of the secret service agents, on his communicator and repeated the message.

Peters slipped into the conference room where the president had just finished giving the opening speech. After the applause died out and the president had seated himself again, Peters leaned over the President's shoulder and whispered in his ear.

—

The president hurried out into the hall and followed Peters to the security room where he picked up the phone and dialed.

Dr. Harris jumped to the phone as soon as it rang.

"Hello, Mr. President?" he asked.

"Yes, who is this? And what is so important as to disturb this meeting?" said the president, his irritation coming through loud and clear to all within hearing distance.

"This is Dr. Harris of NASA, sir. We have a disaster in the making that will literally shake the earth. Two nights ago one of our amateur comet hunters discovered that an asteroid had collided with something else out there. Now it's headed toward Earth."

"No," said the president in pure disbelief. "How could this have gone undetected until now?" He felt his face drain of color as he suddenly realized the magnitude of the disaster suggested.

"It was too close in. Everybody has been looking into deep space lately."

"What exactly will it do to the earth? Will it hit us?"

"We're not sure. We don't think it will collide, but it's big, larger than any of the fragments of Shoemaker-Levy 9. Also, it is carrying a large dust cloud behind. Coming in between the earth and the sun it will shut off sunlight for several days. Maybe even cause a few earthquakes."

Horror registered on his now whitened face as he thought of what an extended night would mean in crime. *Besides that, every bit of operating light would have to be generated. That would put a strain on resources...and the economy. The earth would cool. What else?*

"Gather together a team of astronomers and physicists that you think could help evaluate this problem, and bring them together for a video/phone conference, along with all the information you have. Is 7:00 tonight enough time to get it together?"

"We'll make it enough time."

"How much time do we have?"

"Between twenty-four and forty-eight hours, the crew is figuring it right now."

"Not much time to prepare," said the president, frowning, "Who else knows about this?"

"It was put on the Smithsonian Telegraph system. Astronomers have access to it all over the world," said Dr. Harris.

"So all governments will be alerted?"

"Probably."

"I hope none of them are foolish enough to leak this to the press. We can't afford to have a panic on our hands before we're ready. Let's get on this. I'll see you at seven."

The president hung up and dialed the Pentagon. "This is the President. Get me Dan Jordan right away." While he waited he turned to Peters and said, "Alert my driver and have my car waiting in the underground garage."

A voice came on the line. "You wanted to speak to me, Mr. President?"

"Yes, Dan," he said turning back to the phone. "Call a meeting of the Joint Chiefs of Staff. Tell them to be at the White House tonight at 7:00 p.m."

"What's going on?" he asked, shocked at the urgency in the president's voice.

"We are fixing to have a world disaster. That's all you need to know right now."

"Yes, sir, we'll see you at 7:00."

David, along with the rest of the state's men, listened in shocked silence. Finally, one of the state's security team asked the President, "Sir, what kind of disaster are we facing?"

"Astronomical."

"Like the comet hitting Jupiter?"

"Yes, but this time it's not a comet but an asteroid, and we hope it will pass on by Earth, but we may have to deal with a dust cloud. And I don't have to tell you to keep this thing quiet. Right?"

Peters came back to announce that the car was ready.

Chapter 16

Inside the conference room the speeches droned on. Both Israel and the Palestinians presented their same demands even though they expressed optimism toward a peaceable settlement between them. Everyone knew they were just establishing a base from which to negotiate.

After all the scheduled speeches, the pope gave encouraging words and pronounced a blessing. The secretary of state, who was the MC in the president's absence, casually asked if there was anyone else who wanted to say anything before they adjourned the meeting. He didn't really expect a response, but to his surprise J. Leucus Adoni´ rose to his feet.

"Gentlemen, I have listened to both sides of this issue, and I can't see where either party is willing to change. Changes have to be made if the problem is to be solved." He paused. "May I make a suggestion?" He looked around the tables to see the reaction of the delegates. Seeing some affirmative nods, he proceeded.

"Gentlemen, I suggest that you opposing delegations meet tomorrow morning among yourselves and decide what you are willing to negotiate and what you are not willing to give up. Make lists in order of importance, and come back to the conference tomorrow afternoon prepared to give and take. Both parties must be willing to give up something in order to get something else. This is basic diplomacy. We will strike an agreement somewhere in the middle, no?" Then he sat down.

Haik Ra'amon leaned over to Kutter, one of the Labor MKs, and asked, "Who is that man? I thought he was one of the Arab delegation, but he talks like he's neutral." *And he talks with such self assurance, commanding attention,* he thought.

Kutter replied, "I think that is J. Leucus Adoni´, you know, the one who came up with the solution to the Palestinian refugee problem."

"Oh," he replied thoughtfully. "That must be why they brought him here. I wish we had him on our side."

The secretary of state tapped on the table to quiet the murmuring passing through the delegates. "What do you think of this suggestion?"

—

Jerry, the American secretary to the pope, worried about the Holy Father. Pope Peter had seemed disappointed with the afternoon's offering. He had watched him squeezing his hands in frustration until they were nearly bloodless. He recognized that as a signal of distress The pope leaned toward his microphone.

"I think it's an excellent idea, but the Israelis and Palestinians are the ones to decide."

Jerry breathed easier now that the pope's attitude had abruptly changed and his hands relaxed.

The secretary of state turned to Prime Minister Ra'amon first and said, "We are scheduled to meet in the morning, but if you want to meet among yourselves we can be flexible."

Haik replied, "Of course we are willing to give and take. After all, that is what negotiating is about. But as to a specific list—we haven't exactly made one along those lines."

Nabil Dakkah broke in. "We are willing to try this if the Israelis will."

Haik Ra'amon nodded his agreement, adding, "We don't need to take up valuable conference time. We could make our list tonight at the hotel."

Nabil Dakkah agreed.

The pope turned to his delegation and whispered loudly, "Gentlemen, we also will meet tonight to pray for the delegations."

The secretary of state set the time for reconvening the following morning at 9:00 and adjourned the meeting.

J. Quentin Rice, who had been sitting at the head table, frowned his disapproval at the president's empty seat then muttered to himself aloud, "How could he leave such an important meeting? I can't imagine anything more essential than settling the Jerusalem problem."

Chapter 17

Rachel passed the president's car when she approached the state department building shortly after 1:30. Later she and Hillman delivered the first three speeches to the secretaries. Hillman told her then that David was tied up in other business. She had been disappointed because she had started reading the book he'd bought her and wanted to discuss it with him. Maybe when the conference broke up he would accompany her with the rest of the tapes, at least she hoped. She sighed as she sat in the lobby waiting and watching, where she had been most of the afternoon. She was glad she had the book to pass the empty hours.

The president picked up the direct line to his national security officer in the west corner of the White House. Jack Trent answered on the first ring.

"Yes, sir."

"Come to the office, Jack, we need to talk."

"Right away, sir," he replied. He immediately jumped to the conclusion that a crisis had arisen at the conference. He nodded to Peters standing guard outside the Oval Office.

"Has Israel stalked out of the conference or something?" he asked, knowing that the secret service men saw and heard every-

THE BEGINNING OF THE END

thing that went on. Peters shook his head and gravely added, "Worse then that."

Jack whistled. *What could be worse than that?* he thought as he opened the door.

"Sit down, Jack, I want you to help me think. I got an emergency call from NASA. The Hubble has spotted an asteroid collision that will have repercussions for us on Earth. The collision sent an asteroid of considerable size on a new course headed toward us. They don't expect it to collide, but we can expect some dire side effects from a close call."

"Like what?" asked Jack, astonished; his line of thought was on political problems not a natural disaster. *Besides, he was not studied in cosmology. How could he help the president think?*

"Earthquakes, maybe a blackout of the sun for some time due to a huge dust cloud in space."

Jack breathed out a swear word. *No wonder Peters thought it was worse. It was not a political crisis at all.* Extended darkness could be a thousand times more destructive. His mind raced over some of the more evident effects of such a situation.

The president continued. "Even though this will affect the whole world, we have to treat it like a national security problem. Jack, what will happen if we have uninterrupted hours of darkness?"

Jack's thoughts escalated from one problem to another. After a few moments he spoke. "First, there's the usual problems we deal with on any night: crime, accidents, and such. Of course all light would have to be artificial. If the power drain gets too high there could be brown outs. Could bring all normal activity to a screeching halt. We would definitely have to shut down all unnecessary power use.

"Grocery stores would empty in the first few hours like they do before winter storms. Could be nasty if people panic. We might have riots. Looters could become a major problem if the darkness lasts longer than a day or two.

"Manufacturing plants might have to shut down unless they have their own power plants. We could expect an increase in traffic accidents—due to fatigue since regular timing for sleep would become irregular. Mental depression could set in generally due to lack of light."

Mentioning the light gave new direction to his thoughts as he continued. "Plants would probably lose their leaves. The grass would die. That would be a big problem for farmers. It could even get cold unless the earth heats up from internal friction. That's what I can think of right off the top of my head."

"What if we add several earthquakes?" asked the president.

"Well, sir, that might ignite gas line fires—and fill the local hospitals and morgues with people," he added. "It could be as bad as a war."

"That brings up another question," said the president. "Would aggressive nations take advantage of the situation to expand their territories?"

"Sir, if all this starts happening to us, I don't see how we could worry about the rest of the world. Our early warning systems should still pick up on any missile launches to us."

"Would they? Harris told me that there's a lot of debris associated with the asteroid because of the collision. Could they even tell the difference if meteorites begin falling?"

"I don't know. What can we do about any of this?" he said, dropping his arms to his sides and looking dejected. Jack was woefully aware that such a disaster was well beyond their ability to cope.

"I don't know either," replied the president. "But I've called a meeting of the Joint Chiefs of Staff and top scientists for tonight at 7:00 p.m."

"Can you think of anyone else who needs to be in on it?"

"What about treasury? Financial transactions could be in a mess if the computers of the world start going down."

"Good idea, Jack, I didn't think of that." He picked up the phone. "Get me the secretary of treasury, Ginny," he said to his secretary.

He turned back to Jack and said, "I need you to make a list of what we've been discussing, and anything else you can come up with. It will start the others thinking. And Jack," he added as Jack started out the door, "see if you can organize this meeting to expedite time. I don't want to get into useless discussions."

After he talked to Alec Johnston, the secretary of treasury, the president called Peters and told him to add Alec's name to those expected at the meeting.

Chapter 18

The Joint Chiefs arrived first, a little early. They were directed to a conference room. Like Trent, they assumed the meeting had something to do with the conference. But when they saw a TV monitor with scientists sitting around a table in view, they were puzzled.

At 7:05 the president spoke to Dr. Harris as the camera singled him out and asked, "Are all the scientists there that you called?"

"Yes, sir."

"Okay, Jack, take over."

Jack said, "Dr. Harris, will you brief the rest of us with what facts you have?"

"Certainly," he replied with aplomb then glanced at a paper he held. "Gentlemen, earlier today it came to our attention that we have a maverick asteroid headed close to our place in space. An amateur comet hunter spotted it on a photograph taken three nights ago."

"Three nights ago?" exclaimed the president. "Why are we just now hearing about it?"

"Because, Mr. President, the first night it only turned up as blur on their film, because they were shooting for deeper space. They had to wait another night to focus on that area."

"We trained the Hubble Telescope on it as soon as we heard, and the data we received indicates that an asteroid roughly twice the size of Phobos, or twenty miles across, has been thrown off course by a collision. Possibly more than one, but one that we know of. It now heads on a course between ten thousand to twelve thousand miles from Earth. Coming that close the earth will feel its force, might even capture it, giving us another moon. More than likely the speed generated by the collision will send it on past. But that's not all; it's carrying a lot of space debris from the collision in its wake. That could mean a blackout of the sun for days. We could have some abnormally high tides and maybe some earthquakes. The collision also sent pieces in all directions, so we could have sizable meteorites hit the earth. That's about all we know at the moment, but we have the whole astronomical community monitoring it minute by minute," Harris finished.

"Thank you, Dr. Harris," said the national security officer.

"Gentlemen, the president and I came up with these likely problems." He proceeded to list them. "Now, I'd like to hear first from you scientists concerning what we may have missed. Then we will all discuss with you Chiefs of Staff how to solve the problems of disorder the crisis will generate."

Resting her eyes for a moment, Rachel glanced out the window. Outside the building she could see several groups protesting the conference across the street. State security men lined this side of the street, trying to confine them to the opposite sidewalk. Signs reading "Jerusalem Belongs to Israel" and "Jerusalem, the Capitol of Palestine" projected above opposing sides. The press clogged C Street, waiting like vultures to pounce on the tired delegates. Because of the confusion outside the front entrance, the delegations were instructed to leave via the underground exit.

Haik Ra'amon was tired and disgusted with the conference thus far.

Nothing is really changing. His thoughts were interrupted by a hand on his should. David took him aside to speak to him privately.

"Sir, we have a natural disaster about to envelop the earth. The president has been informed—"

"What kind of a disaster? And how do *you* know?" interrupted the prime minister in an irritated voice. *Captain Solomon is military. How dare he compare the conference to a natural disaster? Is his religious nature trying to influence the outcome? Knowing his background, I should have insisted on Johnny leading this mission.*

David flinched, obviously stung by the slur. "Some kind of astronomical disturbance sent an asteroid off course. Apparently it's headed toward Earth. I just happened to overhear the US President when they told him in the security room."

"Astronomical..." repeated Ra'amon in stunned surprise because of his train of thought.

"Yes, do you want me to contact Jerusalem?"

"What do they expect to happen?"

"I don't know anything else about that, but the president called a meeting of his Chiefs of Staff," David replied lamely.

"Sure, by all means, contact the Ministry of Defense and let them get in touch with our scientists," said Ra'amon. He frowned. *Why should some heavenly phenomenon concern me? Nothing is as important as this conference. Surely it is overblown. At least I won't worry until I hear something official.*

After David spoke with Ra'amon he turned and spoke to two of his men, telling them all he knew. Then he said, "When you two go back to the hotel, inform the others about the disaster. I will try to pick up some survival supplies."

Ra'amon didn't seem to grasp the seriousness of the situation, so David decided to take matters into his own hands. After all, his job was security, even if the threat was not terrorists.

"Is Ms. Lieberman still around?" he asked Hillman.

"She is in the main lobby," he said. "She doesn't have clearance for this hall."

Chapter 19

David went to the lobby. He had been busy most of the day with the other security teams planning for the emergency that only they knew was coming. He was tired and worried, but the thought of seeing Rachel bolstered him up some. When he entered the lobby he saw her reading the book he had given her.

She looked up. Their eyes locked, drawn together like the force of a magnet. She smiled and jumped up, saying, "Do you need your chauffeur?"

"Y-es," he almost sang.

In foolishness and temporarily out of character, Rachel made a low, impulsive bow, swinging her arms behind her spread eagle. "Your wish is my command, mine Saab."

David laughed out loud, saving her embarrassment. He needed that. The laughter medicated his soul, and Rachel's smile was more than medicine. It was pure delight.

She picked up her book and her purse to leave.

"Well, did you hear anything from the meeting this afternoon?" Rachel asked as they hurried down the hall toward the rear of the building. I could use some news. Man, what a boring day."

"Only that the delegates will meet separately to make some sort of list," he said, looking away in a distant stare.

Rachel noticed his distraction. "The president sure didn't stick

THE BEGINNING OF THE END

around long. I saw him leave as I came in," she probed, knowing there must be a reason.

"Yes," said David, now gravely serious. The nagging gloom was back.

Rachel, keenly aware of the silence, glanced sideways at his face. Suddenly she stopped. Taking David's arm she turned him around to face her.

"You know something, don't you? What has happened?"

David was caught by surprise. How could she even suspect there was trouble? "It has nothing to do with the conference."

"But you're worried aren't you? I can tell," she persisted.

"How can you tell? You hardly know me," he said, his mouth twitching at the corners. He studied her earnest face and felt a tugging at his heart, touched by the personal connotation.

Suddenly she turned serious. "I can just feel it. I'm picking up your vibes," she spoke so softly it was a near whisper.

By this time they had reached the exit.

"Let's get to the car where we can talk," David said. He needed time. *What shall I tell her?* Such a curious woman would be difficult to pacify, especially one as intelligent as she was. Yet he didn't think she would panic at the truth or spread it around carelessly. He knew the reason the president asked for their silence was to prevent panic. If he didn't tell her she might be caught unprepared, and somehow he felt compelled to protect her. *David, you're getting involved,* he warned, *watch yourself!*

Traffic was zipping along near the side of the building when they reached her reserved parking place. After they were settled inside, Rachel insisted, "Okay, now we are in the car. Let's have it. Traffic is picking up, so we will probably crawl anyway. You will have plenty of time."

David sighed. "I've been debating what to tell you."

"Why? Does it involve national security?"

"Not exactly, but if it leaked to the public it could cause a panic."

"A panic," Rachel repeated, wondering what could cause a panic that was unrelated to national security. A natural disaster wouldn't cause a panic. The weather people announced hurricanes and tornadoes all the time, and it didn't usually cause panics when they were aware.

"Has there been an accident at one of the nuclear plants?" she finally said.

"Good guess, but it could be worse than even that."

"Well, are you going to tell me or let me die of curiosity?" she burst out, exasperated.

"Okay, okay, a large asteroid is going to graze the earth in a day or two."

"Oh, come on, David. Don't joke with me. I'm completely serious."

"It's no joke," he said gravely. "That's why the president left so early."

"You think a little fireworks in the sky will cause a panic?" she asked.

"It's more than fireworks, Rachel. Like most people you are unaware of the physical damage likely in such an encounter. If it collides, it could destroy the earth. Just coming close might cause earthquakes. Or the dust could block out the sun."

"Oh," she exclaimed. "But how can it be? I thought they tracked those bodies out in space. Besides, why haven't we heard about it until now?"

"I guess they just found out. That's the same question your president asked."

"I don't understand. How can you know what our president knows?"

THE BEGINNING OF THE END

"Not you too! That's the second time I have been berated for knowing what your president knows."

"Sorry, it's just—"

"Your president got a call in the security room," interrupted David. "We all heard his end of the conversation. He called a meeting for some scientists and the Joints Chiefs of Staff for tonight."

"What's supposed to happen to the earth then? And when?" she asked.

"Again the question the president asked. I don't know. That's what they are going to discuss at the meeting. How about you? How are you fixed for an emergency? Do you have adequate food to last for a week or two? The grocery stores are bound to be stripped as soon as the public finds out. What about flashlights and batteries or candles and lanterns?"

"No, I'm afraid I'm not prepared at all."

"Where do you live, with your father?"

"No, I have my own apartment."

"It might not be a bad idea to move home for the duration," David said, his tone deadly serious. "One thing the security group at the conference seemed to agree upon was that the clouds from the collision would darken the earth. Without sunlight for several days, it could get a little chilly if it lasts very long. What kind of heat do you have?"

"Gas."

"That will probably be okay unless we have earthquakes too."

Rachel drove on in silence, thinking. *I probably should go to Papa's,* she thought. She'd have company if she went home, since Dan, her brother, and his wife, Sheila, had moved back into the house with her father after her mother died. At least her family would all be together.

After a long silence, each engrossed in his and her own thoughts,

Rachel said, "But what about you? What will you do? And the delegation?"

"I'm sure the hotel has its own emergency power generator, and I hope a good store of food. If not, we might all end up cutting back on our eating."

Finally they reached the office, and Rachel parked the car. David picked up the final tape of the day.

"I'm going to have to get emergency supplies for the delegation. If you like I will help you pick up some for yourself too. That is if you will chauffeur me around. I could take a cab back to the hotel after I get you settled."

"I wouldn't let you do that."

"But I would insist; it might get late before we finish."

As they arrived on the fifth floor and entered the reception room, David handed Rachel the tape and asked her to take it to the secretaries. He wanted to talk to Feldman.

After she left the room, Feldman smiled, "Enjoying your job?"

David remained silent. Feldman noticed the sober face and forgot his tease.

"What's up, Captain?"

David told him what had happened, and they discussed what they needed to do for the delegation.

Rachel walked into the secretaries' office and handed the tape to Deidrienne, who looked at her first with surprise and then disdain.

"Have you taken over David's job," she said sourly, looking past Rachel's shoulder and trying to get catch a glimpse of David.

"No, just David," Rachel quipped and abruptly left the room, smiling with satisfaction at the look of fury on Diedrienne's face. Rachel couldn't resist tormenting such blatant possessiveness.

"Ms. Lieberman," David said when Rachel came back into the reception room, "Katz and Bader will be spending the night here. How can we arrange meals?"

"We could order in pizza for them."

"Could you do that for me?"

"Sure." Rachel turned to Katz and Bader and asked what they wanted.

David turned back to Feldman and said, "I will get Ms. Lieberman to take me to get the supplies. She will know where to go. I'll get back with you as soon as possible, and we will plan for the emergency as much as we can. But first I need to fax IDF's headquarters in Israel."

When David entered the secretaries' office, Deidrienne smiled, threw her arms around his neck, and cooed, "Are you through for the day so you can go back to the hotel with us? I have hardly seen you since we got here."

He gently untangled her arms and fed a short paragraph he had just drafted to the fax machine then said, "Sorry, Deid, I literally have miles to go before I'll be ready to return to the hotel tonight. Trouble is brewing, and your gallant security officer has many things to see to." He smiled at her as he left the room.

"*My* gallant security officer? Then why is he hanging around with that black-haired American witch?"

Merrill's lips twitched.

"Don't you say one word," Deidrienne said, her eyes flashing a jealous green.

David was relieved to have the fax on its way. He couldn't rely on the US Government for his information. David's fax informed Israel's Defense Force of the disaster and advised them to check with the scientists. The scientists would already be picking up the latest information on the Internet from telescopes around the world. He requested they send a report back and keep the delegation informed. Someone had to be at the offices twenty-four hours a day anyway for security reasons. If anything important came in they could notify him.

Rachel finished the phone orders. Presently David appeared and said, "Let's go shopping."

Deidrienne watched them leave, crest fallen. "Rachel was right," she murmured to herself. "She *has* taken over David, for now, but when I get him home…"

Chapter 20

Haik Ra'amon gathered his delegation together after dinner in his sumptuous suite decorated in Louis XIV style. The room was crowded, and many were forced to sit on the floor, but it posed little discomfort with the thick carpet. Ra'amon opened the meeting.

"Gentlemen, we have a list to come up with," he said with impatience, not wanting to lose a minute.

"Well, I don't see how we can give up anything else," stated Hausan of the National Religious Party, jerking his head in rhythm with his words. "That's all we've done is give, give, give. They won't be happy until they have it all back and push us into the sea."

"And we can't just chop off East Jerusalem either," said Rabbi David Rosenfeld. "We'd lose the Wailing Wall again."

"What are the chances of ruling part of the city jointly?" asked the mayor of Jerusalem. "We could enforce it with a combination of Jews and Arabs."

"I don't know. The last attempt at joint management they ended up killing one another. Which part do you mean?" asked the prime minister.

"Well, I was thinking mainly of the Old City with its religious shrines."

"Might be a consideration if we could get something in return," said Ra'amon. "The Arabs hinted in the preliminary meetings that they might be willing to share the Old City."

"We could put that on our list as negotiable," suggested MK Plaut, one of the Meretz Party doves who was strictly secular. He wanted peace at any price. The Meretz Party thought the religious segment of Israel was a pain in the neck, always demanding a Biblical outcome to everything.

"As long as we do not lose our rights to the Wailing Wall," said the MK from the National Religious Party with a worried look on his face. "You in the Meretz Party must not negotiate away *all* our gains." Appearing to be deep in thought, he stroked his thick black beard.

"We will not give up our sovereign right to the rest of the city either," stormed Goren, the one Likud MK, his beady eyes flashing and competing with the shine from his bald head. "After all, the new settlers in East Jerusalem are still in the city itself."

"Perhaps we could redraw the municipal limits of the city," suggested the mayor weakly.

"No way! The Arabs are already yelling about the Arab settlements that were locked out in the last revision," cried Yudelman of Labor. "Another could really set them off." They had come so close when Peres was leading Labor. "We can't let the peace process fail now that we are back in power."

"Well, we can't let them push us back to the 1967 lines either," said Likud's MK in almost a growl.

"I thought most of this had been already worked out in preliminary committees," Plaut complained. "You sound like we are starting over."

"We are only trying to decide what is negotiable and what is not," said Ra'amon. Then he added thoughtfully, "I don't know if the people of Israel will stand for giving up complete sovereignty over any part of the city."

"Okay, then that is a *non-negotiable* on our list," said Kadima

Party MK Kauferman, a tall lanky man who was acting as recorder for their list.

"But the Arabs are going to demand a portion of the city to be the capital of Palestine. They have already issued business cards from the Orient House giving the address as Jerusalem, Palestine. There's no reason for them to come to the negotiating table if they can't have that. We will never have peace if we can't give them that," whined Ben-dor, the other Meretz MK.

"Couldn't their capital be part of the jointly governed part?" asked David Rosenfeld meekly.

"Yes," chimed Goren in agreement, "that's all we *can* give them—joint administration with their government buildings acting like an embassy in a foreign country. In other words, that's the only portion they could sovereignly control, while all property surrounding their compound would be jointly governed by a council and judicial system. We could even give that portion a new name. It would act as a neutral zone between us."

"It could be a big plus for us," added Kutter, the other Labor MK.

"How so?" asked Ra'amon.

"Because if their sovereign government were located in neutral territory we could keep a close eye on them. We could see who comes and goes. We could easily hold them hostage if the Arabs start misbehaving. It would give us some continuing muscle."

"Now I like that idea," said Goren. "What about giving them a plot for their government on one of the eastern mountains where their flag could be seen from the east. It would give them a close connection to their territory. Just make sure we could surround them if necessary."

They continued to fine tune the suggestion until they had an out and out proposal. They had their so called list.

Nabil Nakkah gathered the Arab delegation after dinner also. Iraq's new king, Hassayni, and King Hassih of Jordan were invited, as well as Leucus Adoni´. Nabil, anxious to hear what Adoni´ had in mind by suggesting that the delegations make lists, hurried everyone to their seats. Then to Adoni´ he said, "You must have some plan, otherwise you would not have suggested a list. What is it?"

"Yes, I've been studying the situation for weeks. As you know I am primarily a business man owning a large bank with many locations throughout the Middle East. It is greatly to my advantage to see peace in the region. Consequently, I have gathered my own intelligence on what the various peoples want. It is clear to me that neither side can have all it wants. The trick is to satisfy each side enough to calm our peoples. That is why I suggested a list. To help each side focus in on what they really want. If the people on both sides receive what is most important to them, we will finally achieve peace. And if I might add, I think we will have to start with religion because this is where the passions are. Once we have satisfied the extremists, the people will settle down, and then we can focus on the economy.

"I also know from my sources that the powerful rich who pull the strings of the Western governments are looking for a religious settlement. So we would gain their support," he said.

"Why do we need them?" asked one of Nabil's delegates.

"Because they can influence the American government and put pressure on Israel to accept our demands," replied Adoni´.

"How can we satisfy Israeli fundamentalists who insist on taking the Temple Mount? It seems every other day they keep trying to enter the mount to pray," queried Hassayni, the king of Iraq. His former country, Jordan, had been favored by the Israelis to hold the authority over the holy sites to the chagrin of the Palestinians, who eventually chipped away the Jordanian authority. They appointed a new Mufti over the mosques to represent them, without consulting Jordan, and had finally taken complete control. He feared that another compromise might put the authority over the sites back in the hands of the Israelis.

"You have a good question, my friend," said Nabil Dakkah. "Adoni´ has told us why we should make a compromise, but he hasn't told us what. Then turning to Adoni´ he asked, "What exactly *do you propose we offer?*"

The preliminary discussion was good, thought Adoni´. Perhaps now they were ready to listen to his shocking proposal. He began cautiously, "I've been following the Jews debate about their temple site. There are four conflicting views. One site lies between the Al Aska mosque and the Dome of the Rock, one on the site of the Dome of the Rock, one including part of the Dome of the Rock, and one beside the Dome of the Rock.

"A few years ago an Israeli Hebrew University professor, a physicist named Asher Kaufman, published a paper concerning the Jewish temple site based on twenty years of study, using archaeological remains and old aerial maps used by German reconnaissance during World War I. Pictures that show features no longer visible. He compared them with descriptions in the Talmud and other ancient documents and concluded that the ancient Jewish Temple stood, not where the Dome of the Rock now stands, but one hundred meters north. That places the location in the middle of an area that is mostly pavement."

He opened up his briefcase and brought out some diagrams. He had one of the delegates hold up the first diagram, pointing to the specific spot he'd mentioned.

"You can see the area I mean. I believe the Arabs would lose little to gain much if you could part with this inconsequential part of the mount."

"We can't give up the holy mount!" cried Hassayni. "All of Islam would be in an uproar."

"Not necessarily," continued Adoni´. "Even though they are in debate as to the true site, they have already prepared all kinds of articles for building and servicing a temple. They have even identified their living priests. Sooner or later they will attempt to take the whole Temple Mount, which could only bring more war. Why not give them a small portion and keep the relative peace we now have? This way we can control what we give them. Besides, this is not a new idea at all. Your great uncle was negotiating with Golda Meir to do just that when he was assassinated."

"Now you want to get the king assassinated?" Hassayni scoffed.

"It's different today. The peace process has changed all that."

"But if we had Jews worshipping on the same mount, we couldn't control it. Soon they would want it all," declared one of the other delegates.

"No, I don't think so. You see we could build walls to separate out a portion just here and here." He switched to another diagram, pointing to the proposed walls. "That way you could restrict your portion of the mount to true believers and close it off to infidels. The Jews could do the same. The southern portion would still give you access to the underground Mosque, Al Aska, and the Dome of the Rock. And the far northern portion would still be yours. Of course they would have to build their own access to the mount. If they entered from the east side it would separate the people coming to worship as well. Each could satisfy his own religious needs in complete privacy and without the mixing of the two peoples. The Jews would focus on building their temple while you build your government buildings in Jerusalem. How could the Jews refuse such an offer?"

"If we give them a portion of the Temple Mount, will we get complete authority over East Jerusalem?" asked Nabil.

Adoni' looked at him kindly. "I am afraid that is too much to hope for, at least at this time, my friend. The Israelis will never give up all authority to the Old City. I think this is one place we will have to meet halfway."

Nabil looked at his delegation one by one. He could see their minds working by the expressions on their faces.

Finally, one of the delegates broke the silence and said, "But it would spoil the beauty of the mount to put walls up."

"This is true," agreed another.

"Could not the remaining space be redesigned to make it more pleasing. We could charge the Israelis for the cost," said Nabil.

"Or perhaps those influential businessmen will pick up the bill for it," suggested Adoni´. "We could make it part of the conditions for giving up part of the mount."

"I like the idea of closing off the mosques from the general public," said one of the faithful of Islam. "Plus, it certainly would calm the differences between us and the Jews, at least for now."

"Yes," added Adoni. "I know Islam wants to control the whole area, but there is more than one way to wage war. A subtle way is through peace."

"Okay, if we offer the mount as negotiable, what do we put as *non-negotiables*"? asked Nabil's assistant, Amral Shaas, who was recording the list.

"The right to place the head of our government in East Jerusalem, with free access to consist of a wide strip of land connecting to the Palestinian territory and full authority of our government to control our portion. Otherwise we would be in a dangerous position, vulnerable to Israeli forces," said Nabil firmly.

"What about all those settlements the Israelis have in East Jerusalem—on the French Hill, Ramat Eshkol, Gilo, East Talpiot, or Har Homa? What can we do about them?" asked the recorder.

"They will be the same as any other Jewish settlement in Palestinian territory," replied Nabil. "I think the important thing to stress is that our government's seat must be part of the Palestinian territory, subject only to our rule. It can't be isolated in the city like an embassy but within our own borders."

"Do you mean annex a section of the city to our territory?"

"Yes."

"Do you think the Israelis will give back more territory?" asked another.

"They will have to if they want the Temple Mount," said Adoni´.

"I believe we can make this work," said Nabil.

All agreed.

Chapter 21

"Hardware first and then the grocery?" Rachel asked as they went down the elevator. "Most hardware stores will be closing soon, but the groceries are open twenty-four hours a day."

David nodded. "Do you have a place where we can get some cellular phones?"

"Yes, but we will have to go to the mall since it's so late."

"Is that a problem?"

"No, not really. We'll just find a grocery store out that way. We can get the hardware items at Sears."

They got in the car and headed for the expressway.

"Why do you want cellular phones?" questioned Rachel.

"Because unless the towers go down, you can communicate with anyone anywhere since your phone is always with you. Overhead wires might not make it. Could be handy in an emergency. I brought mine from home. Because of my job I have a hookup to a satellite. But Johnny doesn't have one that will work over here."

"You could use mine," offered Rachel.

"No, I need phones for the delegation to keep in touch. I don't know why Johnny didn't make arrangements when he first got here."

"What else are you looking for?"

"Flashlights and lots of batteries. Maybe some camp lanterns and some dehydrated food packets and bottled water, or at least the means to store city water. In fact, you need to get some water put up in jugs as soon as you get home. Potable water is crucial in a disaster because it's so easy for public water to become contaminated and spread disease. Do you have any containers?"

"No," she replied, "and I don't know what they have at Papa's, but I think I better go over there as you suggested. How much time do we have?"

"I can't say. We will have to wait until they get back with us from Israel," said David gravely. "That's why we have to get what we need now before the panic hits."

Rachel turned into the mall parking lot. They found all the items David wanted at a sporting goods store in the camping department. Rachel purchased some of the same—several three gallon collapsible plastic water jugs and a butane camp lantern. They paid for their purchases and headed to the mall for the phones.

David purchased two cellular phones. Using his official ID, he arranged for the Israeli Government to be charged through the embassy for a temporary service. Rachel had her family's numbers in her phone contacts. She put David's number in it too. They grabbed a quick sandwich in the food court of the mall and then drove to the grocery store.

"Now," David said, "the trick is to get only what will not spoil without refrigeration, just in case we lose power."

Later they loaded their food cache in the car and drove to Rachel's apartment to pick up her clothes and toiletries. David made a note of the address. Then he helped himself to a cup of coffee while Rachel packed.

Rachel drove to the back of her father's stately house where they could carry the groceries into the kitchen. The housekeeper/cook opened the back door when she saw them coming up the stairs, arms loaded with large grocery bags.

"What on earth, Miss Rachel?" asked Hattie as they came in the door. "And what am I supposed to do with all this?"

"Just put it away for now. Hattie, this is Captain Solomon. He's helping us prepare for a disaster."

"Hello Hattie," said David.

Hattie barely acknowledged him. "Disaster? What's you mean?"

"I'll tell you later. Get Charlie to help David with the rest of those bags, will you? And fill these plastic jugs with water."

"Where is Papa?" asked Rachel.

"In the den I guess."

"Don't need no more stuff in this house," muttered Hattie as she went to call Charlie. "I just got groceries yesterday."

Simon leaned back in a dark well-worn leather Lazy Boy, feet up on the extending portion, with the *Wallstreet Journal* held high, hiding his face. At the sound of a step he peered over his paper and dropped it in delighted surprise.

"Rachel, my love, I didn't expect to see you until after the conference."

"Hello, Papa," she said as she kissed him lightly on the forehead. "How would you like to have a house guest for a while?"

"Who?"

"Me."

"Always glad to get my favorite daughter back," he said with an affectionate smile. "What's the matter, have you overstepped your salary already?" he teased.

"No, David thinks I should be here with you for the next few days. We have a disaster on its way."

"The conference?" he asked alarmed.

"No, nothing to do with that," she said calmly and then explained the situation. "David and I just picked up some supplies—some for us and some for the delegates and his men."

Presently Charlie, Hattie's husband, brought David into the den.

"We've unloaded everything. I need to call a taxi now, to take my supplies back to the delegation."

"No need to do that. I'll take you back to the hotel," said Simon. "I appreciate your caring to look after us. It's the least I can do."

"Well, thank you, sir," said David, relieved. Also he welcomed the chance to get to know Rachel's father. "I wonder, could we stop over to the office first? I want to see if we have heard from home."

"Of course. In fact, I'd like to hear more about it myself," said Simon. When he looked at Rachel he saw her disappointment. "Rachel, you wouldn't begrudge me this opportunity to hear about the conference, would you? Let me do this for him, okay?"

Rachel reluctantly agreed. "It will be good for you to get to know David."

As they drove, David told Simon all he knew about the conference and the president's conversation. When he stopped at the office they carried up a thermos of coffee for the men that Rachel insisted they take.

Feldman unlocked the door after David identified himself.

"Have you heard any news yet?" asked David immediately.

"Yes, and it's all bad. They've checked the major Asteroids, Ceres, Pallas, Juno, and Vester, which used to have closely adjacent orbits—well, something knocked one of them off course, and now they are bouncing around out there like billiard balls. They are way out in space between Mars and Jupiter, but with their new headings, who knows? The present collision is just the beginning. The Internet is buzzing with data flying back and forth."

Suddenly, a Scripture David had often puzzled over came to mind. He voiced it saying, "They come from a distant land, from the end of the sky—the Lord, and the weapons of his wrath—to ravage all the earth! Howl, for the day of the Lord is near; it shall come like havoc from Shaddai."

Simon said, "Where is that from?"

"*Yesha'Yahu* (Isaiah 13:5–6, Tanakh), and the oddest thing about it is that it goes on to talk about the sun and the stars being darkened."

"The *Moschiach* must be coming soon," said Simon, awed by the significance.

David and Simon drove on to the hotel, discussing their own personal study of the Scriptures, each duly impressed with the other.

The meeting at the White House over, the president, sitting in his favorite chair in his private living quarters, bent down to remove his shoes. Then he leaned back, exhausted from the day's trauma. *Well, it's done.* They had given it their best shot. They had ordered nuclear rockets, prepared just in case the asteroid changed to a more threatening course, but most of their preparations were for coping with ground problems. Word went out immediately to all military bases. Troops and supplies were probably already enroute to every major city to help keep order; national guard units already called to active duty; major hospitals notified to put all their doctors on call—all with orders to begin storing water and medical supplies. They alerted utility companies to beef up their emergency crews. They ordered a small detachment of local National Guard troops assigned to each grocery store to ensure against hoarding, where dollar limits would be imposed according to family membership.

Financial establishments were not overlooked but admonished by the Department of Commerce to record all of their data on disks and keep written records as well. The president sighed. He felt good about their preparations. Just one more thing to do. Tomorrow he would prepare his press conference statement and give it to the people. *God, I pray the people don't panic.* He ran his fingers through his semi-silvered hair, catching a glimpse of himself in the mirror across the room and said aloud, "My God, am I just imagining things or is my hair turning white overnight?"

Chapter 22

Ra'amon's meeting was over when David got back. Haik listened as David reported the latest news on the coming disaster. It alarmed him. Somehow the importance of the conference had eclipsed it in his mind. Now this report forced him to realize the ramifications of the coming event. He looked at his watch.

"Eleven o'clock," he said aloud. "That means it's five a.m. at home. I'd better call the IDF and get things rolling for emergencies."

"They are already alerted," said David. "I faxed them this afternoon as soon as the conference was over. In fact, it was they who have been monitoring the Internet and got this information."

"Oh," said Ra'amon, a little taken aback. After all, *he* was the prime minister, David only a security officer. But then he realized it was something he himself had neglected, so he let it pass. "Good work, David, I will still need a report as to how they are preparing our people. Does the Knesset know what is happening?"

"I thought you would want to tell them yourself, sir. The IDF will only organize until you and the Knesset give the orders. Do you think we should alert the Palestinians? They don't have a connection to the astronomical community. They probably know nothing of the coming disaster. They will have to work with the IDF at home anyway, or we could have spreading chaos," said David. "After all, what good is a conference if anarchy breaks out in the disaster? It could be war all over again."

"You are right of course. Do we have a way to reach Dakkah?" said Haik Ra'amon.

"Just pick up the phone and call them. Their delegation is in the West Wing."

Haik called Kauferman, his acting secretary. "Call the desk and get me the room number of Dakkah."

"I'll see you in the morning," said David as he left the room. He still had to brief his men on the situation.

Rachel was up early. It was good to be back in her old room. She had lived in it only briefly after returning home from college. Living at home was too confining after her independence at school, but this time was different. She'd had her taste of apartment living. Being back now was just...nice. *Must be because it is my own choice,* she thought as she descended the stairs, humming a merry tune.

"Good morning," she said brightly as she popped through the kitchen door.

Hattie was looking slightly grumpy. "You want breakfast?" she half mumbled. She hadn't started anything, as it was only six-thirty.

"No, Hattie, I'm used to fending for myself. I'll just fix a quick cup of coffee and be on my way."

Rachel wanted to pick up some rolls and coffee for the guys at the Israeli office so she could get the latest on the disaster before she left for the embassy. She would eat with them. She walked out to her car with a decided bounce to her step.

"I wonder why she's so happy," muttered Hattie as she watched Rachel get into her car. "And us expecting a disaster...humph... Disaster or no disaster, *I take care of this household.*"

Rachel turned on her car radio to CNN. *Might as well catch the news first thing,* she thought.

"...preparations are even now being made. The president is holding a press conference at ten this morning. Everyone is advised to listen. The conference on Jerusalem will continue today. So far there has been no report of any progress. The Dow opened today..."

Rachel switched off the radio. *So they know.*

David phoned the office first thing upon waking. He had worked late the night before, briefing his men and making plans. Because of this he overslept. It was already six-fifty, and he felt embarrassed.

Feldman answered, "Yes?"

"Any news this morning?" asked David without a salutation, expecting his voice to identify him.

"You're late, Captain. The prime minister already called. Didn't he tell you?"

"No, I haven't talked to him yet."

Feldman told David what he told the prime minister. After that David hung up and dialed the number of Rachel's cell phone.

"Hello," said Rachel.

"*Shalom,* are you awake yet?" said David.

"Awake, I'm on my way to your office with coffee and rolls for the guys. Where are you?"

"I'm getting ready to leave for the conference," he said, not letting on to his true state.

"I just thought I'd say good morning."

"Well, good morning to you too. Any news yet?"

"The guys will fill you in when you get to the office. I have to go now." He hurriedly added, "You *are* going to be my chauffeur today, aren't you?"

"Probably, but I have to check in at the embassy first. If I don't show up, give me a call later," she replied gaily. "You have my private number."

After David agreed he hung up. A tinge of conscience hit him.

She's becoming too important to me, he thought as a vision of soft blue-gray eyes floated before him. *I need to concentrate on my job and the importance of this conference.* Yet he knew she was the one he had always hoped was out there, waiting for him. *We have so little time,* he moaned within.

Chapter 23

Milling around the hallway in front of the door to the conference room, excitement stirred the delegates as they anticipated the unveiling of their so-called lists. Both the Israelis and the Arabs showed confident smiles, revealing the upbeat attitude of the crowd. The president arrived late, and the conference was delayed, but the delegations didn't seem to notice.

Curious, David thought as he observed the obvious optimism. *I wonder how many of them are aware of the impending disaster.* He desperately hoped they could finish this conference before it struck. *Would it be bad? The prophets who spoke of the judgments just before the kingdom came made dire predictions concerning the earth. I know some of these things are necessary to prepare the kingdom, but surely the Almighty God of my fathers would not let anything destroy the earth until he has brought forth his Messiah and Salvation.*

The president opened the conference.

"I apologize for leaving early yesterday. I was called away for an emergency meeting. As some of you may already know, the earth is facing a near miss with a maverick asteroid. According to our astronomy community, we can expect a bombardment of dust and meteorites and maybe even a few earthquakes. If you haven't done so, you may want to warn your people back home. Because of this we need to conclude this conference as soon as possible. Due to this crisis, I won't be able to stay this morning either."

After that the president left to meet with the press and address the American people.

All knew of the impending disaster except the religious delegation under the pope, so Pope Peter immediately sent John McCutchen to call Vatican City. Then the meeting settled down to the business at hand.

Filling in for the president, US Secretary of State Russel Hamilton began the meeting with, "Gentlemen, I presume you have your lists made. I think we will start first with the list of non-negotiables. And we will try to negotiate from there." He turned to Israel on his right and asked, "What are your non-negotiables?"

Prime Minister Haik Ra'amon stood and spoke softly but firmly.

"We will not negotiate away our sovereignty over the city of Jerusalem. Jerusalem must always remain under Israeli control." Then he sat down.

"This is your only non-negotiable?" the secretary asked.

"Yes," he replied.

Then he turned to Nabil Dakkah and repeated the question put to Israel.

"Mr. Secretary," Nabil replied, "the Palestinians will accept nothing less than a portion of East Jerusalem to be annexed to our territory for government facilities."

"Do you have a certain portion in mind?" asked the secretary, trying to get more specific.

"Our only condition is that it be adjacent to our territory and become part of it permanently."

"Well, that blows our hopes for an embassy-type concession," said Goren under his breath. "They want us to give up more territory as usual."

An undercurrent of mutterings swept through the Israeli delegation.

"Order, order," called the secretary then proceeded in the ensuing silence.

"Now we will take up the negotiables and see if you can meet halfway." Again he turned to Israel first.

"Mr. Secretary, we are prepared to offer a buffer zone between our two boundaries by making East Jerusalem, including the Old City with its religious shrines, a jointly ruled section with government buildings for Palestine inside this territory," said Haik Ra'amon.

"Where inside this territory?"

"Anywhere they choose," Haik replied.

"But it would be under joint government authority, would it not?" asked the secretary.

"No, it would be like any embassy on foreign soil—subject to the Palestinians alone."

"I'm sorry," said Nabil, rising to his feet. "That is not acceptable to us. Surely you can see we would not be secure. To have the head of one's government surrounded by potentially hostile territory would be indefensible."

"Do you have anything to negotiate that might cause the Israelis to change their minds?" asked the secretary.

Nabil turned and nodded to Adoní, whom he had appointed to present their proposal.

Haik watched as Adoní stood to his feet. *Him again. What is it about him? He's so calm, so sure of himself, and so confident of winning this concession for the Palestinians. What does he know that we don't? How can he resolve this impasse?*

Adoni´ cleared his throat and waited until he had the complete attention of the conference.

"Gentlemen, I have taken the liberty to prepare some diagrams of Jerusalem. If you will permit, our men will set up the overhead projector. While they do that I would just like to say a few words."

Two delegates rolled in a small table containing an overhead projector. Adoni´ met them at the head table as he stepped to the microphone at the rostrum.

"First of all, let me introduce myself to you," he began while the men set up a small screen behind him. "My name is Julius Leucus Adoni´. I represent both delegations, in a sense, as I was born of both peoples who are trying to negotiate this peace. My mother was Jewish and my father a Syrian Arab. I understand both peoples and both religions." He paused to let that sink in. "Our peoples have been dwelling together for centuries, even from the beginning. Is this not so?" he asked, looking first at his own table and then to the Israelis. "It is only the return of the Jews to their ancient homeland in this past century that created this present conflict. And even their return was prophesied centuries ago by the prophets of the Holy Scriptures, so we cannot stand against the word of Yahweh, the God of Avraham our father. But we can stand against the hatreds that have developed. We can replace them with brotherhood and co-operation.

"My brothers," Adoni´ said as he looked both to his fellow delegates and then across to the Jews. "We cannot both have exactly what we ask for. Shall we not meet in the middle?

"Please turn on the overhead," he said as he turned to one of the delegates who'd set it up. "Lights," he said as the other darkened the room.

The diagram projected onto the screen showed the Temple Mount with the Dome of the Rock and the El Aska Mosque indicated by a floor plan to scale.

THE BEGINNING OF THE END

"This," he said with drama, sweeping his hand toward the slide, "is the solution for peace between the Jews and the Palestinians. If the extremists of both peoples can be satisfied, the rest will settle down and live in peace. One of the great problems between us is religion.

"A few years ago Professor Asher Kaufman, a retired Hebrew University physicist whose hobby is archeology and who has studied the position of the ancient Jewish Temple for years, published a paper locating it one hundred meters north of the Dome of the Rock just here." He pointed to a space next to the Dome of the Rock with a wooden wand. "Next, please," he requested. The delegate laid down a clear overlay on the projector, indicating the outlines of Herod the Great's temple superimposed on the floor plan of the Arab holy places.

"If this is true, and Professor Kaufman suggests how it may be verified, you can see there is adequate room on the Temple Mount for both a Jewish temple and the Dome of the Rock."

A gasp of surprised wonder went up from the delegates of the entire room. The Israelis sat in stunned silence. Never in a thousand lifetimes would they have expected the Arabs to make such an offer. They knew of course that there were four viable theories of where the original temple had stood. This being one. But they didn't expect the Arab world to give up one foot of the Temple Mount.

"I propose a great wall be built between the two holy areas with separate access to both places. We do have one small problem, but I believe we can work it out. I'm referring to the Arab cemetery." The delegate put up another slide that showed the wall with steps and a bridge approaching the eastern wall. "You Israelis may have to build a bridge from the east side as shown, so as not to desecrate the Arab burial ground here." He pointed. "Also you would have to help with a new landscape plan to make the Dome of the Rock more balanced in its new confines." Again he pointed with his wand to landscape changes. "The Palestinians offer the rights to the Temple Mount in exchange for their own sovereign part of the city as their capital." Another slide was projected, showing the portion of the city they wanted. Then Adoni´ sat down as dramatically as he had stood. His action adding an exclamation point to his message.

The pope nodded in agreement. He leaned toward John McCutchen and whispered behind his hand. "I can work with this man. A Jewish/Arab cross—what a combination for peace."

Haik Ra'amon could hardly contain himself. *He's one of us. Who would have thought it?* A Jewish mother determined one as a Jew in such a marriage, according to Halacha, the body of the law as practiced by the Orthodox Jews. Whereas a Jewish father and an Arab wife would not. The prime minister was not at all religious, but he *did* know *that. It should satisfy the religious parties and seal the peace. And I will be the prime minister to finally achieve it.* Haik stared at Adoni´ with unmasked admiration. The delegates began to buzz with excitement.

J. Quentin Rice smiled and said to himself, "Not even the powerful 'establishment' dared hope for such a breakthrough." He looked over at the pope and nodded, acknowledging a secret between them as well. Rice, besides being a member of the powerful US CFR, was also a Knight of Malta, an ancient organization that was sworn to uphold the power of the papacy. They also meddled in the politics of the world, promoting Vatican affairs.

Secretary Russel pounded the gavel, calling for order. As the delegates quieted down, he turned to the Israelis.

"Do you need time to confer with your delegation?" he asked.

"Yes, Mr. Secretary, but we could reconvene this afternoon since the time is short," said Ra'amon.

"Shall we say 3:30 p.m.? Will that give you enough time?"

Haik looked at his watch. It was nearing 12:00.

"I think so, Mr. Secretary."

THE BEGINNING OF THE END

After that the Secretary adjourned the meeting.

"We'll go over to the office and look at this proposal," Haik said. "Have David bring the tape of this morning, while I see Mr. Adoni´ a second." He walked over to where Adoni´ was gathering the papers at the overhead projector.

"Mr. Adoni´, Haik Ra'amon," he said, extending his hand and flashing his friendly smile. "I was wondering if you have any copies of the diagrams you flashed on the screen for us to study?"

"Of course, of course, delighted to meet you, Mr. Ra'amon. Yes, I anticipated your need for them and brought several copies. I made them for both delegations." Then pointing to the papers he said, "This is the present state of the mount. And this is the proposed change. But of course you may come up with a better approach to the mount than I have shown. It's only a suggestion."

"Tell me, how did you persuade the Arab delegation to give up part of the mount?" Haik asked with interest.

"We had to offer something so both parties could gain," he replied, showing great wisdom for a man so young and at the same time melting Haik as he gently gazed at him with those rich mahogany eyes. Haik was mesmerized. His emotions churned with a strange passion he had never felt before. His admiration grew with each word Adoni´ spoke. He took the diagrams and returned to his delegation, but his mind was still fixed on Adoni´'s gaze—a hypnotic gaze.

Chapter 24

The pope was waiting to speak to Adoni´ after Ra'amon left. Pope Peter II extended his hand and said, "Bless you, my son. I believe you've hit upon a solution. The God of all peace is with you."

"Thank you, Holy Father, I believe the time for peace has finally come. I am honored that God can use me in some small way to work his will," replied Adoni´.

"If this proposal is accepted and worked out to the satisfaction of all, I think it deserves to be called a Holy Covenant."

"Yes, it truly would be that to the Jewish people. I think it would turn their eyes away from war and defense and toward peace and security as they rally around their temple building project," said Adoni´.

"Yes, yes," said the pope, unable to discern the full intent of Adoni´'s words.

Adoni´ intended to re-focus Israel entirely. He wanted peace so he could further his own growing empire.

David looked up in surprise as Labor MKs Yudleman and Kutter burst into the security room and asked him to bring the tapes.

"We've had a breakthrough," Kutter explained. "The Palestinians offered us part of the Temple Mount."

"What!" exclaimed David. "Will you repeat that again?" He was not sure he heard right. *Can it really be so?* This was his heart's desire. His pulse quickened.

"That's what I said. They've offered us a portion of the mount so that we can rebuild our temple in exchange for a section of East Jerusalem. Now we have to meet in the office and talk. So let's get going. There is not a minute to lose."

David gathered the tapes in a daze. Perhaps this conference was prophetic after all.

Rachel caught up some paperwork that had accumulated during the last two days. The ambassador stopped by her desk to ask how she liked being a chauffeur. She laughed gaily and said, "I never thought I would like it, but I really am enjoying it."

He smiled knowingly. He saw a sparkle in her eyes.

"Are you chauffeuring today?"

"David said he would call."

"David?" asked the ambassador, raising his eyebrows.

Rachel felt the heat creep up over her face.

"Rachel, you are actually blushing," teased the older man as he looked at her laughing.

"Can't help it," she said, then she decided she didn't care who knew. She was so happy. After he walked away, she glanced at the clock.

"The morning is gone and part of the afternoon. I wonder why he hasn't called," she said to herself. "They usually take the tapes to the secretaries before now."

The delegation arrived at the office complex and immediately retired to the conference room. David was told to deliver the tapes. Landau and Hillman, David's men from the conference, joined Feldman and Bader in the reception room.

Feldman looked at them questioningly. "*Mah ha'inyan* (what's up), Landau?" he asked.

"I'll let the captain tell you."

When David came into the reception room, Feldman asked him.

"All I know is the Palestinians have offered part of the Temple Mount in exchange for part of East Jerusalem." All the way to the office David had thought about the offer, and suddenly he felt a chill. *What if it was just a clever ploy to weaken the Israeli hold on Jerusalem as a whole?*

"*Nissim v'niflaot* (Miracles and marvels)!" said Feldman.

"Do you think they will refuse it?" asked Bader.

"I don't know. I didn't hear any of the particulars," said David absently, his mind obviously occupied.

"What's the matter, Captain? I thought that was what you wanted," declared Feldman, recalling a former conversation on religion.

"Yes, it is, but I have a feeling something is not quite right here," said David.

Why am I troubled? I haven't any reason to feel this way. Yet somehow I feel it is a trap.

His cellular phone rang. David knew it must be Rachel. He hadn't called her, and she would be wondering why.

"Do you need your chauffeur yet?" asked Rachel brightly.

"No, I'm afraid not. I just now came to the office with the rest of the delegation."

"Why?" Rachel resounded with disappointment.

"They had some proposal to talk over," he said, sounding vague, deliberately hiding the reason from her. "It doesn't look like I will be needing you at all today unless they return to the conference later. If I need you I will call your cellular. You do keep it with you, don't you?"

"Yes, but..." She wanted to know about the proposal, but David cut her off.

"All right, I have your number, bye now."

David didn't want to talk in front of his men, and besides that he would have sounded his worries to her if he had kept her on the phone. No, that was something he wanted to talk to her about in private. *She will understand. I just know she will. I am already accepting her as a sounding board—needing her. David, you are getting carried away,* he chastised himself. He had never before wanted to share such feelings with a woman. *It's just that she is interested in the same things and comfortable to talk to,* he rationalized. It had been all he could do to keep from spilling his guts to her.

Looking down at the phone in her hand, Rachel felt rejected by David's abruptness. It was an entirely new emotion to her. *That's what you get for running after him like a foolish school girl. Well, who needs him and his phone call?* she scolded herself, anger flaring. She walked out of her office stinging, deliberately leaving the phone on the desk. *I'll just grab a late lunch before I finish this paperwork. It will help stretch out this boring day that started out with such promise.*

Haik Ra'amon could hardly contain his excitement. *This is too big for us to decide alone.* He was feeling generous enough to share history with them all.

"The whole Knesset needs to vote on it, don't you think?" he said to the delegates.

They agreed wholeheartedly. He called direct to the Knesset building in Jerusalem and received no answer. *Of course there's no one there; it's 8:00 p.m. at home.* In his excitement he had momentarily forgotten that Israel was seven hours ahead of Washington time. He called Mordecai, his finance minister, at home.

"Hello, Yesha, this is Haik. Listen, the Palestinians have offered us a portion of the Temple Mount so we can rebuild our temple. Call a special meeting of the Knesset immediately. Do you not think the whole Knesset should vote on this?"

"How is it possible?" Yesha said. "What do we have to give up?"

"You'll find all the details in the proposal," Haik answered.

"Yes, I suppose everyone would like to be included in such a momentous breakthrough."

"The religious parties will think this is a miracle. I'll fax the diagrams and a written copy of Adoni´'s speech to your office at the Knesset building. I think everyone needs to hear it before they vote."

"Who is Adoni´?"

"He's with the Palestinian delegation as a negotiator, but he's also one of us. He may be the Messiah for all I know. I believe he has given us the solution to the problem. He is definitely a peacemaker."

"I didn't know *you* were looking for the Messiah, Haik?" said Mordecai.

"Well, I never have been before, but don't the religious parties expect him to rebuild the Temple? This man is offering us a chance. He must have mesmerized the Arabs to get them to agree to give up part of their mount in compromise. I'd say that would take a very special person."

"I don't believe in such stuff."

"Listen," said Ra'amon sharply, "this is just what we need to satisfy the right-wing extremists. Don't knock it."

"All right, I'll call the Knesset together so they can vote. Is everyone there in favor of it?"

"Of course," Ra'amon replied.

Mordecai hung up. *Sounds like this Adoni´ has mesmerized Ra'amon,* he thought. *Messiah, indeed. If they get the temple site back that would be just another expensive project.* Maybe the Palestinians meant to bankrupt them; with all the rebuilding as a result of the Katyusha explosions and the attempted clean up of Tel Aviv, money was tight as it was. He called his secretary and asked him to call the Knesset Ministers to a special meeting.

―

David's father, Jesse Solomon, was surprised to get an automated phone call summons to the Knesset building. Not much was happening with the prime minister out of the country. He walked in with several others, all questioning one another as to the reason for this meeting.

Yesha Mordecai strode into the room and called the men to order.

"*Rabotai* (Gentlemen), I received a phone call from the prime minister about an hour ago. The Palestinians are offering to give up part of the Temple Mount so we can rebuild our temple, if we give them a section of East Jerusalem to be their capital. Here are the diagrams, and here is the proposal that was made by a Julius Leucus Adoni´, who, by the way, Ra'amon thinks may be the Messiah." Then he laughed. "Nevertheless, he wants the whole Knesset to vote on this. I'll read Adoni´'s speech and then the proposal."

After he finished reading the proposal, the room came alive with everyone talking at once. Those in the religious parties were thrilled. Only a few were wary—those who represented the new settlements in East Jerusalem and some of the orthodox MKs. The Arab MKs were surprised. How, they wondered among themselves, had the Palestinian delegation been persuaded to give up part of their holy mount? But the vote proved to be overwhelmingly for the proposal. Only a very few dissented—mostly the very religious who maintained that the Dome of the Rock was the site of the original temple and therefore the offer meant nothing.

Jesse Solomon, excited beyond belief, left the meeting with a determination to reach David immediately. *What a breakthrough*, he thought. For years the faithful had struggled with the Arabs for their own land, their own identity, and their own religion. Now the ultimate goal seemed attainable—their rebuilt temple. Finally, the holy mount, or at least a part of it, would be theirs. Peace, that elusive dream, would come at last. Who could doubt the Messiah was near—maybe even that fellow Adoni´?

He smiled. Ra'amon, who was strictly secular, acclaiming the Messiah? Knowing Ra'amon it was probably a political move to appease the religious segment and strengthen his position. But it was impressive that a Jew, at least a Jew according to Halacha, had persuaded the Arabs to give up part of the mount. Before leaving the Knesset building Jesse called the embassy in Washington to get in touch with David. Though it was late in Israel, it was the middle of the afternoon in the US. They might not locate him right away, but when they did he would leave word for David to call home immediately despite the time difference.

Ambassador Levy's secretary took the message at the embassy and called directly to the temporary Israeli office. Upon receiving the message David dashed out of the office to find a private place to use his cell phone. What could have happened at home that his Abba wanted him to call so late?

Meanwhile, the Israeli delegation came out of their conference room all smiles. Finding David gone they rushed back to the State Department without him. He wouldn't be needed any more today anyway. He could go back to the hotel with rest of the office personnel.

David's palms sweat as he waited for the call to go through. Finally, a voice answered.

"Hello, *Abba*, is any thing wrong?" The worry was clearly evident in his voice.

"Wrong? How could anything be wrong with all that's happened?"

"But you wanted me to call, I thought..." David trailed off.

"Oh, I did, but only because I wanted to know what you thought about what is happening."

"What's happening?" asked David, relieved but slightly confused because he didn't expect his father to know anything about the conference.

"I'm talking about the Palestinians offering the Temple Mount."

"How did you know about that already?"

"Haik Ra'amon faxed the proposal for us to see and vote on. And we voted overwhelmingly in favor."

"I knew they made the offer, but nobody told me any details. I'm just getting bits and pieces of what is going on," said David, wondering why he was still feeling uncomfortable with the proposal.

"David, I thought you would be excited," said Jesse. "Now we can become a whole nation with our spirituality restored."

"I don't know, Abba, I have this strange foreboding like something is wrong."

"Nonsense! How can anything be wrong if the Messiah has come?" said his father jubilantly.

"Messiah?"

"Yes, Haik Ra'amon told Mordecai that he might even be the Messiah."

"Who?"

"This Adoni´ who made the offer."

"Why should the prime minister think an Arab is the Messiah?" asked David, totally confused.

"Because he is not an Arab; his mother was Jewish."

"You mean the offer didn't come from the Palestinians?" asked David.

"Yes, he was in their delegation, but as he said in his speech, he is the offspring of both peoples. He is trying to bring peace to us both."

"I'll see what I can find out about him." Then he changed the subject. "Father, are you aware of a possible physical disaster from the heavens?"

"Yes, we have all been alerted."

"Have you stored up some food and water just in case? Also batteries and lights?"

"Yes, Son. Don't worry about us, but before you hang up, let us ask the Master of the Universe to keep us all safe through it." After that he offered a prayer and then a blessing.

David hung up and dialed Rachel's cellular. It rang and rang, and finally a voice came on the line, but it was not Rachel's.

"Yes," said a male voice.

David said hesitantly, "Have I reached Rachel Lieberman's cellular?"

"Yes."

"Is Rachel not there?"

"Evidently not. Who is this?"

"David Solomon, and you are?"

"Avraham Lechtman. Rachel went out and apparently forgot her phone. I can't even imagine why she needs one. She doesn't do much of importance around here."

"If she comes back in will you ask her to call me?" he asked.

"If I remember," he replied.

"Okay...um, thanks anyway." Stung, David hung up. *What a jerk!* But David's concern turned back to Rachel. He was puzzled. *Why didn't she keep her phone with her?*

Chapter 25

Adoni´ noticed right away that the prize was won. He could tell by the jubilant mood of the delegates as they milled around in the hall prior to the opening of the session. Nabil nodded to him knowingly as he and the king of Jordan approached from across the room.

"It looks good, no?" said Adoni´. Nabil agreed as they entered the conference room and settled into their chairs.

The president, who was back in charge, opened the meeting by addressing the Israeli delegation.

"I understand you Israelis have been considering a Palestinian proposal."

Haik Ra'amon stood.

"Mr. President," he said, "we wholeheartedly accept the Palestinian proposal. It has the endorsement of the entire Knesset." His eyes singled out Adoni´'s, and he smiled warmly as he sat down.

Turning to the Palestinians the president said, "Have you any thing to add?"

Adoni´ whispered to Dakkah, the head of the Palestinian Authority.

"Yes, Mr. President," he said, as he rose to his feet. "We also gladly accept the Israeli offer of a buffer zone between our two territories with all the religious sites and the joint authority they proposed."

"Wait a minute," shouted Gormen. "We just gave you several dunams of East Jerusalem free and clear when we accepted *your* offer. You can't expect us to yield any more authority to you."

Shock registered on the Israelis' faces, then anger. They had chosen to give up their proposal and accept the Palestinians', not to put both into effect. Pandemonium broke out as each Israeli delegate vented his frustration.

"Order, order," called the president.

Haik was red faced. He had accepted too readily. He had naturally assumed their own proposal would be replaced by the Palestinian one. Now he was made to look foolish.

The pope slowly rose to his feet and lifted his hand, signaling the delegates to silence. The noise settled down as the delegates realized he wanted to speak.

"My brothers," he said, using a gentle tone, "we are *so* close to a wonderful peace. Shall we not calm down and think this through? A temporary buffer zone will indeed profit both sides, enabling everyone to get used to the new boundaries."

Haik stood up slowly. He had been out-maneuvered. He needed to regain his composure, so his words came deliberately.

"That may be true, Holy Father; however, we gave them complete authority in the portion ceded to them, which, let me remind you, was our *non-negotiable*. We can *not* give them any more authority in Jerusalem."

"What if the authority of the buffer zone was given to a neutral country for a limited time?" suggested the pope.

"You mean like the UN?" the prime minister asked warily.

"No, I had in mind my Swiss Guard from the Vatican."

"But surely you don't have enough to patrol such a large area. This is much bigger than the Vatican."

"Oh, but we have many who are in reserve. We can easily handle it," said the pope eagerly.

"For how long?"

"Six months, one year—whatever is agreed upon."

Haik huddled with his delegation. "I'm afraid if we don't agree, the Palestinians will withdraw their offer of the Temple Mount," he warned them.

"Then we will withdraw the offer of East Jerusalem," said Gormen, determined not to capitulate to the Palestinians completely.

"We could agree, if it is only temporary. What could it hurt?" asked another.

Meanwhile, in the Palestinian delegation Nabil whispered to Adoni´, "That was a stroke of genius. I was ready to settle for their acceptance of our proposal."

"Well, we probably won't get any authority, but they will lose some. We take it a little at a time, no? make a *hudna*," Adoni´ said, making himself their ally. Then he added, "Ask for the time to be three and a half years."

"Any particular reason for three and a half?"

"No, but that gives us more time to work on something else," he said and smiled.

Finally Ra'amon stood and was recognized by the president. "The Israeli Delegation will agree if the time is temporary and the Swiss Guard is the authority. Except that we stipulate that each religion will have complete authority over their own sites."

Dakkah looked first to see his delegates' response then he stood.

"We will relinquish our claim to joint authority and agree to the clause on the religious sites if the time can be set at three and a half years. If we begin the time in June and end the half a year at the beginning of the calendar year, it will give us two months to set everything up. That should give us both time to settle into the new arrangement."

The president turned to Haik, who nodded.

Seeing the nod, the pope stood again.

"I would like to make a motion that we call this agreement The Holy Covenant."

"Very well," said the president. "I have a motion to call this agreement The Holy Covenant. Do I hear a second?"

"I second it," said Adoni´.

"I now ask for a vote of the two delegations to accept Pope Peter's motion to name the said agreement The Holy Covenant," said the president.

The vote was unanimous. By 4:30 the president was asking the delegations to form the committee to write the wording of the covenant.

"We will reconvene tomorrow morning at 10:30 with just those you choose. The rest of you enjoy some sight seeing in our capital. By tomorrow afternoon we should have a document ready for signatures."

—

After Rachel finished her late lunch she sat in the restaurant, leisurely drinking a cup of coffee. Over and over she thought of her humiliation as she held the warm cup to her chin. She had always been so cool, so in control, and now she had started acting like a silly, no, outright giddy young girl. *What is wrong with me?* Never had she allowed herself to feel any attachment to anyone. Never had she cared whose hopes *she* dashed. Now the shoe was on the other foot. It hurt to care.

Maybe I'm not the iceberg everyone thinks I am. Her heart softened as she thought about David's smile. The way he brushed his hair out of his eyes, such tender eyes. But most of all she thought about his passion for the Moschiach. That was her problem; she cared about him—to be honest, she couldn't wait to see him again.

How childish for me to sit here feeling rejected, she thought, as reason finally began to take precedent over her emotions. *He probably couldn't talk when I called. I should have waited for him to call me.*

Casually she looked out the window. It was getting dark. *How long have I been sitting here nursing my wounded pride?* Alarmed she looked at her watch. It was late afternoon but not *that* late. Strange, the forecast that morning had been for fair skies. She hurried out to her car. Studying the sky she realized it was no ordinary storm. In fact she could see very few clouds, but there was a black section of the sky. One side of the sky had a dim light. The other half in deep twilight was being overtaken by the encroaching darkness.

It's happening, she realized, *and I foolishly left my cellular in the office.* She raced back to the embassy as fast as traffic would allow.

When David came back to the office he learned that the delegation had left him stranded. Trying to decide whether to walk, he hesitated. He wasn't worried that he would get lost—they had driven it so often the last two days, but was he really needed? Surely not, now that the conference was all but over. He needed more time with Rachel before he had to leave. He wanted to talk to her about his fears. *What would possess her to go off without her cellular?*

Diedrienne, realizing she had David to herself, came up behind him and slipped her arms around him.

"Finally a reprieve. Shall we go back to the hotel and rest?" she asked seductively.

David gently unclasped her arms and started to turn toward her when Bader, who was reading a magazine, said, "Hey, who turned the lights down?"

David ran to the window. "It's started," he said.

"What?' asked Bader.

"The darkness," he replied. Now he really was concerned for Rachel. Ignoring Diedrienne he called her cellular again. Still no answer. He called Johnny at the hotel.

"Yo," said Johnny.

"Johnny, have you looked outside lately?"

"No, why?"

"Because it's getting dark, and it's only 4:45."

"What do you mean?" Because he was inside he could not see the creeping darkness.

"I mean the cosmic rain is about to fall."

"*Oy vavoi!*" he whistled, "I better alert the guys. Is everybody there with you?"

"No, the MKs went back to the State Department with Landau and Hillman. I had to call my father, and they left me behind. Can you send a van right away to pick us up here at the office? I'm afraid the traffic is going to get fierce. I think it is best that we all be together there at the hotel where all our supplies are. No need to secure the office anymore anyway since the conference is all but over."

"*Be'seder* (okay), I'll try."

Deidrienne opened her mouth to speak just as David tried Rachel's number again. Before she could speak she heard him say, "Thank the Almighty, Rachel. Where have you been? I've been worried sick." Deidrienne was crestfallen.

"I'm sorry. I forgot my phone," said Rachel. "And I had to fight traffic to come back for it. Do you need me?"

"Johnny is sending a van for us. Where are you?"

"About halfway between the embassy and the State Department. I can be at the office in about twenty minutes if this traffic keeps moving."

David didn't protest even though he knew he should send her straight home. He wanted to see her. How could he manage that with his responsibilities to the delegation? Was he being selfish? *Yes*, he thought. *She has become that important to me.* "Yes, come on."

"Okay, I'll get there as soon as I can," she said and hung up.

"He said a van was coming for him," she whispered to herself.

But he didn't tell me *not to come* when I offered. "He's worried about me."

Ambassador Levy, having heard a report on CNN concerning the imminent darkness, had already taken steps to get the office people back to the hotel. He knew the delegation had its own transportation. He did not worry about them. But the office secretaries and the security men would not get back if he didn't get them early because the traffic was going to be horrendous. He walked into the office just as David hung up from talking to Rachel.

"I've come to take your personnel to the hotel."

"Ambassador, you are an angel sent from God," David declared. "Can you take everyone?"

"Yes, of course. Let's get out of here as quickly as possible."

"Let me call Johnny and cancel the other van. They probably haven't left yet."

He dialed Johnny's cellular and heard his familiar, "Yo."

"Johnny, the ambassador has come with a van. Can you stop the other one?" David asked.

"I was just going to call you. We can't even get out. The streets are almost to a standstill. The drivers are acting crazy."

David turned to Ambassador Levy and said, "Rachel is on her way here. You go on ahead. I will wait for her."

"I don't like to think of her being out there in panic traffic. A woman alone… I hate to think of her out there alone, that's all."

"She has her cell phone. I just talked to her. We can call her," said David.

"Good. Dial her number. I want to talk to her."

Rachel picked up the phone.

"This is Ya'cov, where are you now?"

"Just approaching DuPont Circle. I plan to stay off New Hampshire and just take 19th Street up to Swann. Why?"

"Because I'm here to pick up the ones at the office. Johnny's van can't get out because Wisconsin Avenue is clogged. David will start down 19th on foot to meet you. Watch for him. We don't want you out alone in this panic."

"I'm okay, but some of the drivers are getting irritated. It's just that I have to go so slow."

"If you get stuck, call David. He can hurry his steps. I definitely don't want you alone in your car in a stand still."

"Okay, but I'm still moving right now."

He hung up and said to David, "She's all right for now. Go ahead and take her to her father's home. You won't be needed in your official capacity. Johnny can handle the security at the hotel, and your men at the conference can take care of the delegation. She's almost like a daughter to me, and I don't want to worry about her safety. Maybe later after the traffic dies down we can get you back to the your hotel."

"I'm not concerned for myself," said David. Then he added, "Ambassador, I think it would be wise to take the fax machine and the computers back with you to the hotel. We don't know for sure if we will be able to get back out here. That way we can at least keep in touch with home."

"Good idea."

The office crew rounded up the equipment and all their important papers then they all climbed into the van, except David. Diedrienne stared blankly. The look on David's face told her he didn't mind his new assignment.

"*Mazel tov*," said David as they drove away. Then he started west toward 19th Street.

Chapter 26

By this time it was completely dark and only 5:00 p.m. He rang Rachel again.

"I'm just a block away."

"I'm coming down Swann," said David just as he caught a glimpse of a car entering his block. As it came closer he recognized it as hers. He waved and she pulled over.

"Finally, I made it," she said as she got out of the car. "Just let me stretch for a few minutes."

"I wish I could drive for you, but I don't know the streets," he said, showing compassion as he climbed into the passenger's side. "I should have told you to go straight home. I'm just being selfish...I wanted to see you again, and besides, I was worried about you." He tried to hide the emotion that was creeping into his voice. "No telling what people will do when they're scared."

"That's very kind of you. Are you always so gallant in caring for defenseless females?" Rachel got back into the drivers seat. "You know, David, I'm not completely defenseless. I always carry mace in my purse, and I took a basic course in Judo when I was in college."

"Yes, but do you remember how to use it?"

"Oh, yes, I had to throw a coupla guys that got fresh with me."

"Remind me to behave myself," said David, amused. "Maybe

you should come to Israel and apply to the Mossad. They could use your talents."

"I bet that would be exciting," she said, trying not to show how tired she was. She hadn't worked that hard. It was just the waiting and the emotional stress that made her so tired. "Where are we off to?"

"My orders from the ambassador are to get you safely to your father's house."

"Oh really?" She thought for a minute and said, "Look, I need a rest. Besides, it's too far to try to get to Papa's in this traffic. Why don't we try to make it to my apartment, at least until it clears some?"

Rachel turned the car around and headed up 18th Street. A couple of turns later, when she reached the Duke Ellington Memorial Bridge, David said suddenly, "Look at that! There's another."

"Falling stars are supposed to be good luck, but I bet it doesn't mean that tonight," said Rachel. "What *does* it mean?"

"It's a meteor shower, probably from the asteroid collision."

Rachel shuddered. "What if one hits Earth?"

"Trouble...big trouble. Lots of damage if it hits a city."

They traveled on in silence. There was little traffic on the streets leading from the office, but Connecticut Avenue, the main thoroughfare heading northwest, was bumper to bumper. The traffic light offered their only opportunity to access the main street. Even then the steady stream of traffic only obeyed the red light when there were cars entering from the cross streets.

"Is it far to your apartment from here?"

"Only about five miles. It's in Wesley Heights near the American University. We'll get there eventually. All I can think about right now is a hot shower and a cup of coffee," she replied with a sigh.

"When we get there, show me where you keep your bowls and pans, and I'll make you a nice omelet and coffee while you bathe."

"A man who can cook," she commented lightly.

"My wife taught me," he said, watching her face fall.

"Just kidding. I'm not married," he said, his eye twinkling with mischief. "I was just checking to see if you cared."

"That's not fair," said Rachel. She felt her face blush. She had noticed that he didn't wear a wedding ring, but sometimes that didn't mean a thing.

David saw the relief pass over her face in spite of its color. So he switched subjects.

"Oh, I forgot to tell you all that happened at the conference today."

"At the conference?" repeated Rachel, also relieved at the change of subject. She turned off the main street and threaded her way west.

"Yes, the Palestinians offered Israel a portion of the Temple Mount in exchange for a whole section of East Jerusalem."

"Really? How could you forget to tell me such wonderful news? You know how much I care," exclaimed Rachel, her embarrassment forgotten in her excitement.

"I would have told you on the phone this afternoon, but I wanted to talk to you privately about it."

Rachel nodded. *So that's why he was so abrupt. I was right; he couldn't talk.*

"According to my information, someone named Julius Leucus Adoni´ made the offer. The prime minister called a special session of the Knesset to vote on it. My father called to get my feelings about it. He said Haik Ra'amon thinks this Adoni´ may be the Messiah."

"The Messiah? Oh you mean the *Moschiach*. I just knew he was around somewhere."

"Yeah, but is he really?" He paused. "This is everything I have ever hoped for, but somehow I have this—I don't know what to call it—a kind of gut feeling that something is wrong. That's what I've been wanting to talk to you about."

"Why me? I don't know anything," said Rachel. "This business about the temple is outside my understanding."

"Because I feel comfortable talking to you. We have the same love for our people and the same hopes of the Messiah. There have been so many false hopes through the ages. What if this is another one? As to the question, why you, none of my men are very religious, and somehow I feel a kinship with you. I guess I just need someone to sound off to now...here, today. You don't mind do you?"

"Of course I don't mind," replied Rachel. Actually it made her feel good that he wanted to share his fear with her.

When they stopped at a stoplight, Rachel looked over at David's dead serious expression and thought what lovely kind eyes he had.

"What?" he said, questioning her look.

"You have the heart of a leader. Do you know that?" she said softly, more a statement than a question. "Oh, at last my own street." She sighed her relief before he could give her an answer.

Rachel put her keys and her purse on the kitchen table and opened an upper cabinet.

"Up here are the bowls; down here are the pans. The eggs are in the fridge. Onions are in this cabinet..." She opened it. "And peppers are in the bottom of the fridge, if you need them. Coffee is here in a canister. I use instant. You see, I fully intend to take you up on your offer."

"Okay, go get your shower. I'll manage fine."

Rachel luxuriated in the steaming hot water and eventually emerged from her bedroom in a clean pair of jeans and a sweatshirt and sneakers.

Refreshed, she exclaimed with delight, "What a wonderful smell! It can't just be an omelet."

"I found some potatoes and combined them with onions and peppers. Are you ready for your omelet?" David's eyes swept over her. Even in jeans with no makeup she was stunning. He felt his baser emotions stirring. In the past he had worried whether he was normal because of his lack of lust or even interest in the opposite sex. He would worry no more.

"Yes, I'm famished."

"The coffee water is ready. You can fix that."

"Yes, sir, Captain, sir," she said, playfully saluting him.

By the time he had the omelets ready, Rachel had set the table and fixed the coffee.

"There must be some bread in here somewhere," she said as she rummaged through the freezer. "Surely we didn't take it all to Papa's. Here we go…English muffins." First she nuked them in the microwave to thaw them. Then she pried them apart with a fork and dropped them into the toaster.

"Now, back to the subject in the car," said Rachel after they offered a blessing over the food. "Why do you think this Adoni´…" she stopped. "What an odd name. Adoni´… That's too close to Adonai, which means Lord in Greek. Is he Greek? Is there such a surname as that?"

"No, he's not Greek. Now, I've made you suspicious too. Maybe I should have kept my fears to myself. But I couldn't talk to my father and dampen his spirit. He's so excited and says Haik Ra'amon is positively enamored of the guy."

"Do you know the prime minister?"

"Only by reputation and what I've read until this trip. The man has political savvy or he couldn't have that position, as young as he is. But I've heard rumors of his ambitions. He's too smooth to suit me."

"What do you know about Adoni´ besides his name?" asked Rachel.

"Only what my father told me. I don't even know which one he is. Father told me that Ra'amon says Adoni´ is one of us, according to Halacha, because his mother was a Jew. He is the one who persuaded the Arabs to give up part of the Temple Mount."

"Hey, do you suppose it is on the news?" asked Rachel. "It's nearly seven. The world news will be on soon."

They picked up their dishes and carried them to the sink. Rachel turned on the TV then they both sat on the couch to wait for the news. David reached over and took Rachel's hand and pulled her closer. Their eyes met and it was like a caress. Rachel tilted her head back as he leaned down and kissed her lightly on the lips, his hands now gripping her shoulders.

He had been wondering for a couple of days how she would taste. Her mouth was delectable with a slight lingering taste of their supper. Rachel responded by slipping her arms around his neck. His arms dropped to her back as he drew her closer, and he deepened the kiss. His temperature began to rise. He felt her shyness melt into passion. He was right about the fervor of her ideology translating into passionate emotions at the sensual level. Then slowly he released her, searching her eyes for her reaction. Her normally grey-blue eyes darkened to a dark slate blue. Satisfied that his kisses were welcomed, he straightened, but kept one arm around her shoulder as the news began.

Rachel was silent, quietly savoring the experience. *So this is what passion is,* she thought. *All this time I thought it was just romantic dribble.* Never had a kiss generated such feeling. Was it because it was David? Was she falling for him? Then startling headlines of the newscast caught her attention.

"The headlines tonight are the darkness and the great breakthrough in the Jerusalem conference. First the darkness… Scientists have been warning us of meteor showers, and now it seems they have begun. Several small meteorites have hit around the world. So far the damage has been minimal, falling mostly in uninhabited places or farmlands. The tracking stations in Canada followed one down."

Next the cameras focused on eyewitness accounts of seeing it fall.

Then the commentator said, "Scientists are warning coastal dwellers of potential high tides. Evacuation should be considered. The president ordered the Coast Guard to put on all personnel for the week. Also the population is advised to store water and grocery supplies for several days.

"The government orders us to conserve electricity. Each household must use lights in one room at a time. Neighbors are asked to cook jointly. The order is conserve or we may have brown outs. The scientists tell us that a giant dust cloud in space is the cause of the darkness. They don't know how long it will last, so conserve where you can.

"Also a warning has been issued concerning crime. The National Guard is on standby to help local police in case of earthquakes or damage to businesses as a result of meteorite falls. Looters will be shot on sight. I repeat, looters will be shot on sight. No one wants a repeat of what happened in New Orleans in 2005.

"Now the news concerning the conference ... The conference on Jerusalem took an exciting turn today as the Palestinian delegates presented a surprise move. J. Leucus Adoni´, an invited member of the Palestinian party, offered Israel a solution to a major problem of the conference—the religious problem. He did this by offering part of the holy Temple Mount to the Jews so they could rebuild their temple.

"Taking the Israeli delegation by complete surprise, the offer called for a wall to be built between the Arab section with the Dome of the Rock and the pavement where the ancient Jewish Temple is alleged to have stood. The Israeli Prime Minister called for an emergency meeting of the Knesset to vote on the issue. It was overwhelmingly accepted by them. After this commercial break we will bring you an interview with Israel's Prime Minister, Haik Ra'amon, the head of the Palestinian Authority, Nabil Dakkah, and his friend J. Leucus Adoni´."

David looked at Rachel and said, "So far he hasn't said what we have to give up to get the mount."

"It's called managing the news. Israel is always getting the shaft in the media. You watch, what's given up will be minimized."

"Well, at least we will get a look at Adoni´," said David.

The news commentator came back on.

"And here is Andrea Morgan with a personal interview with the principals in this negotiation on the Temple Mount."

A young attractive blonde sat facing Haik Ra'amon, J. Leucus Adoni´, and Nabil Dakkah.

"Mr. Prime Minister," said Ms. Morgan, "can you tell us your reaction to this astounding proposal."

"At first we were all in shock. Somehow I guess we assumed that the Palestinians would never relinquish any part of the Temple Mount. Our government has always bent over backward not to offend in this area. Sometimes it's been difficult because of our own zealots."

"I'm sure you are referring to the Temple Mount incidents."

"Yes," replied Ra'amon.

Turning to Dakkah the reporter asked, "And what made you come up with such an astounding offer?"

"It was my friend Leucus who really came up with it," he replied, nodding toward Adoni´.

"Mr. Adoni´?" she turned to him in surprise.

As the camera zeroed in for a close-up Rachel gasped. "Well, he certainly is a good looking man."

"Well, sir, tell our listeners a little about yourself. How did you happen to be involved in this conference? I understand you are not even a Palestinian yourself."

"This is true," he replied calmly, completely confident. "My role in this conference is strictly as a negotiator."

"But what is your background that caused the Palestinians to ask you to their delegation?"

"I'm a Lebanese banker who is used to making deals."

"And you made another so-called deal for the Palestinians."

David said with disgust, "He's too smooth. I don't like him. He's not the Messiah—no way."

"I helped them find a solution to the refugee problem in Lebanon, yes, I guess you could call it a deal." He smiled, giving the impression of modesty.

The camera backed off, showing a shot of both Ra'amon and Adoni´. It caught an expression of pure admiration on Ra'amon's face as he looked at the middle-man like one worshipping a god.

"Look at that! Father was right," David exclaimed. Somehow he felt revulsion, and then he wondered why.

Andrea Morgan turned back to Ra'amon.

"And what did Israel bring to the negotiating table to make this deal, Mr. Prime Minister?"

"We gave up several thousand dunams of East Jerusalem, from the north wall of the Old City, including the section with the Orient House then extending into the Judean Desert toward Jericho, along the Jericho Road, which will be the southern border. Then we negotiated a temporary buffer zone between our two territories, including the Old City with the religious sites of all three major religions."

"And who will rule in the buffer zone?" she asked.

"Israeli law will continue, but it will be enforced by the neutral Swiss Guard for three and one half years. This was the pope's suggestion."

"Oh," she asked, surprised, "and what else did the pope suggest?" She had not heard of his participation.

"He called for the agreement to be called The Holy Covenant."

"What an apt title. When will this covenant be signed?"

"Tomorrow."

"Gentleman, thank you for coming."

They all nodded.

Andrea Morgan turned back to the camera and said, "And there you have it—a conference that will no doubt go down in history as a tremendous step toward peace in that part of the world."

"Thank you, Andrea Morgan," said the CBS anchorman whose face now filled the screen. "After the next commercial break we'll come back with the latest news of Congress and special reports on the market due to communication gaps."

Rachel stood to switch off the TV.

"We lost a lot," said David sadly. "I hope it is worth it. I don't think they intended to give up any more territory."

"You don't think getting access to the Temple Mount is worth it?"

"I don't know," replied David, lost in thought. *The city will be divided again.*

Rachel arose and went to the window. "The traffic is about back to normal. Shall we get back on the road?" She made the suggestion, but in her heart she wished they could stay so she could explore the feeling his touch had aroused. Rachel had never gone through the giggly, young, "hung up on boys" stage. Instead she was a serious "little miss adult." In fact, she angered and intimidated the young boys in her synagogue when she bested them at the Torah studies Papa allowed. Even the boys in public high school who pursued her were cut down by her biting tongue, as she deemed them "stupid *Goyim.*" So emotions aroused by David felt surprisingly wonderful.

But Rachel would never initiate a romantic gesture. She didn't even know how.

It was just as well. The news cast had broken the spell. David had directed his mind to weightier matters.

"Let me just rinse off these dishes so I don't come back to creepy-crawlies," she said lightly.

Chapter 27

Back in the car David remained quietly thoughtful.

"You're worried about what will happen to your people, aren't you?" Rachel said.

"Yes, somehow I'm anxious about the covenant. Even though I thought getting the Temple Mount back would be a good thing before we came. It's costing our sovereignty over the whole city."

"Look," said Rachel, "the traffic has died down. Why don't I just find you a taxi so you can get back with your men. I can get home just fine. It doesn't seem to be any more dangerous now than any other night."

Just as he said "Maybe you are right," a giant flash of lightning spread over the entire sky. Suddenly the car seemed to lift off the road, straight up. Rachel and David momentarily floated above their seats.

"What's going on?" Rachel screamed, her knuckles white from gripping the steering wheel.

David grabbed the dash and quickly assessed what was happening.

The buildings on either side of them trembled ever so slightly. The streetlights jiggled, and some of them popped like a blown fuse. Nothing swayed like in an earthquake. The next few seconds seemed interminable as the car wheels spun, making little headway against the pavement.

"It's a tidal action," said David finally. "I'm glad we are not near the ocean. There's bound to be flooding. The earth is reacting to the asteroid. It must be a doozy to lift the ground this way, and the lightning... Could it have been a thunderbolt?"

"What's a thunderbolt?" asked Rachel.

"A spark of electricity passing between two charged bodies...like that kiss on your couch." David laughed, seeking to calm Rachel.

Slowly she relaxed and smiled. "It was like that, wasn't it?" She stopped the car.

He was pleased with her admission. "Still want to find me a taxi?" he asked, chuckling as he reached over and pulled her against his shoulder, wrapping his arms around her.

His calmness reassured her. She felt safe in his arms and was reluctant to part from him. "I'm okay for now, but why don't you call and see what's happening at the hotel. If they are okay, I'd just as soon you stayed with us at Papa's tonight."

"All right," he said, glad for an opportunity to prolong his time with her. "I'll call Johnny." He released her and dialed.

"Yo," said Johnny in his usual manner.

"Did you shake, rattle, and roll over there?" asked David

"Sure did, ole buddy, but it seems to have stopped."

"Anybody hurt?"

"No, just some broken glass and scared people."

"Is the prime minister back?"

"He's been here all evening."

"What about the news interview?"

"Oh, it was taped earlier, after the conference was over."

Suddenly a long piercing sound like a trumpet swept through the car, drowning out their voices. The sound seemed to go on forever. Rachel covered her ears.

Minutes later David said, "Did you hear that, Johnny?"

"Yeah, man, that was awesome."

"Did you hear it through the phone?"

"No, man, it was here, all over us. What was it?"

"I don't know, but it must have something to do with the asteroid. Listen, I'm still trying to get Rachel home, but if you need me I'll just bring her there."

Rachel and David were still in the vicinity of Rachel's apartment. Small apartment houses interspersed with older houses of a generation ago lined the street. In response to the lifting, people were leaving their houses and apartments to get away from the structures, and the street was filled. Rachel stopped the car again. She couldn't proceed. It was pandemonium. Finally, she rolled down her window and asked, "What's going on?"

"What's going on?" cried a woman. "Can't you see it's the end of the world?"

The sound like a trumpet began again, changing in pitch, up, down.

"Johnny," David shouted, "I don't think we are going anywhere. The streets are full of people. We can't move. They must think it's an earthquake."

Rachel watched and listened to the bazaar scenes around them. Little groups huddled together. Parents clutched their children. One woman was frantically saying her rosary. Rachel caught a few phrases. "Holy Mother of God, save us..."

"Okay, ole buddy, I'll call you if anything changes here," said Johnny.

Earlier in the afternoon, standing by the window, Simon Lieberman sighed as he looked at the sky. *It has finally begun,* he thought. *I better dismiss the office personnel so they can beat the traffic home.*

"Libby," he said to his secretary as he flipped the switch on the box. "The clouds are starting to roll in. Call Dan on his cellular and tell him to drop whatever he is doing and head for home. Tell him not to expect me. I'll wait until traffic clears." Then he switched to the office intercom and announced, "Listen up, everyone, the darkness caused by the asteroid is imminent. Leave everything and get on home before panic strikes and traffic jams up. We'll send voicemail tomorrow as to whether to come to work."

Libby spoke through the box. "Dan says he will see you at the house."

"Good, I think I will stay here and catch up on some paperwork while it's quiet. He stood at the window watching as some of his office staff drove out of the parking garage. *I wonder what this means. Is G-d warning the world? Could it be the kingdom coming—the Moschiach? Did not Rebbe Menochan Schneerson, when he was alive, say it was time for Moschiach to appear? Rachel and I thought this conference would be a sign, but this—this is truly a sign of...what?* He smiled. *We Jews always need a sign.* Then he sat down at his desk and tackled the huge pile of incoming bills in need of his authorization for payment.

■

Albar Nassum paced back and forth in agitation. "Where is he?" he questioned out loud.

The American agent was two hours late. The attack had been set for the day of the signing to gain the most in psychological effect. It would be impossible to try anything at the actual signing because of the security, so they opted for taking out the whole Israeli delegation just before their departure. Knock them down just when they think they have won. But the evening news had just announced a breakthrough, and now the signing would be tomorrow, days earlier than he had thought. They had only the night to finish getting ready.

They had planned to bring in the weapons and the explosives

just before the attack, to minimize detection. The American would bring the explosives in boxes marked as detergent and the AK 47s in boxes marked sheets. Actually the guns would be individually wrapped in sheets inside the box with a layer of folded new sheets on top. (The rest of the bomb making ingredients had been brought in piecemeal as the terrorists came and went to their third-floor rooms.) The American would transfer the final pieces—the wiring to Agor, their man employed by the hotel for room maintenance. Agor would then put them in his laundry bag on his pushcart and bring them up in the service elevator to the third floor where they would assemble them during the night. When they were ready, Agor, who had been making friendly with the Israeli guards daily, could approach them without suspicion. He could easily take them out and get their coded card, giving them access to the second floor from upstairs, coming down the stairwells. The card would be used to open the stairwell door at the far end of the hall. Then with those security guards taken out first with silencers and that end of the hall secured with two of their men, a third would return with the card for the other stairs, and they would take out the two in the main hall, leaving the way clear for their suicide bomber, who waited in the housekeeping room beside the service elevator. The rest would be history.

After three hours and an empty incoming bill basket, Simon stood up from his desk and stretched. It was completely dark, not at all like a normal spring day. From the window he could see that the traffic was lighter; he could try to get home now. Suddenly a white flash illuminated the streets below. The building bounced slightly. Books fell. Pictures on the wall vibrated. Then a deafeningly loud trumpet-like blast sounded with the force of a shock wave. The room filled with a blinding bright light—like the sun viewed directly, unprotected. Simon groped for the desk with one hand and shielded his eyes with the other. But before he could find the desk, he suddenly collapsed to the floor as if his muscles had melted to molten wax.

As he lay face down on the carpet, a voice with the sound of great authority called out his name.

"Simon, Simon..."

"Who's here? Who...who are you?" Simon stuttered, not daring to move because of the absolute authority in the voice. Then he felt a touch on the back of his head.

"I am *Yeshua*, your *Moschiach*. Take off your shoes and stand up. You are on holy ground."

Immediately his strength returned. Simon removed his shoes. *It must be the G-d of our fathers.* He dared not speak. He stood up, trying to see into the light, carefully shading his eyes with his hand. But he could make out but a vague form.

The voice spoke again. "I have called you to be my witness. I anoint you with the Spirit of my Father. You will go to your brethren and to the Gentiles and tell them that I am coming to set up my kingdom. You are but one of many I am calling throughout the world. You must preach that the Lamb of God has come and is coming again soon, with the wrath of judgment. Warn the people to repent of their sins, because if you do not I will require their blood of you as I also warned Ezekiel, my watchman."

"Who is this Lamb of God?" he asked timidly. His heart was racing. The *Moschiach...here? Talking to me?*

"You will read about him in the book of *Jochanan*," said the voice. Then the light vanished.

Slowly Simon's eyes adjusted to the florescent light in the room. After a while he sat down at his desk, still in his stocking feet. The clock on the desk read 7:40. Resting his elbows on the desk, he put his head in his hands. *What does it all mean? I have been* chosen—*just like Moshe and Yoshua? They too were asked to remove their shoes when they met G-d. But why me?*

THE BEGINNING OF THE END

Is the Moschiach God Himself? he suddenly questioned. *Yeshua*—that is what he said his name was. "A *Moschiach* named *Yeshua*," he said out loud. "But who is this Lamb of God?" Read about him in the book of Jochanan he had said. The Tanakh has no book of Jochanan. Did he mean the book of John in the Christian New Testament? Where could he find one? Probably any bookstore, but they would be closed by now. He had to find one. He had to know what it meant.

Wait a minute, didn't one of the secretaries have a Bible in her desk? Kent Davies was always making fun of her because she would read it on breaks. He would say she should have been a preacher in the Salvation Army. They take fanatics like her. Encouraged, Simon bent down and put on his shoes. Then he walked out of his office, turning on lights as he went. Janet's desk was in an alcove outside of the leasing department. As he approached he noticed how neatly everything was arranged on her desk.

Curious, the difference in secretaries, Simon thought. Janet had always seemed a pleasant, cheerful person, but he had not noticed her neatness before. *Her Bible must be here somewhere, unless she carries it home every night.* But somehow he didn't think so, at least he hoped not. Opening one drawer after another, he *thought, this is the perfect time to research this matter while I'm here at the office alone.* Finally, he opened the bottom drawer and there it lay—a small New Testament. He snatched it up and looked in the front for the contents.

Matthew, Mark, Luke, John...he stopped. *Here it is,* he thought as he quickly scanned the rest of the names. He frowned when he found three more Johns. He wondered which John the voice meant. He couldn't quite call the voice by his name. It seemed irreverent somehow.

"Well, I guess I'll just have to read them all," he said aloud as he shut the drawer. He took the small leather book back to his office, switching off lights as he went. But as he reached his desk the power went off everywhere.

—

The phone finally rang. Albar snatched it up. "Hello."

"I'm sorry, I've been tied up in the worst traffic jam I have ever seen. My cell phone went down and I had trouble recharging it, so I couldn't call, but I'll be there in about ten minutes. Make sure the way is clear," said the voice on the phone.

"Okay," replied Albar.

"Jazal, go alert our man downstairs and distract any who are curious while they unload the stuff. Blend in, whatever you do."

Jazal went to do as bidden.

Ten minutes later the whole room shook. Lightning shone through the windows and then came the loud trumpet sound that vibrated Albar's skin.

"What's going on?" he cried. Then the lights went out. *Praise Allah, what a plus for the transfer downstairs,* he thought. *By the time the generators kick in, they should be ready for the elevator.*

Chapter 28

Darkness surrounded a small chapel enclosed by an iron fence behind the St. Mary of Zion Church in Aksum. The guardian, Gebra Makail, stood looking outside at the unusually dark night. Hi. Unable to sleep, he had gotten up to check the lamp in front of the ark. Not that he thought it had gone out but to relieve his endless tossing and turning. *Why am I so restless?* he wondered. Except for his studies and prayer, his uneventful life consisted of various rituals he performed. He arose each morning, lit fresh incense, prepared his meals, and generally looked after the Ark of the Covenant, the most precious artifact in the world and, more importantly, *the* treasure of Ethiopia. Within it were the actual ten commandments placed there by the ancient patriarch Moses himself.

The service of the ark was the sum total of a guardian's life. His social life ceased at the death of the former guardian monk, when he was appointed to take his place. Nor would he ever have more than superficial contact with others as long as he lived. He was a living sacrifice to God and to the Coptic faith, as were all guardians before him for centuries. No one but he and the head of the Coptic Church were ever allowed to view the ark.

Until the trouble between Ethiopia and Eritrea, he had accompanied the covered ark in procession on Timkat, the most important festival of the Ethiopian Orthodox Church. But due to the present political instability it remained in its chapel, guarded by the guardian and the fierce devotion and tradition of the people. The danger of it being ambushed by terrorists or zealots of other religions was too great. So a replica was used for the holy day processional on Timkat. The religious crowd knew it was not the real ark because the guardian was not in the procession.

A reporter, curious to see the ark, once asked what would happen if he forced his way into the chapel. He was told he would be immediately killed, not by the guardian but by the people themselves.

Gebra Mikail started back to bed when suddenly a blinding light flashed through the chapel. Then came a thundering shockwave, causing the little chapel to tremble. He ran to the door. *Was it an earthquake?* The loud blast of a trumpet sounded menacingly and lasted for a minute or two.

Suddenly it was quiet. The lightning flash had shorted out the town's transformers, making it pitch black. Awakened by the tremors and the trumpet blast, the people of Axsum stumbled out of their houses in confusion, still in their night clothes. In a panic families groped for one another and called out in the darkness. Above the din, a voice in the crowd near the Church of St. Mary cried out, "Fire!"

The crowd turned toward the voice and saw the little chapel. It burned a bright orange in the darkness. The noise stopped. The crowd forgot its fear in concern for the chapel. A large burly man said, "We need light to gather fire-fighting equipment." He shouted to the women to get flashlights or lanterns—candles even—whatever would give the men light. The men scrambled to bring water as soon as they could see. But as the people approached the iron fence that surrounded the chapel, they realized the fire had no earthly origin.

"It's the eternal fire!" one observer shouted in exclamation.

"The *Power* has returned!" rippled through the gathering crowd.

The women with lights joined the rest of the people. Mothers searched for their children. Families searched the crowd for one another. Then they discovered that many were missing, mostly elderly parents, but a few could not find spouses or children. They began to take stock of who was present and who was not. "What could it mean?" questioned the crowd in whispers, a new panic rising. Where were their missing family members?

"We must ask the Nebura-ed," declared a young man earnestly. The Nebura-ed was the chief priest of the St. Mary of Zion Church. "Perhaps their disappearance is connected to the fire."

"Where is Gebra, the guardian?" cried another. "Why does he not come out?"

The self-appointed leader divided the people—some to stay at the chapel and some to petition the Nebura-ed.

A procession formed. Those with lights distributed themselves among the others more or less evenly as they made their way slowly toward the Nebura-ed's dwelling. The others stationed themselves around the fence to keep watch.

On the way to Nebura-ed's house, the people made another discovery. Those family and friends who were missing were of the old faith, those who had been thought of as traditionalists, not taking into account the modern philosophies of religion. They were considered more ignorant, stubbornly clinging to the old ways. *Where were they?* members of the crowd wondered. Were they still in their homes oblivious to what was happening? Surely they of all people would be interested to know the celestial fire had returned.

Arriving at their destination, the burly man who had taken charge knocked loudly on the door. The house was dark and still. After some minutes the crowd began to murmur. Someone shouted to the burly man, "Go inside and see what has happened to Gamiel and his family. Perhaps they are injured."

The man in charge appointed three men and beckoned for them to come up onto the porch while he quieted the crowd in front of the house. He tried the door. It was locked. Then he tried a window. Feeling it give way, he motioned to the men to enter. Taking flashlights the three men climbed inside and disappeared into the house. The crowd watched as the flickers of the flashlights appeared in first one window and then another. Some minutes later the three men emerged alone. A hush quieted the crowd as they waited for news. The eldest of the three men spoke in quiet whispers to the man in charge

"They must have vaporized. They are not here, but the clothes they were wearing are."

"What do you mean vaporized?" the burly man shouted loud enough for the whole crowd to hear.

Hago, the tallest of the three men explained. "Gamiel and his family's night clothes are in their beds. They lay in different positions as if their bodies passed right through them, and their undergarments were inside of them."

Confusion shown in the leader's eyes as he tried to comprehend the significance.

Meanwhile the small crowd left behind at the chapel called out to Gebra Mikail, the guardian. Still he did not appear. A daring young man climbed over the iron fence and approached the door of the small building. Cautiously he reached for the door handle. Suddenly a flash of light engulfed him. He screamed and dropped like a limp puppet whose strings were let go. Those closest to the fence watched in absolute horror as his body convulsed and his clothes burst into flame as if electrocuted. The burning stench of singed hair and burnt flesh sickened the whole crowd. Stunned to silence they stared at the charred clothing and still body. Awe swept over them as they realized the Power *was not* to be trifled with.

Chapter 29

When Pope Peter and his small band left the conference in the darkness, they were so elated with the outcome they didn't noticed the darkened sky, probably because they entered the dark-glassed limousine inside the building. Then they had entered their special quarters the same way. But when they reached their suite, the pope first noticed and remarked about the gloom.

John McCutchen walked to the window and looked out. Most of the sky was black. The rest was twilight.

"We must have talked longer than I realized. I thought it was only five o'clock," he said.

"It *is* only five," said Jerry.

"Well, just look how dark the sky is."

The others joined him.

"It must be the physical phenomenon the president told us about," said the pope.

"Oh dear," said John, "is there anything we should do?"

"Yes," said the pope. "I think this calls for prayer. If you will excuse me I will attend to it right now." He then retired to his bedroom down the hall from the sitting room. Taking the pope's cue, John McCutchen did the same. Jerome McFarland, the American secretary, stood by the window watching.

Placing a pillow on the floor, Pope Peter sank to his ailing knees beside his bed. He began by appealing to the Holy Mother for mercy for the world. Praying in each of the many languages he knew, he made supplication for his people, his cardinals, and his staff. After nearly two hours he rose up, stretched, and turned on his light. It was completely dark by now. He washed his face and went back to the sitting room.

"Tony, will you make us some coffee?" he said to his Italian secretary.

"Good idea," said Antonio Cirillo. "Espresso or cappuccino?" He laughed, knowing their Italian preferences could not be met by their room's coffee machine. They would have to settle for American coffee. "Would you like something to eat from room service? We've eaten."

"Yes, thank you. Just order something light like a ham sandwich. Where is Jerry?" asked the pope while Tony called room service.

"He went downstairs to get something. What was it, John?"

"I didn't pay attention," replied John, looking up from his *Washington Post*.

"Shall we see the evening news while I wait on my sandwich? I want to see how they report the conference," said the pope. "Does the Post mention the conference?"

"No, the conference ended too late to make this addition."

The news report of the meteorite fall brought home to them the danger of the darkness. But the interview with Adoni´ and Ra'amon really captured their interest. They were especially pleased that the media had given Pope Peter credit for his part in the conference. After the news report ended they realized that Jerry had not returned. Visibly alarmed, the pope said, "Why is he not back? Tony, go downstairs and see if you can find him."

It was after Tony left the room that the blinding lightning flashed across the sky. The building trembled noticeably as pictures thumped against the wall. Pope Peter, who had just lifted his coffee cup to his mouth, spilled coffee down the front of his new *cossak*.

"What is this?" he exclaimed as he started to rise up to brush himself off and was lifted out of his chair. Standing, John felt the floor lift under his feet.

"This is very strange. Not like an earthquake, at least the ones we have back home," he said. Then the blast of a trumpet sounded long and loud. The pope felt his way down the hall because the building seemed to reverberate and tremble in the sound. He was going to his room to change his soaked robe. It finally stopped as he reached his room. But when he opened the door he faced another surprise. There standing in the center of the room bathed in a soft light stood the Virgin Mother. He fell at her feet.

"Rise up, my chosen, I have much to tell you," she said softly.

He stood trembling and wondering at the sight of her young and beautiful face. She was clothed in royal blue silk with a white overshawl covering her head and shoulders, like some painting of the masters. Around her neck hung a rosary with a cross dangling from it that was encrusted with diamonds that sparkled in the unearthly light.

"Trying times have come to the earth. It is time to separate the wheat from the chaff. I have much for you to do. But it cannot be done with the church in its present condition. Those ahead of you have allowed the faithful to wander far from the safety of the church. The rules must be obeyed if your flock is to find salvation.

"It is time for my Son's kingdom. He will not tolerate the insubordination any longer. You must see that the traditions of the past are restored. When you have restored all the holy laws to the church, you must purge all heresy from it. There is only one way to God and that is through *his church*. And there is only one universal church, which you will restore. Those who will not come to his church will be destroyed so that my Son's kingdom can be established in truth. I now endow you with the power and authority to carry out God's will."

A feeling of supernatural power surged through the pope's body, and with it came a strange light-headedness. When his head cleared he saw what he must do, almost as if he had an entirely new mind. The Virgin disappeared. *Well, of course,* he thought to himself. *I have followed the trend of those before me at the II Vatican Council who thought that modern man had changed and the old rules were for old times. Not so. I see that now. I will rise to the occasion since my mandate comes straight from the Queen of Heaven.* He looked down at his robe to find it dry and without stain.

Anthony Cirillo searched the hotel lobby before reaching the door to the street. Caught in a gusting wind, the door flung open with a bang, hitting the outside wall. Debris flew past him in disarray. What was happening? He glanced up and down the street. He couldn't see far because some of the lights were out. Hearing a clunking noise, he turned toward it. Then he saw them—Jerry's cowboy boots, which he always wore with his *cossak*. They were the one vestige of his western American heritage. They skidded along the pavement in jerks as the wind caught them. Cirillo was puzzled. Jerry never went anywhere without his boots. He ran into the street and scooped them up, calling Jerry's name. Hearing no response he carried the boots inside and up to the pope's suite.

"This is the only trace I could find of him," he said.

The pope stared at them in disbelief. "Jerry would never take off his boots outside."

"Especially not in the dark," added John McCutchen. "There's something very strange going on here."

Pope Peter said, "Holy Mother of God, what has happened to Jerry?"

—

J. Luecus Adoni´ watched the news in his room alone. When he

THE BEGINNING OF THE END

saw the clip of his interview with the reporter, his heart swelled with pride. He had been known among the Arabs for some time. Now he was known all over the world—a world player. He liked the idea. Where would it lead, he wondered. Perhaps bringing peace to the Middle East was his destiny. It was obvious that the Jewish leader, Ra'amon, would support him. But that didn't satisfy him. He had seen what it was like to have raw power when he had been with Saddam's elite. Someday he too would have such power, he just knew that somehow. He could feel his destiny beginning to shape.

In the midst of his reverie it started. The building trembled and shook only slightly. Everything rattled. He felt a slight lifting, and then came the noise. The trumpet sounded, drowning his senses. He clamped his hands to his ears and clenched his eyes shut. Suddenly he became aware of a presence. He opened his eyes. In the corner of his room stood the powerful figure of a...man? At least he seemed human, but his clothes were strange, not western apparel (pants, shirt, and tie) but a short tunic of ancient times, perhaps Roman or Greek, cinched at the waist with a gold band. Upon his head a small crown of gold laurel leaves circled, reminiscent of some Greek god. Golden straps laced his sandals, and in his hand he held a golden scepter that emitted flashes of light. His muscular body rippled as he crossed his arms and leaned against the wall, his scepter dangling from his hand in a casual manner.

Adoni´ stood speechless.

"You are thinking of your destiny," the figure stated, showing his clairvoyance. "I will tell you of your destiny. His voice dropped then he unfolded his arms, strode toward Adoni´, pointing with his scepter, and loudly proclaimed, *"You* will be my representative on the earth." *Look at him. He's not even afraid of me. I've chosen the right man for my purposes.*

"Just who are *you* to speak to me with such authority?" asked Adoni´ boldly, fascinated with the powerful creature in front of him. *Yes, powerful, that is an apt description,* he thought. *Herculean even. Is he a god? And if so, which god? The god of my mother, the god of my father, or someone else?*

"I am Lord Ashtor, in answer to your questions, the god of heavenly fortresses. Both the gods of your parents are minor gods, subject to me! I am the supreme god, and you would do well to respect me," he snapped.

"Ashtor... Is that related to Astarte?" asked Adoni´ meekly, searching through his knowledge of ancient gods and goddesses. He was excited. *Is this my destiny?*

"Yes, that was one of my female names. Ancient men seemed to prefer goddesses." The figure immediately began to change form. He became a woman with a fortified tower for a headdress. Multiple breasts tiered down her front. Adoni´ recognized Diana of Ephesus. *Does the tower headdress refer to the heavenly fortress?*

"This is how some of the ancients knew me," Ashtor continued. "Others as this." He changed into an Egyptian image. "Now I am Isis," the figure said. "But this is how I have appeared to modern man."

His form changed again. Adoni´ recognized the form as a UFO alien like many that adorn the cover of cheap tabloids. He had huge eyes in an enlarged head on a small body.

"But I thought the form of a man would appeal more *to you*."

"So you can take any shape you choose," said Adoni´, ignoring the inference but definitely impressed with the power of the being.

"Of course...I am god," he said as he returned to the Herculean image. It is I who am responsible for this display of power upon the earth. I have directed these asteroids right into the earth's path to establish my presence to modern man. You see, they have forgotten me. They have given another god my place, and they worship him—a god of softness, mercy, and *luuuve*," he sneered. "The ancient peoples knew me and worshipped me. They knew my mighty power.

THE BEGINNING OF THE END

It's time this world returned to worshipping the true power. *You* will make it possible. You desire the kind of power I can give. You will do great deeds for me, my son, after you decide to serve me."

"Are you talking about real authority or just supernatural tricks. I'm not interested in becoming some circus freak. What kind of political power is in it for me?" asked Adoni´, his audacious nature reasserting itself.

"I'm talking about *absolute* political power...*and* the religious status of a demigod," said Ashtor with firmness. "So you'd best change your attitude, or I'll choose someone else for that glory."

"How do *I* know you can do what you say?" bargained Adoni´, not completely convinced.

Ashtor's eyes flashed angrily as he set before Adoni´ a vision of dignitaries bowing before Adoni´ as Ashtor's representative.

"All right!" cried Adoni´, trembling with excitement. He thrust his two thumbs upright and punched the air. "What do I have to do?"

"Fall down and worship me." demanded Ashtor. "After that I require absolute obedience."

Adoni´ was more than willing to obey. He bowed himself to the floor. "My god," he said in obeisance, "and my master."

The golden-clad creature threw back his head and laughed out loud. "Yes, yes, this is what I long for. Soon the whole world will do the same."

Then he was gone.

In a daze Adoni´ lay on the floor, wondering if it had been a dream. So the god of this world is really Ashtor, the god of fortresses—heavenly fortresses—whatever that meant. The thought excited him. I like that—a mover and shaker. A holder of real power.

Slowly he got up. Adoni´ never could quite believe in the god of his mother, Jehovah, or the god of his father, Allah. Actually, Ashtor had predated both his parents' gods, he mused, staring out the window and mentally replaying the "who are you" incident.

I am chosen...me. Chosen to speak directly to god, to serve him, to speak for him—only me. But my secret shall remain until my unveiling after he has given me his power, he plotted, his pride not willing to suffer any embarrassment until Ashtor proved himself. *Besides, the other religions are too strongly entrenched right now, especially those Jews. And to think that I was the one who helped them. But I will win their hearts. I'm already on my way in that respect. Yes, this is a god I can follow.*

Another vacillating trumpet blast vibrated everything in the room. Adoni´ smiled. It was his *god* at work. Then a wind of near-hurricane force ripped through the neighborhood. Another flash of lightning swept the street below, momentarily lighting flying objects. Strangely enough no rain accompanied it. It was just a mighty wind. The air filled with debris: roofing, trash, boxes, papers, even clothing. Someone's laundry, thought Adoni´. Then the lights went out all over town.

Awesome display of power. I wonder if this is happening all over the world.

Chapter 30

When the wind came, the street cleared quickly as people scurried for shelter. Rachel started the car and was proceeding down the street when the flash came again, lighting everything, including objects in the air.

David frowned in puzzlement. "I don't understand why the air is full of clothing. It's almost like a clothes dryer." Then he thought, *this is very strange. A storm with wind and lightning, but it's dry. Not a drop of rain.*

A shirt blew against the windshield, forcing Rachel to stop. David jumped out to remove it when suddenly all the lights in the neighborhood went dark. Using the light from the car's interior to see, he picked off the shirt. He started to discard it when he noticed something unusual. The buttons on the shirt were all buttoned. He instinctively lifted it to his nose to see if it had that freshly laundered smell, but it had a distinct odor of recent occupancy, along with a slight scorched smell.

It's like it was torn off someone a minute ago, except it's not torn. Still holding the shirt, he got back into the car. *How did the shirt come off the man still buttoned?* The only thing he could think of wasn't possible, was it? The mystery of it sobered him. He said nothing to Rachel, but his expression evoked a response.

"What's wrong?" she asked, sensitive to the change.

"Take me to the hotel," David said abruptly. "We will find you a bed in one of the secretary's rooms. I need to be at my post."

Rachel couldn't understand the change in his plans, and she was disappointed since now she would have to share him. Why would clothing in the air make a difference? Still puzzling she turned the car around, paying close attention to the street titles illuminated by the car's headlights. Then the problem of navigation superseded all other thoughts. It was not easy to navigate with the lights of the whole city out. David helped her by calling out the street names as they passed and watching for the traffic since traffic signals were dark also. But the strangest thing of all was that every other car they saw was stopped and without lights. The people milled around outside with hoods up, stunned faces, some frantically trying to make their cell phones work. Forty-five minutes later, when they finally approached the hotel, they saw a few soft lights burning in some of the second floor rooms. The only lights to be seen.

"Good, they've lit my lanterns," said David.

Two armed men stepped forward as they entered the hotel.

"Oh, it's you, Captain," said Landau.

"Yes, and I see you made it back from the conference all right," replied David. "Everyone else here?"

"Yes, and we are all mighty glad you got those flashlights and lanterns."

"What about the emergency power?"

The hotel is saving most of that for the normal daylight hours. We just have the hall emergency lights."

"That's wise. We may have several days of this. But what about their freezers and refrigerators?"

"They are on a separate generator."

"Did Johnny assign you?"

"Yes, we are here till midnight."

THE BEGINNING OF THE END

David found Rachel a place in Merrill's room since the other two secretaries roomed together. Then he went looking for Johnny.

The men all huddled around a battery-operated shortwave radio David had picked up.

"...and that is all that has come in so far," the broadcaster's unmistakable, thick British accent sounded. "Stay tuned. We will keep you posted on the news as we hear new developments. Cheerio."

"What's the news?" David asked. "We didn't even try the car radio."

"You couldn't have picked up anything anyway. Nothing is on the air around here. The strange lightning must have zapped them. We were picking up London," said Johnny as he turned it off.

"They said they think several planes are down, because they are over due and don't respond by radio. The rest are grounded. Even so some of the people on the planes that made it apparently vaporized in the lightning. Strangest thing. It didn't burn their clothes. Just left them on the seats slightly scorched," continued Johnny.

"That's what I thought must have happened," said David as he remembered the shirt.

Johnny looked at him with a question mark on his face.

"There was a lot of clothing blowing in the wind where we were. A shirt landed on the windshield. It was still buttoned and had a scorched odor."

"Poor devils," said Johnny. "I've heard of certain people who have burst into flames spontaneously but never anyone who was vaporized by lightning."

"Anything happen besides the planes?" asked David.

"Yeah, man, there have been earthquakes everywhere. Millions of people are dead and missing. Thousands of people dead in transportation accidents because the drivers vaporized in the lightning."

"Has anyone tried to contact home?"

"I don't know. You'll have to talk to the prime minister."

After finding Ra'amon's suite, David tapped on the door.

"Enter," called Haik. "Oh, you're back, Captain Solomon. Come on in," he beckoned, showing a friendlier face to David than before.

"I was just wondering, sir, have you called or faxed home to hear of the damage there?"

"Yes, we have. It's bad but not as bad as some places."

"I was worried about the fault in the rift valley," said David.

"Strangely, it didn't seem to affect the big central fault, only the lateral faults extending out from it. For instance there was some movement in the fault under the Mount of Olives. Carmel shook some, but the worst was farther north."

"Good, that means the phones are still working."

"Not necessarily all of them. It took some time for us to get through."

"That stands to reason, with all the falling meteorites. They are bound to take out some of the satellites."

"Still, I think I will try to call home and see what happened there," David said. He left to go to his own room.

Rachel caught up on the disaster by talking to Merrill, who had just returned from the room with the radio. Then she tried to dial home to check on her family on her cell but was unable to get through.

"The lightning must have got the towers," she said. The regular ground lines were underground, so the room phone worked. They told her that Simon had arrived and everything was fine. They were thankful for the emergency items she and David had supplied.

It took David twenty minutes to reach his father. He had finally switched to the military satellite to get through. He understood why Ra'amon had said what he did. The lightning must have zapped everything electrical that was exposed to the atmosphere.

He praised G-d that somehow it had missed Rachel's car. He also wondered what was different about the electrical makeup of those vaporized people.

"Shalom," said his father.

"Father, this is David. How are things there?"

"We are all right. We shook, but it was rather gentle compared to some places. Actually Jerusalem fared pretty well. We hear it was really bad to the north."

"Did you have lightning?"

"Yes, it lighted the whole sky. You too?"

Uh-huh, it must have been worldwide. I think a thunderbolt passed between the earth and the asteroid. Was it followed by a lot of wind, blowing around a lot of stuff, even clothing?"

"Yes, some, now that you mention it. I thought it was strange at the time. What does it mean?"

"We think certain types of people were vaporized by the lightning. People disappeared on in-flight airplanes, leaving their clothing on the seats."

"How can that be?"

"I don't know."

"Strange," said his father thoughtfully.

"Well, I'm glad to hear Jerusalem is spared, and you and the family are safe. Now I can retire while others keep watch. It's been a long day for me."

After David's father pronounced a blessing over him, he hung up. He knew it would be hard to sleep. He sensed a new era had begun, perhaps one that had been prophesied for centuries, in which he had already been called to take part.

Chapter 31

Rachel slept fitfully, not being used to a strange bed. When she was awakened by the call of nature, she grasped for her small flashlight to find her way to the bathroom. Once inside the bathroom, she looked at her watch—7:00—time to get up anyway. How strange it was to be in darkness in the morning, especially in the spring. *Time is distorted without sunlight,* she thought then shivered. The temperature must have dropped as well. I'm glad I wore my jeans and sweatshirt. David said it would probably turn chilly. When she came back into the bedroom to dress, Merrill stirred.

"Is it time to get up yet?" she asked sleepily.

"It's seven," replied Rachel as she quickly dressed.

The secretary unwittingly reached for the switch on the lamp by the bed.

"Hey, all right," she exclaimed as the light came on. "The power's back on."

"Good, let's see if the thermostat will turn on some heat. It's cold in here," said Rachel as she moved the indicator. She wrapped a blanket around her and went to the window. She couldn't see any street lights outside, but across the street a large floodlight with a generator shone light on a pole where workers struggled to bring light back to the street. "The city lights are not back on. Our light must be on a generator," she said. Noises of activity began to sound throughout the floor as toilets flushed and showers roared. "At least the water still works," said Rachel. "I'm going to see if I can get some coffee."

She left the room and made her way down the lighted hallway to the stairs. She didn't trust the elevators. Who knows when the power will go out again. She also carried her flashlight and her phone in her purse. Somehow they made her feel secure. She kept the light folded blanket around her shoulders just in case it was cold downstairs.

When she reached the breakfast room, she found it bristling with activity. It was comforting to hear the clink of dishes and smell the coffee brewing. When Rachel got her tray, she walked to an empty table since she didn't recognize any of the faces present. She had just sat down when she heard a muffled ring. Opening her purse, she pulled out her phone and answered.

"Good morning, are you up yet?" asked David cheerfully.

"Up? I am sitting this minute in the breakfast room with a mug of steaming coffee in front of me," she replied, wondering how he got through to her. Maybe some of the phone towers were fixed.

"Good, I'll be right down."

Minutes later David appeared in the door. He smiled and waved to Rachel across the room then picked up his coffee and a roll. But before he could bring his tray to her table, the prime minister took him aside to talk to him.

After a couple of minutes, David came to the table.

"I hope my coffee isn't cold," he said as he sat down.

"Is that your only problem?" asked Rachel, concerned about his conversation with Ra'amon.

"No," he groaned. "We're going home."

"When?"

"Right after they sign the covenant this afternoon. I have to make the arrangements."

"I was afraid that was what you were talking about," said Rachel. "You won't need your chauffeur anymore, will you?"

David looked straight into her eyes, dead serious. "I will need my chauffeur long after I leave here. Rachel, I'm going to miss you something awful."

"I know what you mean," she said under her breath.

"You feel it too, don't you? Tell me it's not just me," said David earnestly, his eyes glowing with feeling.

She nodded her head slowly.

"Listen, this is too precious to lose. We have to keep this thing going between us. I've known only a few women in my time, never anything serious, but this—I want this to last forever." At that he reached over and took her hand.

She squeezed his hand, feeling joy and contentment, her eyes revealing the full depth of her feelings.

"How can we feel so strongly about each other in just five days?" she asked. "How am I ever going to bear your leaving? It was hard enough to be apart from you during this week, but think about weeks and months of it," she said in an almost groan, a tear escaping from the corner of her eye and wetting the thick black lashes.

"Let's get out of here," said David suddenly.

They left the coffee shop, walked through the lobby into the hall, David steering Rachel with his hand on her arm. When they reached an alcove leading to a powder room, he pulled her to him and enclosed her with his arms. Their lips met, need answering need as they satisfied their longings in a deep sensuous kiss. Finally, David dragged his mouth from Rachel's and dropped kisses down her temple to her throat, murmuring her name. Once again he captured her lips, sending a shudder of passion through them both. Then they just stood there, Rachel's head against David's shoulder and his head leaning against hers, enjoying the oneness. Enclosed in an aura of wonder their joy mingled with the sense of belonging.

The noise of approaching steps separated them, and they walked on hand in hand.

Rachel broke the silence first. "What do you have to do to be ready to go?"

"I have to file a flight plan as soon as it's cleared with international. Then I have to order our plane ready for flight. It's in a hanger at Andrews. Ra'amon checked with the airport, and they said the meteorites have stopped. Somehow I can't imagine that the encounter was that short."

"Well, remember the original forecast was that the asteroid would only graze the earth," said Rachel.

"I know, I guess I'm just looking for an excuse to stay longer." David sighed. "Look, I have to go do my job now. I'll call you as soon as I can be with you."

With that he kissed her lightly on the lips and said, "*Shalom*, my *hamoodah* (darling)."

Rachel shivered as she watched him walk toward the elevators. She must have left the blanket in the coffee shop. In the excitement of David's presence, she hadn't notice the chill. She went back to get it.

Most of David's men had eaten breakfast and were back cloistered in Johnny's room, listening to the radio report of the aftermath of the disaster. David arrived just in time to hear the announcer speak of the Middle East.

"Nablas, in the Palestinian territory, was hit hard, as well as the area east of the Dead Sea in Jordan. In Jerusalem, the Mount of Olives moved slightly, causing slight damages to three churches and a hotel.

"Scientists are speculating that the lifting of the earth's crust caused earthquakes in the areas of the east/west lateral faults connected to the greatest crack on the entire earth. The one that runs north and south through the Jordan valley, down the Red Sea, and south into the horn of Africa. Damage farther south has not yet been determined, but latest reports indicate a change in the headwaters of the Nile.

"Because of this, reports from Egypt say the river is reduced to a trickle, making a canyon of mud and rocks. In upper Egypt the people of the west side are stranded and unable to reach the urban areas on the east side. Cruise lines lament the damage to their ships. Helicopters rescued passengers on the ships scuttled mid-river.

"The Egyptian Government is struggling to quiet a panic. Agriculture and fish industries dependent on the water will be particularly hard hit. Egypt has appealed to the nations of the world for help. The US Army Corp. of Engineers in the Middle East is sending pontoons and crews to help erect temporary bridges across the mud canyon, but they worry that the loss of water may be permanent. All of Egypt depends on the river to exist.

"The scientists believe that the asteroid that caused this catastrophe has passed on out of the earth's influence, and things should calm down. They expect the darkness to last for a while since the dust that blocks out the light of the heavens remains in its orbit. Gradually, they feel it will thin out, and we will see the sun again. In the meantime, we will need to conserve energy as the earth cools.

"In the US, farmers expect to cut into the nation's grain reserves for animal feed until the grass revives. It is hoped they won't have to slaughter too many livestock, driving the prices down.

"In fact, the whole economic picture for the world looks bleak, since most of the money will be used by the governments to rebuild. That will make money very tight.

"A mystery still remains concerning what happened to thousands of people who literally disappeared, leaving behind their clothing. The popular theory is that they vaporized in the thunderbolt that passed between the earth and the asteroid, but scientists say there is no basis to such a theory."

Finally, the commentator ended on this note. "I'm sorry to say there doesn't seem to be any good news. All we can say is we must be citizens of the world together and try to work ourselves out of this mess."

Someone switched off the radio. David said to his men, "Listen up, guys." As soon as it got quiet he continued. "The prime minister wants to leave for Israel as soon after the covenant signing as possible. We shouldn't encounter any difficulty with security if we all stay inside the hotel until time to leave. Arab fundamentalists who don't go along with the Temple Mount concession might try something in this darkness. I don't want any of the delegation wandering around outside the hotel. See that they don't." He continued with his instructions until every man was assigned to his guard post then he tackled the problem of getting them home.

He called Andrews Air Force Base. Yes, they thought the meteorite falls were over, but FAA would have to give the go ahead.

"When will they know?"

"As soon as the astronomers clear them…maybe six or seven hours."

"Thank you, I'll get back with you," said David. *Maybe we won't go today,* he thought. He looked at his watch. Only 9:15. He wondered if they had left for the conference yet.

He went to the prime minister's suite and knocked. Kaufman opened the door.

"Is the prime minister still here?" David inquired.

"Yes, come in, Captain," called Ra'amon.

"Sir, the FAA won't know about making overseas flights for another six to eight hours. We can't leave without their clearance," reported David.

Ra'amon turned to Kaufman. "Let them know in Israel we

can't be back until tomorrow at the earliest. Thank you for trying, David." Then he turned to the others. "Let's go finish this historic conference."

Chapter 32

Simon Lieberman woke up late that morning, if you could call it morning, since only the clock said so as he lit his lantern. He had spent a good part of the night reading the New Testament taken from Janet Stewart's desk. He jumped up, refreshed in spite of the lack of sleep. His heart sang with joy.

Because of the darkness and the lack of traffic lights he had reached home quite late last night. Dan and Sheila were waiting up for him and told him the news about the Temple Mount. He received the news gladly, but the overwhelming curiosity about the Lamb of God dismissed it from his mind. He couldn't wait to get alone with the New Testament, which beckoned from his pocket. Neither could he tell Dan and Sheila of his experience, at least not yet. He needed to know what it meant himself first.

"Do you want a flashlight or a lantern to take to your room?" asked Sheila, who had the equipment ready, awaiting his arrival.

"I want a lantern," he said, "but first I need a cup of coffee and a sandwich from the kitchen before I retire."

"Do you want me to fix it?" she asked.

"No, no, you go on to bed. I'll do it myself," he said, anxious to be alone. Hattie had long since retired after Sheila finally calmed her down.

Simon hurriedly made his snack and took it with him to his

bedroom. His hunger and thirst for knowledge far outweighed his hunger and thirst for food. He opened the little book, finding the page number for the book of John. He sipped his coffee as he turned the pages. Leaning down close to the lantern he began to read, nibbling away at his sandwich at the same time.

"In the beginning was the word and the word was with God, and the word was God. All things were made by him; and without him was not anything made that was made."[1]

He stopped. *Yes, that's true. The Torah says, "G-d said and it was..." He even spoke his word aloud giving the law at Mt. Sinai.* But why was it calling the Word a *him*? He read on.

"He was in the world, and the world was made by him, and the world knew him not. He came unto his own, and his own received him not."[2]

His own. Why, that's us, the Jewish people. We didn't receive the Word. Many times in the Tanakh the prophets accused the people of refusing the word of G-d. Just like olden times, he thought.

He read on. "And the word was made flesh and dwelt among us..."[3]

Simon was repulsed as he realized this was referring to Jesus, the god of the Goyim. Jesus couldn't be the Lamb of God. Jesus was the one who had caused untold misery for his people for centuries. Besides, the voice said his name was *Yeshua*, not Jesus. He read on.

"For the law was given by Moses, but grace and truth came by Jesus Christ."[4] Yes, it *is* talking about Jesus. The voice said the Lamb had come and was coming back. He read on with suspicion. Was Jesus ever called the Lamb of God?

Then he saw it.

"The next day John seeth Jesus coming unto him, and saith, 'Behold the Lamb of God that taketh away the sins of the world.'"[5] Simon frowned. How could a *man* take away the sins of the world?

Only G-d could do that. Continuing on he came to another disturbing sentence.

"And I saw and bore record that this is the Son of God."[6]

"This is blasphemous," he said out loud. "No one can be the son of God without being a god himself. Does not the law say 'Hear O Israel! The Lord our God, is One'?"[7]

Silently an unbidden thought entered his mind. He remembered a reference to a Son of God in the Hebrew version of the Scriptures—Psalm 2. "Kiss the son lest he be angry..."[8] He went to look it up in the Tanakh. Translated into English the Tanakh didn't mention the Son. Instead it translated the word for son as "Lord" and footnoted the passage, saying it was of uncertain meaning. But *I know I read it.*

He got out his Hebrew Bible. Turning to Psalm 2 he found it and wondered why they changed it in the Tanakh.

נַשְּׁקוּ־בַר פֶּן־יֶאֱנַף וְתֹאבְדוּ דֶרֶךְ כִּי־יִבְעַר כִּמְעַט אַפּוֹ אַשְׁרֵי כָּל־חוֹסֵי בוֹ

The Hebrew translated read, "Kiss the Son/the heir lest he be angry perish ye (from) the way, when is kindled but a little his wrath. Blessed are all they (who) in trust him."[9] That was the last verse. Then he read the Psalm from the beginning in the Tanakh. He stopped at verse two where it said, "...kings of the earth take their stand, and regents intrigue together against the Lord, and against his anointed?"[10]

Humh—his anointed? I wonder if it means the Moschiach. Reading on he stopped at verse 6. "But I have installed My king upon Zion, My holy mountain!"

Yes. It is the Moschiach *as king,* interpreted Simon. He read on. "Let me tell of the decree: The Lord said to me..."

That must be G-d speaking to the *Moschiach*," Simon said again reasoning out loud.

"You are my Son, I have fathered you this day."

He frowned. *Why have I not seen this before? The book of John calls Jesus "the only begotten of the Father."*

He looked back at the New Testament page. Where had he read that? Oh, yes, verse 14 and again in 18. He read verse 18 out loud.

"No man hath seen God at any time; the only begotten Son, which is in the bosom of the Father, he hath declared him."[11]

The only begotten means the only one to come from the loins of God and be born as a man. He knew the Christians made a big deal of the birth of Jesus. Was this why? Where could he find out about the birth of Jesus?

He looked in the beginning of the New Testament. It seemed only logical that it would begin with his birth. It began with a genealogy starting with Abraham. But it ended with Jesus called the Christ. There was a note on the word Christ. Looking at the bottom of the page he found that Christ meant the anointed one. Christ is Greek for our Moschiach. The book of John said that Jesus was the Moschiach *and* the Son *and* the Lamb of God. He wondered how many other parts of the Tanakh spoke of these things. Time for that later. He needed to read this New Testament while he had it.

He turned back to the book of Matthew. He read the account of Mary and Joseph. So that's how he was considered the Son of God. Again it said that Jesus would save his people (*that's us*) from their sin. *Yeshua* means Salvation in English. I wonder if Jesus means the same in the Greek?

The footnote at the end of the genealogy mentioned a separate genealogy in the book of Luke. As Simon read Luke's account of Jesus' birth, he came to a dead stop when he read the angel's message. He reread it aloud. "A savior which is Christ the Lord."[12] Lord was the English word for Aden in the Greek, and Aden in the Greek was the word for G-d in the Greek translation of the Hebrew Scriptures, the Septuagint. Again that meant the writer considered the savior both Moschiach and G-d.

Mary's son was called Immanuel—God with us. The prophet Isaiah predicted it.[13] *I wonder why the rebbes have not taught that the Moschiach was to be the Son of God. I'm asking more questions than I'm answering,* he thought.

He realized at this point that maybe the rebbes were afraid the people would believe in Jesus, so they ignored those parts. From then on he read with more interest and less suspicion, finding yet another Scripture from a footnote in Luke mentioning G-d as the Son. "...For unto us [*that is us Jews*] a child is born, unto us a Son is given."[14] Before he quit reading he had definitely decided that the powerful voice that spoke to him must have been that of the Christians' Jesus. With that decision made, he went on to read of his death and Resurrection. Simon began to understand how Jesus became a kind of Passover lamb to the world—one that substituted for the sins of all mankind. Was this the reason he referred to himself as the Lamb of God?

To avail oneself of this forgiveness from God, all one had to do was to admit to himself that he was a sinner and repent of his sins then accept Jesus' death as a sacrifice to God for him or her. Simon had fallen on his knees and done just that when he understood the plan of God. At that very moment he had been filled with a sense of God's love and acceptance, which he had never known in all his life despite his studies.

The feeling had lingered on until this morning, and he was so full of joy that all he could do was sing. He came down the stairs singing Psalm 27. It seemed appropriate somehow.

"The Lord is my light and my salvation..."

The rest of the family was in the breakfast nook. They heard him coming down the hall. "Therefore will I offer in his tabernacle sacrifices of joy; I will sing, yea I will sing praises unto the Lord," sounded out the loud baritone voice. He opened the door.

"Good morning," he said cheerfully.

"And what have you got to be cheerful about this gloomy morning?" asked Sheila in surprise.

"The best of all reasons," he replied as he set down his lantern and helped himself to scrambled eggs in a chafing dish on the buffet. "I have met the *Moschiach*."

"Oh, Papa, get real," Dan said. "Nothing you say can cheer us up in this gloom."

"I *am* being real. He came to me at the office last night. Remember when the shaking came? And the lightning?"

Dan nodded.

"After that the loud trumpet sound?"

"Yes, yes, go on."

"Well, when the trumpet sounded a blinding light appeared in my office, and all of a sudden my legs turn to jelly and I collapsed to the floor. Then this voice told me to take off my shoes and stand up because I was on holy ground. When I asked who was talking to me, he said, 'I am *Yeshua*, your *Moschiach*.' Then he said he had chosen me along with several others and anointed me with the Spirit of his Father. I was to tell our people and the Gentiles that he is coming to set up his kingdom. He said I must preach to them that the Lamb of God has come and is coming back again soon with the wrath of judgment. He said to warn the people to repent of their sins. If I don't, he will require it of me."

"And just who *is* this Lamb of God?" asked Dan. "Are you sure the lightning hasn't addled you senseless?"

"That's what I asked," said Simon, ignoring the crack about his senses. "He told me to read about him in the book of *Jochanan*."

"But there's no book of *Jochanan* in the Tanakh," protested Dan.

"That's right," said Simon. "It's in the New Testament."

"But the Jewish *Moschiach* would not direct you to the Bible of the Christians," he cried.

"*Unless* the Jewish *Moschiach is* the God of the Christians."

"Wait a minute!" Dan was almost shouting. "Are you saying that the hated Jesus is our *Moschiach?* You must be crazy."

"I went through the same feelings that you feel now, but I discovered some things the rebbes haven't taught us."

"Such as..." said Dan sullenly.

"Did you know that the *Moschiach* is the Son of God?"

"Where does it say that?" he asked with unbelief.

"In Psalm 2," Simon answered in triumph. "The Almighty seemed to bring that Scripture to my mind when I was asking the same question. The voice said, 'I anoint you with the Spirit of *my Father*'. You see, the first chapter of the book of *Jochanan* says that Jesus is the only begotten Son of God; he is the Christ. That's the Greek word for Messiah. *And* that he is the Lamb of God. Remember, he told me that the Lamb *had come* and was coming back."

"How can a man be a Lamb?" asked Dan, starting to show interest.

"Because Jesus is the real Lamb of Passover. Just as the blood of the Passover lamb in the Exodus diverted the angel of death, so does the blood of the Moschiach cover the sins of those who believe. In fact, Yeshua, that's his Hebrew name, died at the same time they killed the official Passover lamb in the temple. His one death paid for the sins of the whole world because he was God, whose life is infinite. He took the death penalty for sin for every man."

"But," protested Dan, "If you keep the law you are not a sinner."

"You can't keep the law perfectly. You know that. Did not the prophet say, 'Come, let us reach an understanding, says the Lord. Be your sins like crimson, they can turn snow-white; Be they red as dyed wool, They can become like fleece'?[15] Come, I will show you from the Tanakh." He picked up his lantern from the table where he set it and led the way back to his bedroom where Simon preached his first sermon to Dan and Sheila.

———

The pope kept hoping that Jerry would return. Jerry was his favorite, always showing an uplifting spirit, and his joy lifted all their spirits. He was always singing or whistling the new Scripture choruses of the Charismatic branch of the Church. He had such a good manner for dealing with the English-speaking peoples. Everybody seemed to love him. What could have happened to him?

On the morning news (one emergency station was broadcasting locally) the pope heard for the first time about the missing people who had left their clothes behind. Since he had Jerry's boots, he concluded he must be one of them. Jerry's with the Lord now, he thought and crossed himself, but it was strange not to have a body to bury. He was saddened. He would miss Jerry.

Knowing Jerry's fate, Pope Peter turned his attention to his assignment from the Virgin. *No more Mr. Nice Guy,* he thought. He would have to get tough, especially with the Holy See and all those trying to modernize the Church. (The Jesuits had been in rebellion against the last three popes.) He was the pope. He had the power; the Virgin had given it to him. He would use it. First, he would gather the conservatives around him who were against all the changes Vatican II had made. He was sure Opus Dei would help. The Opus Dei was a large organization in the Catholic Church made up of powerful lay people. When he was ready, he would call for a consistory (the pope's mandatory recall for every cardinal to meet with him in Rome). Then he would purge the Church of her modern garbage and prepare her to rule.

Chapter 33

The State Department briefed the other security teams on procedures for the signing at the White House. So far no protests had been raised. Probably because making the Temple Mount available to the Jews had caught everybody by surprise. But even so, neither Hizbullah nor Hamas's Izzadin Kassam announced their responsibility until after a tragic attack.

The plan called for men with bomb-sniffing dogs to mingle with the small crowd inside as well as outside. Strategically placed marines patrolled the grounds outside, while two helicopters circled overhead in constant contact with them. (The military had immediately gotten its communications towers up and running.) The Secret Service would surround the president and other US officials. David and Johnny's men would protect the Israeli delegation. The Arab security team would do the same for their delegation, and the State Department would look after the pope. Through it all, the media would try their patience with their usual circus atmosphere.

Those writing the covenant finished about noon. The signing was set for two o'clock inside the White House. Usually these type of agreements were signed on the White House lawn, but the inside was easier to secure in the darkness. By one o'clock the security was well in place, as evidenced by the beating of helicopter propellers.

The time of the signing was given only to select media. The news would run a tape of it for the public later on.

The delegations began arriving at one-thirty. The actual signing began as the media took charge, staging each step for the camera. First, the pope made his way to the front. Standing at a small podium he proudly proclaimed, "Fellow citizens of the world, we few meet today for a momentous occasion. The beginning of true peace in the Middle East. It has cost dearly, but at last we can say thanks to the God of Abraham for it." He purposely addressed God thus to include the Arabs. "I believe this signing marks the dawning of a new age for mankind. I think it rather significant that we agree to this Holy Covenant in darkness, for when the sun does shine again, it will shine on a different world, a world of peace."

Afterward, Haik Ra'amon and Nabil Dakkah also gave short statements. The camera turned to the table that held the documents, a copy for each participant. Haik Ra'amon signed for Israel, Nabil Dakkah for the Palestinians, and the pope for the Vatican, which had agreed to provide the neutral Swiss Guard in the buffer zone.

The president, US secretary of state, and J. Leucas Adoni´ stood behind until it was their turn to sign as witnesses.

"Now shake hands," commanded the press coordinator. Cameras flashed and TV cameras rolled, recording the historic event—the signing of the Holy Covenant. By three o'clock it was all over without any incident. Security concentrated on safely returning the delegations to their hotels, and they all began making arrangements for departure to their own lands.

David used his cellular to call the base before he left the White House.

"David Solomon here, of Israeli Security, have you heard anything from the FAA yet?"

"Yes, the astronomers gave the go ahead just an hour ago. They said reports coming in mention only small meteors that burn up in the upper atmosphere. Nothing that we know of has reached the earth in the last six hours."

"Can we schedule our flight now?"

"Yes."

"Good. Put us in your flight schedule for Ramalla, the new Israeli/ Palestinian International Airport."

"When do you want to leave?"

"Six p.m.," he said decisively.

"I'll see how close I can arrange it. The FAA is being bombarded with requests from the commercial airlines to restore their regular flights, so it's going to be a scramble for a while as we try to squeeze you in."

David gave his cellular number so they could reach him anywhere. Then he advised the prime minister that they should all return to the hotel until the flight plan was approved. On the ride back to the hotel, David ordered their plane serviced and ready for take off.

Rachel hung around the hotel all morning. She wouldn't leave until she saw David again, no matter how brief a time it might be. She wondered if he had made the flight arrangements and how long it would be until he left her life feeling emptier than it had ever been before this week.

The only love that Rachel had known until now was from her family. She was either too religious or too aloof to attract even the Jewish boys during her teenage years. She was only really close to her papa because of their religious bond. The rest of the family did not share in it. When she was just a tiny tike, he would fill her head with stories of the coming Moschiach and his wonderful kingdom. Growing up with them as she did, those stories were more real to her than life itself.

All through school they set her apart. When others shunned

her because of her beliefs, she would tell her papa, "*Goyim*, who needs them?" Her mother protested his filling her head with religion. Being more of a socialite, she belonged to Hadassah and other Jewish women's associations. Society bored Rachel. Like Yental of the movie, she would rather study Torah with her papa.

Dan took more after his mother in that his devotion to the faith lacked fervor. Even so he and Sheila had begun going to the synagogue on *Shabbat* with her father for the sake of appearance, since they had moved in with Simon after his wife died. Compared to Rachel they were but nominal believers. Her papa had instilled in her a genuine love for God and his righteousness.

For Rachel to find a man like David, a man whose ideals and passions were identical to her own, was overwhelming, almost too good to be true. Her past experience with the opposite sex had always ended up in a wrestling match. Men, she had concluded, had one mind—to take away her purity. *But David,* she smiled, *is a real gentleman.*

It was obvious that Rachel was euphoric. So obvious that Merrill commented, "You are *for sure* gone on the guy, aren't you, honey?"

Rachel blushed. "Is it so obvious?"

"Yes," replied the secretary. "You are positively glowing."

Rachel laughed. "It has never happened to me before. I feel like a little kid who has just received a wonderful present."

"You have, my dear. I don't know how many of the girls have tried for David, but the only one he ever noticed even slightly was Deidrienne. Even they only went out a few times, but she thinks she has her mark on him, but he is just being nice to her."

"I didn't think it could happen this fast," said Rachel, ignoring the reference to Deidrienne and glad for an opportunity to express the feelings bursting inside.

"Honey, all it takes is the right chemistry. I've been there many times," said Merrill.

THE BEGINNING OF THE END

"You mean it won't last?" asked Rachel, doubt clouding her eyes for the first time.

"It all depends. When you first meet a guy, you only see the good stuff. Later, when the faults start showing up, things seem to cool off."

"Oh," Rachel replied thoughtfully, trying to imagine David with a fault.

At that moment her cellular rang. She let it ring until she could step into the hall. She knew it was David. When she answered he said, "Where were you? I thought you left your phone somewhere again."

"No. I just didn't want Merrill listening in," she replied. "Do you know anything yet?"

"I'm waiting for them to call. Do you want to wait with me?"

"Oh, yes, where are you?"

"I'm in the lobby. Remember that alcove in the hall? I'll meet you there."

Rachel hurried down and rushed into his waiting arms. He crushed her to him in a long, satisfying kiss. Then he turned her head up between his hands and said, "My *hamoodah* (darling), we have to make some plans, and we haven't much time. As soon as they call back, I may be too busy to see you." Then he kissed the end of her nose and said, "Come on, let's get a cup of coffee."

When they had decided on a table in the corner, David took out a pen and searched through his pockets for something to write on. Finding nothing, he looked at Rachel.

"Paper?"

She looked in her purse. Taking out one of her cards from the embassy, she handed it to David. He wrote down his address and phone number in Jerusalem on the back.

"I'll be writing to you, but I don't want you to have to wait to write to me. We won't be able to keep using these telephones overseas." He laughed. "At least not on my salary."

"Nor mine," replied Rachel.

"How do you feel about moving to Jerusalem to live?" asked David, searching her eyes to see how deeply she would commit to him.

"You know I love the land, but how and where could I get a job?"

"Through the embassy maybe. Think about it."

"I know it is going to be exciting over there. They will be building the temple soon. Maybe Papa will be going over..." Rachel's voice trailed off. *Surely he doesn't mean...*

David charged right on, not noticing the change in her expression.

"I like your father. We had a great discussion the other night when he brought me back to the hotel. Do you think he would approve of me as a son-in-law?"

"Ar Are you asking me to marry you?" asked Rachel, her voice subdued. Rachel was thrown into a turmoil. She thought she loved David, but this was happening too fast. Never had she had these wonderful feelings. Nevertheless she was used to working things out with her mind. She couldn't make a decision with her heart, at least not one that important, could she? What if Merrill was right? She didn't really know David. How could she answer him?

"Yes," he said, searching her eyes again. The silence seemed to go on forever.

She could see that David read it as doubt, because she saw his face fall. She knew she was hurting him, but she couldn't seem to help it. *Here I go breaking another heart.* She twisted her napkin, searching for words to end the awkwardness.

Finally, she spoke. "I'm sorry, I've never felt this way toward anyone else. But how can I give an answer to such an important decision in an instant, especially in all this emotion. I'm used to thinking things through. I don't even know your faults yet. How do I know you won't be a wife beater?" she said, remembering what Merrill had told her about feelings. Then she laughed, trying to lighten the moment.

David looked relieved. "There's plenty of time," he replied. "The trouble with me is I've been waiting so long to find you. I was prepared to love you before I even met you. You are the woman of all my dreams. I recognized that right away."

"I do care for you, David. Of that much I'm sure, but is it just a feeling, just chemistry, like they say, or is it the real thing? I can't sort it out in all this emotion," she spoke honestly.

"We'll sort it out in time," David replied, taking her hand. "It's just that it would be so much easier if we were in the *same* place."

His cellular went off, ending the precious moment.

"Yes," answered David.

"We have you a flight scheduled for 7:15 p.m. That's the best we could do."

"Good. We will take it," replied David and pressed the off button.

"Seven fifteen," he repeated to Rachel.

"So soon," she cried. "That's less than two hours. I—is this good-bye?" she faltered

"I need to tell the delegation. Wait here until I know if I'm needed. If I can't get back I will call you." He stood, leaned down, and brushed her lips in a brief kiss then left the table.

Rachel followed the movement of his body as he walked away. Back in his khakis today for the signing, he looked neat and lean in the close military fit. She admired the cool self assurance that emanated from his walk. As he rounded the corner to the hall, he turned and threw her a kiss. Then he was gone. A feeling of gloom settled over her. Soon there would be an ocean and a sea between them. Could she marry him? She didn't know. Right now all she felt was misery.

Chapter 34

Before the elevator reached the Delegation's floor, David heard gunfire. What was happening? Had he been derelict in his duty by spending time with Rachel? But there was no time to feel guilty. His training kicked in as he readied himself to fight. Drawing his ever-present nine-millimeter Beretta, he flattened his chest against the buttons to the right of the elevator door, making himself invisible. He also poised his finger on the door's close button just in case. When the door opened bullets sprayed inside, narrowly missing him. David quickly closed the door. Praying no one had pushed the button in the lobby to recall the elevator, he pressed for the next floor. The elevator went on up, thank the Almighty. The door opened. He glanced right then left, his gun ready. Nothing. After checking to see if enemy perpetrators were lurking in this hall, he darted to the exit stairs. Using the same caution as before, he quietly made his way down, hugging the wall until he reached the platform where the stairs reversed. Then, gun in hand, he dropped to the floor and peered through the banister to see around the corner to the lower level. The stairs were empty. He hurried down the rest of the steps.

All was quiet in the hall as he looked through the small window in the door. He could see a couple of crumpled bodies at the juncture of the two halls in front of the elevator—the security guards.

He also saw two perps with AK 47 machine guns hiding at the corners on either side of the delegates' hall. He realized that the security teams must be pinned in their rooms with the delegates. That meant that the terrorists blocked the other end of the hallway as well. He had to take out those on this end and to give the rest of his men a chance. As he readied himself, a man carrying a large knapsack on his back lumbered by, obviously carrying a heavy load. He headed toward the other terrorists. At that instant David understood their plan. If the suicide bomber reached the center of the delegation's hall they would all be history. He had to act fast. Inserting his coded card, he opened the door just a crack and braced it with his foot. He had to be accurate because if he happened to shoot the knapsack the whole floor might explode anyway. Taking careful aim he shot at the man's head. The man slumped to the floor.

Surprised by the gunshot in what they must have considered a safe hall, both men turned their AK 47s on David. He let the heavy security door slam shut just in time, and then he shot out the glass in the exit door window and returned their fire. He couldn't let them reach the bomber. They might yet detonate the bomb, but every time he chanced a shot, he exposed himself. *G-d of the Universe, protect me,* he prayed.

With the shooters concentrating on David, the other end of the hall erupted with gunfire. From the time they had become aware of their peril until they began to fight, the team had gathered their own assault weapons and planned their strategy. They rushed the far end as soon as David had drawn the fire on his end; some spraying covering bullets so others could advance. Katz and Matza came out of the elevator just in time to take out the men shooting at David. After making sure they had killed all the terrorists, the security team released the prime minister and his delegates. They had saved the delegates but lost at least three of their own, maybe more.

THE BEGINNING OF THE END

No one knew the fate of those guarding the service elevator in the basement.

Landau was the most seriously injured with a wound in his shoulder. Others had suffered superficial flesh wounds in the ensuing battle. Johnny's men had been guarding the two ends of the hall. Finding pistols with silencers on the terrorists, they knew how the guards had been taken out, evidently both posts at the same time. It had all taken place within ten minutes.

When David reached the prime minister's suite, he walked into a bustle of excitement.

"Where have you been?" Haik Ra'amon demanded.

"In the dining room downstairs. I had my cellular. Nobody called except the airport. I came to tell you we leave at seven-fifteen."

"Good, the sooner we get out of here the better," said Ra'amon, relieved.

"And thank you for saving my life," said David to himself out of earshot. "Oh well, I was just doing my duty."

Katz tapped him on the arm. "Someone sent a terrorist threat."

"Who? When?" David asked.

"We were bringing it up to you when the shooting started. Here, read it for yourself." He handed David the note. David read, "You will never leave the country." Signed, Hizbullah.

"That doesn't sound like Hizbullah. They don't announce their attacks. How did this come?"

"They sent it to the lobby with the prime minister's name on it."

"How long ago?"

"About ten minutes."

David frowned. "We weren't supposed to get this in advance. It was left to give them credit after we had been blown to bits. Katz, how was the note delivered?"

"No one saw it delivered. The desk clerk found the envelope on the desk face down."

"Who came in during the last ten minutes?"

"No one came in the front door, Captain," said Matza.

"What about hotel personnel; have any waiters or others been at the desk?"

"No, only the desk clerk."

"Wait a minute," said Katz. "Someone did check out."

"I'll go talk to the desk clerk." David raced down to the elevator and then to the desk, Katz and Matza following close behind. Speaking to the desk clerk he said, "Who checked out last?"

"A Mr. Musgrave from room 302."

"Did you leave the desk at any time when he was checking out?"

"No, but he was clumsy and dropped some of his change. Some coins rolled off the desk on to the floor. I had to pick them up."

"That's when he delivered the note. How long did he stay?"

"He checked in on the fifth."

"The day before we arrived. He's been here all the time. I wonder how they knew where we would be staying? That means one of their team got away. I wonder if they have a contingency plan if plan A fails?" David turned to the desk clerk and asked, "How do you get to the roof?"

"Take the elevator to the eighth floor. There are stairs at the end of the hall, but the door is locked."

"Let me have the key," demanded David.

"You have to see the manager for that."

David sent Katz for the key and Matza to the basement to check on the security team, while he went back upstairs. The delegates were all packed up and standing around in Ra'amon's suite when he came in.

"We've had a security breech," said David. "Open all your luggage and make sure there is nothing in it that should not be there—like a bomb. They may have a plan B. All of you, including security," David commanded. "Hillman, you go through Johnny's and mine.

THE BEGINNING OF THE END

Call me if you find anything suspicious. Johnny, you come with me, but leave your cellular with Hillman." He headed toward the door.

He took Johnny to the eighth floor where Katz was waiting at the open door leading to the roof. David led the way to the top. They walked out and looked around.

Johnny had been frowning the whole way. No doubt David would blame him.

"How could there have been a breech in our security?" he asked. "I took every precaution here at the hotel." He felt threatened, as if David didn't trust his work.

"They couldn't have pulled this off unless they had a sleeper here in the hotel," said David as he walked all over the roof.

"What are you looking for anyway?" asked Johnny.

"I just wanted to see how much room we have for helicopters to land up here. What do you think?"

"The roof may not be able to take the weight, but it could hover, say four or five feet above."

"Didn't you check for that when you set up the escape routes?"

"Not the strength. I didn't think it would be necessary," said Johnny with downcast eyes.

David sighed, then he whipped out his cellular and called Ra'amon's suite. "Did you find anything?"

"No, nothing," said Hillman.

He hung up. "No bomb at least," he said. "The only other way they could hit us is on the way to the airport or later on the plane." He called the State Department security.

"David Solomon, Israeli security here. We just suffered a terrorist attack here in our hotel. We were able to take them out, but they may have a plan B. We are going to need a couple of US Army helicopters over here to take our delegation to Andrews as we planned for in case of an emergency. I'm glad we had this plan in place. Send some medics along too. We have some wounded. Oh, and some way to pick up the dead perpetrators."

"Will do."

"Thanks."

"Can we land on the roof?"

"You could hover low enough to load. There's plenty of room, but we don't know the strength of the roof."

Then he called the security at the hanger where the plane was.

"Is the plane serviced yet?" David asked, not bothering to identify himself.

"Yes, they just finished fueling it."

"We have had a terrorist attack. I know the plane should be secure there at the base, but get someone with one of those bomb-sniffing dogs to go over the plane just in case."

"Okay, Captain. Did we lose anybody?"

"Yes, unfortunately."

David had just clicked off when the phone rang.

"When do you want the choppers?"

"Now," said David.

"Will do," said the voice.

"Okay, guys, let's roll. Get everybody up here with their luggage and the bodies of our comrades. I still have a few calls to make."

Johnny and Katz hurried down to get the others while David called the embassy and made arrangements to return the cell phones. Then he called Rachel.

"Hello, David," she answered.

"Yes. Listen, we have had a terrorist attack. But the threat is not over, and I am completely tied up. I'm sorry, but I won't be able to see you again before I leave. I love you, my *hamoodah*. Please write soon."

"I heard the noise, and then I saw you at the desk and I knew something was going on. I'll write right away. I'll miss you...I—"

"Sorry, got to go. Bye."

David could hear the helicopters coming. The delegates began filing out the door onto to the roof. Some came with doubled-up luggage as others lumbered under the weight of the bodies of their comrades. David looked at Matza. He shook his head. That added two more to the total. What a cost! But at least the delegation had been saved, as well as the peace process.

—

Rachel picked up her purse and went out to her car. As she reached it two helicopters flew over, and she could hear them hovering above the hotel. *They must have come for the delegation,* she thought. She stood listening for about ten minutes. An emergency vehicle pulled up in front of the hotel. Then she heard the helicopter motors take on a high-pitched whine and saw the lights of one as it lifted off. It banked away from the building. Then the other followed shortly. *That's it,* she thought. *He's gone.*

"Will I ever see him again?" Her shoulders slumped with more than fatigue when she climbed into her car and drove for her father's house.

Chapter 35

Hattie had kept her supper warm. The others had already eaten. She was so tired she just minced over her food, shoving her fork around on her plate. Her papa came into the kitchen as soon as he knew she was home.

"Rachel, how did things go for you today?" asked her papa cheerfully.

"Okay, I guess," she said in almost a sigh.

"You sound tired," he said.

"Yes, I spent the day waiting."

"How boring. Has the Israeli delegation left yet?"

She nodded. "Almost an hour ago. They had a terrorist attack and had to take army helicopters to Andrews."

"I'm sure your Captain took care of them. He's such a capable young man," he said, watching her carefully.

"Yes." She sighed. "He did. Did you watch the signing ceremonies?"

"Yes, isn't it exciting?"

"Do you still think it's time for the Moschiach to come?"

"Oh, I know it. I've met him," he said, smiling.

"You met Adoní? You think he's the *Moschiach*?" she said, lifting her voice in alarm.

"Who's Adoní?"

THE BEGINNING OF THE END

"I thought you were watching the signing. He was the negotiator from Lebanon."

"Why should I think he is the Moschiach?"

"The prime minister thinks he is."

"Why?"

"Because he made it possible for Israel to build their temple again. And besides he's a Jew, according to Halacha."

"Rachel, the Moschiach is not a man, but God."

"What do you mean?" she asked in a slow, incredulous voice. "You sound like the Goyim." She knew perfectly well what they preached. She had heard it often enough.

"Maybe that's because they were right all along."

"Right about what?" Now she was getting angry.

"About the *Moschiach*."

"What has *happened to you*, Papa? Has this darkness caused you to lose your mind?" she shouted, a surge of adrenalin canceling her fatigue.

"No." His voice gentled. "It has enabled me to light up my life. Rachel, he came to me in the darkness."

"Who?"

"The *Moschiach*. He said his name was *Yeshua*. And he told me to preach to the world about judgment and his coming kingdom."

"Then why do you say that the Goyim are right?" She frowned.

"Because the Moschiach turned out to be their Jesus Christ."

"No, no, no-o-o-o-o," she cried and covered her ears. "I...will...not...listen to any more of this." She ran from the room.

"Rachel," Simon called after her, but she refused to stop, escaping to her second story bedroom and slamming the door. Simon stood in the resounding silence. He sighed. As he watched Rachel flee from his presence, he felt like cursing himself for not being a little more subtle. *I should have realized what a zealot I have made of her. Now she will be twice as hard to reach. Would there have been an easier way to break his news?* he wondered. *We have always been so honest with each other.*

—

In her room Rachel stewed. *How could he? Her wonderful Papa, whom she had always loved and respected. How could he believe such a thing?* She felt betrayed. She sobbed as the pain gripped her heart. David was gone, and now her papa was dead to her. She knew the tradition when orthodox Jews turned to Christianity. *How could he turn away from his heritage—his people—and especially the Torah? How could the Goyim's Jesus be our Moschiach? How I hate that name. How many times have I suffered because of it.*

She remembered the first time; she was only eleven. Mrs. Hill, her sixth grade teacher, had assigned the class to write a report of their choice on current affairs. Rachel chose to write about the newly passed laws of the Likud government, which had just come to power in Israel a few months past—laws that forbade the airline and other government-owned companies from working on the Sabbath. She was delighted to be the first one chosen when the teacher told her to please stand and read her report.

Rachel stood. Her paper trembled slightly as she began to read.

"Last year Menachen Begin, the prime minister of Israel, formed an alliance with some of the small religious parties who are run by Orthodox rabbis. This week they passed new laws, telling the El Al Airlines and others they can't work on Shabbat. This is good because if the people don't start obeying God's law, the Moschiach won't come. Some of the people got mad because they don't want to obey. Also, archeologists are digging in the city of David. This upsets the rabbis because they are disturbing Jewish graves. I'm glad the rabbis have the power to do this because my papa and I want the Moschiach to come. And he won't come if the people don't obey God."

Rachel sat down, flushed and proud to speak up for her Moschiach. Mrs. Hill said, "Thank you, Rachel. That was very nice, except you didn't explain who this *Moschiach* is you are expecting?"

Rachel jumped to her feet again. "The great Jewish king who will rule the whole world and bring peace," she answered then dropped back into her seat with the smile of one satisfied with herself.

The class began to snicker. Mrs. Hill clapped her hands, and the snickering stopped.

"Are you referring to what we Gentiles call the Messiah?" she asked with a soft, understanding voice.

"I-I guess so," said Rachel, no longer so sure of her words.

"You sound like you expect him to come right away."

"Oh yes, ma'am," replied Rachel, eyes sparkling. "He's probably already here somewhere in the world," she said with a wide sweep of her hand. Of course she was only spouting the opinion of her papa, but the Moschiach was the center of all her dreams, so naturally she was excited to tell them about him.

Once again the class began to murmur. Mrs. Hill silenced them and called upon other students to read their reports.

After school a small group from a local fundamental church confronted Rachel as she attempted to leave the school yard.

"Rachel," said one of the girls. "Don't you know the Messiah has already come. Jesus Christ is the Messiah. Everybody knows *that*, except maybe you Jews."

"Yeah," said one of the boys. "You are the ones who killed him."

"Jesus was an impostor," Rachel hurled back angrily. "He is just the Goyim's god. We are the ones with the Scriptures. We know better than you what's what! You can't even read them in Hebrew."

"Neither can you," the boy accused, leaning forward with his hands on his hips

"Yes I can!" she retorted, eyes flashing as she placed her hands on her hips, taking the same stance as the boy. "My papa is teaching me."

"Jesus is the Lamb of God...your Lamb, who takes away the sin of the whole world," interrupted another one of the girls who was anxious to get her word in and proud to testify for her Lord. "He's the one who's coming back to be your king."

Whirling around to face the new attack, she spat, "That's ridiculous! How can a lamb be a king? Jesus is nothing but a false god, and his followers are Jew killers and trouble makers." Her normally gray-blue eyes were blazing a bright neon blue.

"And you are nothing but a dirty Jew," retaliated the budding female fundamentalist.

Rachel fled as they called after her. "Dirty Jew!" "Christ killer!" Tears of anger and frustration streamed down her cheeks.

She flung open the door as soon as she reached the house.

"Papa. Papa," she cried as she ran into his arms.

"There, there, what's the matter, my darling?" he asked, patting her on the back as he held her close.

She stepped back and said, "The Christians are saying that Jesus is our Moschiach. They called me names. They said I was a 'Christ killer' and a 'dirty Jew.'" She sobbed as she buried her head against his chest.

"There, there, Rachel," he said, comforting her, "You have just suffered what we Jews have suffered for centuries. What do *they* know? We have the true Scriptures, right?"

She nodded, wiping her eyes.

"We have the Tanakh, the true word of God, with the Torah and the writings of the prophets, again, right?"

"Yes, that's what I told them," she stated soberly.

"Someday our Moschiach will come and show *them* the truth."

Her mother couldn't keep quiet any longer. She said to her husband, "Now see what you've done! Filling Rachel's head with all that religion." She took Rachel out of his arms and soothed her, pushing her dark hair back out of her eyes. "There, there, baby, you're safe from them now." Turning back to her husband, she scolded, "She shouldn't have to face religious opposition at her age. Heaven knows she will face it soon enough. I've always said she should go to the Hebrew school. At least there she would be with her own people. Besides, she needs the social support of the extra curricular activities."

"Now, Em, we've been over this time after time. I want her to stand her ground in the real world. My teaching is quite adequate. The Hebrew school would not prepare her for Harvard. They teach the girls other things. Rachel's faith is strong enough to stand a little persecution," he said proudly.

Rachel beamed as she left to go wash her face. She felt better. She had stood up for her Moschiach. Of course, her papa was right. *He* was proud of her. She could always trust *him*. Her mama didn't know anything about Torah or the Moschiach, not really. She was just a socialite. But she and her papa, *well*, they were true believers.

Rachel sighed at the remembrance. The operative word here was *were*, but not anymore.

He was mad. He must be. Surely it had to do with the darkness. She fell onto her bed. She was completely used up, too tired to go back to the apartment tonight, but she would go first thing in the morning. She would not stay in this house one moment longer than necessary. *I'm all alone now. All alone*...It hit her full force. David is probably headed over the ocean by now, and her papa was a stranger. Tears of exhaustion and bitterness streamed down her face as she undressed. She cried herself to sleep in despair.

Chapter 36

True to her intentions, Rachel left at six the next morning. She simply packed and left. She didn't even see Hattie.

As she made her way back to the apartment, she thought, *how eerie is this darkness, and so depressing. Would they ever see the sun again?* She shivered and turned on the heater. After she reached her apartment she carried her suitcases up the steps. Thank heavens it was only one floor up. She still didn't trust the elevators.

Once inside she realized the lanterns were all over at Papa's. *But maybe the lights will work.* They did. They must have fixed whatever damage the lightning caused. She went straight to her closet and got out some winter slacks and a sweater. The air was definitely getting colder. Then she went to the kitchen to fix breakfast. Her apartment looked so depressing. *Was this the same place she had experienced such joy in David's arms? Would she ever know joy again?*

As she worked she began to go over the events of yesterday. But all of her precious moments with David were overshadowed by the despair of last night. She thought about her papa. How he had carefully taught her the Torah and some of the Nevi'em (Prophets). How could he betray her and turn to the Goyim's God? How could he? Now she would have to study alone. Study alone... She would be alone except for David, and he was thousands of miles away.

She dropped an English muffin into the toaster and scrambled an egg. How could her papa even imagine their Moschiach was the cursed Jesus? Rachel again recalled that childhood incident that had poisoned her heart toward Jesus, the so-called Lamb of God. He was the one who had caused all the suffering of the Jews throughout history. She had been greatly offended when they called her "a dirty Jew." She had asked her papa many times, "Why did they say I am dirty? Papa, I am not dirty." Similar incidents had hardened her heart against Christianity. The Christians did not show love, only disdain. How she hated them.

She sipped her coffee and finished her breakfast. Papa had heard the Moschiach—no way! The lightning must have affected his mind. *I will talk to Dan about this later,* she decided. It was time to head for the embassy anyway. She put her dishes in the dishwasher.

Once in the car, Rachel turned on the radio. It was mostly silent. An occasional burst of sound indicated that a few stations were on the air. Finally she found news.

"One of the biggest problems of the darkness is the crime rate. Authorities estimate that thefts are up by 50%. The city governments are relying more and more upon the military to help to control it. State authorities in Virginia found out this morning that several semi-truck loads of groceries have been hijacked. They urge the public to buy food from legitimate grocery stores only. Officials have announced that from now on they will send army escorts with the new food shipments.

"NBC has learned from an interview with helicopter pilots that the Israeli delegation narrowly missed being blown up by a suicide bomber. In the terrorist attack five security men lost their lives, enabling the terrorists to pin the delegation in their rooms. Captain David Solomon saved the day when he took out the suicide bomber single-handedly. He drew the fire of the terrorists, freeing the rest of the security so they could end the scuffle. The delegation managed to get off safely from the roof in helicopters. Hizbullah is alleged to have been behind the attack."

"Good news at last, and I don't need any more bad," she said aloud. Rachel switched off the radio. Her David was the hero. He must have encountered the terrorists as soon as he left her.

Her reverie ended as she looked to see people hurrying along the dimly-lit sidewalks. *I guess everyone is trying to go on with their lives in spite of this darkness.* Traffic forced her to slow down. Finally, after forty minutes of stop and go, she pulled into the embassy parking lot.

Rachel greeted everyone as she walked to her desk. She was glad her work had piled up. It would keep her mind off her losses. Both loves of her life, gone—in a matter of hours. Ambassador Levy stopped by her desk.

"I hear the Israeli delegation got off safely."

"Yes, I heard it on the radio this morning."

"You did a good job, Rachel," he said, noticing the dark circles under her eyes.

"Thank you, sir," replied Rachel. Her voice sounded low compared to its usual cheerful lilt. "Have you got a minute to talk, sir?"

She looked up at him with such despair it startled him.

"Sure. What's wrong, my dear?"

"It's my papa."

"Simon Lieberman?" he asked, shocked. "He's not injured, is he?"

"Not physically, but I fear he has lost his mind."

"Why, Simon Lieberman is one of the most stable men I know. What makes you say that?"

"He claims he met the Moschiach in the darkness. He says our Moschiach is Jesus Christ of the Goyim."

Ya'cov caught his breath. "Are you sure you didn't misunderstand?"

THE BEGINNING OF THE END

"No, he stated it quite plainly. And now David has gone back, and I don't have anyone to talk to about it," she said, choking back tears.

"You can tell me," he said soothingly. "Maybe I need to have a talk with Simon, myself. He won't stop coming to the synagogue on Shabbat, will he?"

"I don't know," she said, wiping her eyes.

"What does Dan say about it?"

"I haven't talked to him about it yet."

"Maybe you should."

"Yes," she said. "I think I'll try right now."

Ya'cov nodded and left the room to give her privacy.

Rachel dialed Dan's cellular. She didn't want to chance getting her father on the phone either at home or at the office. It was the same as if he were dead, which was the usual custom in such circumstances. Orthodox believers treated family members as dead when they turned to Christianity. That's why it was so costly for Jews to convert. The Jewish Christian lost his entire community life.

Dan answered brightly.

"Dan, this is Rachel."

"Hey, you left early this morning."

"Yes, I couldn't face Papa. What's happened to our papa, Dan?"

"He met the Moschiach," he said matter-of-factly.

"No, that couldn't be. What *really* happened?"

"I wasn't there, but he told us a blinding light came into his office and knocked him down. Then a voice told him to take off his shoes because the ground was holy. He said he was Yeshua, his Moschiach, and that he was coming back soon to set up his kingdom. He asked Papa to preach to others about the Lamb of God."

"Lamb of God... Who's that?" Rachel asked, but she already knew, didn't she. She had been trounced with that name before.

"According to the study he did in both the Tanakh and the New Testament, *it is* Jesus Christ."

"Surely you don't believe that," she said, voicing incredulity.

"I do now," he declared. "Lot's of things in the Tanakh the rebbes do not explain at all. Papa showed Sheila and I some yesterday. When you look at them objectively, the Moschiach *has* to be Jesus Christ. It's the only way it makes sense."

"I can't believe this! My own family!"

"Rachel, at least let us show you what we've found, because it changes your whole life. Sheila and I are so..." The phone went dead.

Rachel threw it across the room and flung herself down on the desk, sobbing uncontrollably.

Ya'cov heard her all the way down the hall. He rushed back in and put his hands on her shoulders, trying to console her.

"What has happened?"

"Dan and Sheila have turned too. Now I'm all alone," she blubbered. "All alone. It's like I've become an orphan."

"Rachel, I think you had better come home with me. I'll call Rose and tell her you are coming. I don't think you should be alone at this time."

Avraham witnessed this display of emotion from his office across the hall. "So, she's not made of ice at all. It was religion that kept her stiff. That must be how Solomon reached her," he muttered.

Chapter 37

After an uneventful journey, the delegation from Israel landed at the refurbished Israeli/Palestinian International Airport in Ramalla. (The airport at Lod was no longer safe because of radiation from the destruction of Tel Aviv.) Even before they landed, a great crowd of people had gathered to welcome them back, anxious to proclaim their delight over the outcome of the conference. Floodlights illuminated the pavement where they taxied to a stop, highlighting an unprecedented welcome. Banners stood above the crowd reading, "Peace at Last" and "God has Given Back our Temple Site." Black Hasidim hats could be seen mingling throughout the crowd. David recognized this as soon as he came out of the plane. *Will this truly unite our people and close the great yawning chasm so wide between the religious and the secular people?* he wondered. He and his men herded the delegates toward microphones that were set up by the Israeli Government.

The prime minister raised his hand and the crowd quieted.

"Indeed this is a momentous time for our people. The Knesset will drop everything else to plan our next move. I suggest that you of the religious parties and various sects meet together and decide the particulars, according to Halacha and the Scriptures.

"Chief rabbis Hacohen and Shapiro, I ask you to see to this. Be sure you include everyone, every sect of Judaism."

Then he added, "Oh, it's *so* good to be home!" With that he waved and left the microphone.

The crowd began to lock arms and dance for pure joy. Some left, but others who did not participate watched in wonder.

"*Hava Nagilah…Havah Naailah…*" Song filled the air, and small groups of six or seven moved as units, back, forth, around, feet keeping step to the song. The rejoicing would continue on into Shabbat that evening. *What rejoicing will go on in Jerusalem's synagogues tomorrow,* thought David.

David's father found him in the crowd and gave him a big hug.

"My son, I can't believe the joy this country feels. Isn't it wonderful? Our God is so good! You must come home tonight and celebrate Shabbat with us."

"Yes," said David, "I would like that as soon as I get a little rest. I was so pent up with the events of the last hours I wasn't able to sleep much on the plane. Did you know we had a terrorist attack before we left?"

"Yes, we heard about that. I understand you saved them from the suicide bomber. I'm proud of you, my son. Thank the Almighty you are safe."

"I only did my job," said David. I have some important news to tell the family, but I need to be refreshed first."

"Good, I will let you go now, but we will expect you this evening."

David arrived at his father's house shortly before six. He had no more than reached the door when the shofars began to sound. They blew them at six o'clock since there was no sunset. That heralded the beginning of Shabbat in every household of the faithful. The mamas would be lighting the candles and beginning the meaningful ritual that took place every Sabbath in devout Jewish households.

David smiled, touched the mezuzah at the doorway, and rushed

THE BEGINNING OF THE END

in to greet his mama. When she saw him she jumped up from the table and ran with outstretched arms.

"David, my David, at last you come home. And nearly you are late already. Hurry now. We must begin."

"Yes, Mama," he replied as he slipped into his place at the table.

David's two younger brothers and his only sister rolled their eyes and winked but remained silent until the opening ritual was complete and it was time to eat. Then everyone began to talk at once.

"Hey, David, what did you think of America?" asked sixteen-year-old Jonathan.

"Did you get to see anything before the darkness came?" chipped in the older Malcomb before David could answer.

"Boys, boys, one at a time," said his father.

"I didn't see much of America, period," replied David, answering both questions at once. "We were too busy protecting the delegates."

"Well, what did you like best of what you did see?" asked his twelve-year-old sister, Sarah.

"Rachel," replied David.

Everyone looked at David with a questioning expression.

"Mama, I have finally found the woman for me."

Esther Solomon frowned. "An American girl? We don't have enough nice Israeli girls already for you to choose from?"

"A Jewish girl, Mama," replied David. "You didn't think I would pick from the Goyim, did you?"

"What does she look like?" asked Sarah with a twinkle in her eyes. Is she as pretty as Deidrienne?"

"She's absolutely beautiful. Tall, about five foot seven with dark brown, almost black hair and gray-blue eyes. You are going to love her if I can ever get her over here."

"I hope her beauty isn't all just physical," said David's father, thinking of the spiritual aspect.

"Father, she's of the Chabad Lubavitch Hasidim. And she is fervently looking for the Moschiach."

"Where did you meet her, if you were so busy protecting the delegates?" teased eighteen-year-old Malcomb.

"She was an aid at the embassy and became my chauffeur as I took the tapes back and forth from the conference. We had a lot of time to talk while we were driving."

David answered many more questions from the family about Rachel all through dinner.

After dinner Jesse Solomon asked his son to step into his study for a private evaluation of the conference, which gave David a chance to tell him of his apprehensions.

When he left at nine-thirty, he dreaded returning to an empty apartment. He was glad to be home. He loved his country and his religious heritage, but now that he had found Rachel he felt like half a person. He would no longer be content with just his work. He needed her. He felt warm as he thought about her passion for the Moschiach. He wrote her his first letter before he went to bed.

Pope Peter had been silent the whole trip back to Italy. Everyone thought he was grieving for Jerry. Actually, behind his closed eyes he planned his strategy as he focused his mind on the monumental task he had been assigned. He would tell no one of his heavenly visitor, no, not until the right time. As he thought on the Virgin's words, he realized the problems that had severed the Church from holiness. Ever since Pope John XXIII and the Vatican II Council, the Vatican had let the Church slip toward modernization. It had continually gone downhill. Now it was to the point that it no longer resembled the Holy Catholic Church of the past. Listing the problems in his mind, they were: the Mass, which had drastically changed; there were homosexual churches; the priesthood chafed against celibacy; women demanded ordination; the layman practiced birth control or worse, abortion; the pope was no longer considered infallible; the Jesuits, who were sworn to uphold the papacy, had been in rebellion against the papal office since the 1960s. Then there was the scandalous affair of the Vatican Bank and Roberto Calvi in the seventies that ruined the Vatican's good name. At that time the Extraordinary Section of the Patrimony of the Holy See and the Vatican Bank had joined forces with the Italian Mafia and the Masonic lodge P2 of Switzerland through some unsavory friends of Pope Paul VI in Milan. The result was to ruin the financial reputation of the Church. Millions of dollars of Mafia money were washed through Church investments. The next pope had let the decay continue while he waged a political war against Communism in Poland. Next came the sex molestation scandals of priests in the early 2000s. Then the pope before him had died shortly after taking office. It was still the Catholic Church, but it was no longer holy, at least not by past standards. No, he agreed with the Virgin. The present Church is not fit to reign. He would handle it by calling a consistory. Calling all the cardinals back to Rome would be expensive, but necessary if he were to take the keys of Peter as they were meant to be taken.

As he thought on these things, he realized he would have to be careful. One other pope had decided to change things too quickly, and he died mysteriously after only thirty-three days in office.

Rachel followed Ya'cov home in her own car. Rose greeted her with open arms.

"Rachel, my child, how good it is to see you."

"Thank you for having me, Mrs. Levy," said Rachel.

"Make yourself to home. There's a powder room just down the hall if you would like to wash up while I finish the Shabbat meal."

"Thank you," replied Rachel, glad to be among friends.

Later at the table, after the usual Shabbat ceremony, Ya'cov began the conversation.

"Rose, Rachel says Simon has converted to Christianity."

"Oh, my poor, poor dear, no wonder you are so upset," said Rose sympathetically. "What a terrible shock."

"And that's not all. He has also converted Dan and Sheila," said Rachel.

"What will you do?" asked Rose.

"I guess I will go and talk to the rebbe tomorrow after meeting."

"Do you think your papa will come to the synagogue?"

"I-I don't know," she replied. "Surely not, since he is no longer one of us."

"Would you like to sit with me tomorrow since you won't have Sheila?

"Yes, I would like that."

Rachel was grateful to spend the evening in the company of such kindness and understanding, but by nine o'clock she rose up, intending to go home.

Ya'cov protested. "Rachel, I will not hear of it. You must spend the night and go to the synagogue with us tomorrow. It's not safe for you to be out driving alone or even in your apartment for that matter. With all the crime being reported I wouldn't feel right with you home alone. Why don't we go to your apartment early tomorrow and get your clothes and things. You can stay here until the darkness lifts."

"Yes, yes, dear, you must listen to Ya'cov," Rose insisted. "It would be good to have you in the house—like family. Our two children live in Israel, and we miss them."

David was in Israel too, and already I miss him. Rachel was tired and depressed. She smiled, her relief clearly evident in her face.

THE BEGINNING OF THE END

"Thank you so much," she said. "I was definitely dreading being alone. I would have stayed at Papa's if this hadn't happened."

The next morning Simon Lieberman, with Dan and Sheila, entered the synagogue in their usual manner, greeting everyone with bright smiling faces. Sheila looked for Rachel in the women's section as soon as she entered, but she had not arrived yet. Simon was filled with such excitement that everyone seemed to notice. The rebbe embraced him and asked, "How can you be so cheerful in this depressing darkness?"

"The Lord God of our fathers has given me a special light," Simon replied with a positive lilt in his voice.

"What kind of light?" asked the rebbe, surprised. He had known Simon for many years, and he had always been optimistic—looking for the Moschiach more fervently than the rest—but this morning he was different. He just seemed to glow.

"Spiritual light in here," Simon replied as he thumped his breast with his closed fist. "It just fills you with joy and makes you want to sing all the time."

"Well, Simon, why don't you read from the Tanakh this morning and tell us about this light."

"I would be glad to, Rebbe," he said with a twinkle in his eye.

"Good," said the rebbe and turned away, shaking his head in wonder. *Something's surely happened to him. He's changed somehow.*

Rachel and Rose slipped into a seat in the back, while Ya'cov made his way to the men's side. Rachel gasped.

"Papa's here, and so are Dan and Sheila."

"See there, dear," said Rose. "It's all just a big misunderstanding."

"Maybe his madness is past," said Rachel, hoping that was the explanation.

The service began. When time came for the reading of the Tanakh, Rachel was surprised to see her papa stand to do the reading. He turned to the book of *Jeshayahu* (Isaiah) and read from the fiftieth chapter:

> Who among you reveres the Lord,
> And heeds the voice of his servant?—
> Though he walk in darkness
> And have no light,
> Let him trust in the name of the Lord
> And rely upon his God.
> But you are all kindlers of fire,
> Girding on firebrands.
> Walk by the blaze of your fire,
> By the brands you have lit!
> This has come to you from My hand:
> You shall lie down in pain.[16]

Simon closed the book. "For years we have waited for the Moschiach. Rebbe Schneerson excited us with his conclusions that the time for his appearance has come. The servant in the passage I just read refers to him. It says who among you fears the Lord and obeys the voice of his servant? During the darkness, when the lightning came, I heard the voice of the Servant. Today I am obeying that voice.

"When the darkness overtook us I was in the office waiting for the traffic to clear out so I could go home. A great light blinded me and dropped me to the floor. My friends, I didn't just fall. I had *no* power to stand. Then this voice commanded as he touched me, 'Take off your shoes and stand up, for this is holy ground.'" Simon spoke the quote loudly for emphasis. "I did what I was told because the authoritative voice compelled me. I asked, who is speaking? And the voice said, 'I am Yeshua, your Moschiach. I have called you to be one of many witnesses. I anoint you with the Spirit of my Father. Go to your brethren and to the Gentiles and tell them that I am coming to set up my kingdom. Preach to the world that the Lamb of God has come and is coming back soon with the wrath of judgment. Warn the people to repent of their sins or I will require it of you.' So you see, my friends, I must obey the command of the Servant.

"Then I asked him, who is this Lamb of God? He told me to look it up in the book of Jochanan."

At this point a loud murmur ran through the auditorium. Rachel frowned. She knew Jochanan was not in the Tanakh. Where on earth did he get that?

"Yes, yes," shouted Simon over the din. "I know exactly what you are thinking. *So did I.* But I obeyed, and I found some things in the Scriptures I never saw before," he said, holding up the Tanakh. "For instance, Rebbe, did you know that the Moschiach is the Son of God, making him very God as well?"

"Where does it say that?" the Rebbe asked, demanding proof.

"Two places...actually three...You know God's requirement of at least two witnesses." He held up the Tanakh and then turned several pages. "First in Psalm 2. These are the words of the Moschiach, the king who will put down the rest of the kings of the world. Is he not the Moschiach, yes?" Simon paused and looked around for their assent then went on. "He says, 'Let me tell of the decree: "The Lord said to me..."' The me here refers to the Moschiach. 'You are My son, I have fathered you this day.' Later at the end it reads, '...pay homage in good faith, lest he be angered, and your way be doomed in the mere flash of his anger. Happy are all who take refuge in him.'"

"Is that your two references?" asked the rebbe, becoming disturbed.

"No, the other is in Solomon's book of wisdom."

Finding it in the Tanakh, he read:

Who has ascended heaven and come down?
Who has gathered up the wind in the hollow of his hand?
Who has wrapped the waters in his garment?
Who has established all the extremities of the earth?
What is his name…?[17]

At this point he beckoned for the men to answer the questions. They all replied, "God of our fathers, of course."

Then Simon finished reading the passage.

"…or his *Son's* name, if you know it?"

Half the men sat in quiet reflection. Others began to show anger on their faces.

"Please, listen another moment," pleaded Simon, looking over the men. "The voice said to me, 'I will anoint you with the Spirit of my *Father*. He also said that the Lamb of God had come and was coming back soon. I looked up the Lamb of God in Jochanan."

"But that's in the Bible of the Christians," one of the angry men shouted.

"Yes, that's true, but it was written by a Jew. Just because the Christians didn't obey their own Scriptures doesn't mean they're not true."

"Let him tell what he found. Does not the book of wisdom say that he that answers a man before hearing him out is foolish and disgraceful?" asked one of the reflective Jews.

"Please continue," said the rebbe, calming the congregation.

"I found that Jochanan stated that Jesus is the Lamb of God who takes away the sins of the world, and he is also the Son of God."

THE BEGINNING OF THE END

The congregation erupted in angry cries.

Simon threw up his hands and waited until it was quiet once more. "I had all the same feelings you have. I was repulsed when I realized John was talking about Jesus being all these things. Especially, the part about the Son of God. I said, 'This is blasphemous,' until I saw the plan of God. You see, the Moschiach had to be the Son of God in order to be the Savior of the world. All those animal sacrifices in the Torah were not true substitutes for men. We look forward to redemption. This is redemption, right? Having our sins all carried away. Only an infinite life of a *man* could pay for the sins of the whole world. Only a sinless life could be a blemish-free Passover Lamb, not just for our nation but for the whole world. Only the Son of God could be sinless. When I realized this, I knew why I was asked to preach about him. He is coming back to reign, but if you want your sins forgiven *now*, you must believe he is the one. I did, and now joy unspeakable flows out of my being. Not only that, but many Scriptures that were obscure are now becoming plain. It is because he *is* our Moschiach! Remember the Scriptures I read in the beginning? If you walk in darkness (and we literally do right now) we should obey the voice of his Servant. The Servant is the Moschiach. If we do this we have light. Already, I understand more passages in the Tanakh than ever before. That's light—understanding—and great joy. But if you insist on walking in your own light, your own sparks, you shall lie down in pain. Does not the book of wisdom say, 'Do not rely on your own understanding'? Anyone who would like to study this with me is welcome to come to my house." With this he said, "Omen," and sat down.

The group was divided. Some wanted to hear more; others left the meeting disgruntled.

Rose looked at Rachel. "You did *not* misunderstand, my dear, he *has* turned."

"Yes," she said quietly. "It would do no good to talk to the rebbe.

He has heard for himself. She wished she could talk to David. *I'll write him a letter today*, she thought.

On the way back to the Levy's, Rachel thought about what her papa had said. It was clear the people were divided. Many had clustered around him after the meeting. She had always trusted her papa, but now she didn't know what to think. She wasn't familiar with the passages he read. She promised herself she would begin the studies David had suggested. Maybe that would help her understand what had happened to her papa.

Keeping to a routine schedule was hard because of the constant darkness. But Simon arose early, 6:00 a.m., according to the clock. He spent an hour and a half in the Scriptures. It was Sunday, the Christian Sabbath, and he was feeling the need to go to a church where he could openly worship Yeshua. He looked in the Washington Yellow Pages to find the nearest one, which happened to be a Protestant church.

He went alone. He entered the auditorium and found a seat in the back. It was a modern building with a large altar area with an ornate pulpit in the center. Draped over the pulpit was a purple cloth with gold letters embroidered on it. A table with lighted candles and a large flower arrangement stood in front of the pulpit. He looked around as people began to drift in. Families sat together instead of being separated as was the Jewish custom. Soft organ music played until the service began. Finally, the minister mounted the platform and opened the service. It began with a hymn.

"Please turn to number thirty-four in your hymnal: 'All Hail the Power of Jesus Name.'"

By the second verse Simon picked up the melody and sang lustily, "Ye chosen seed of Israel's race, Ye ransomed from the fall, Hail him who, saves you by his grace and Crown him Lord of all."

Simon's voice stood out as he thrilled to the words he sang.

Those around him looked over at him, startled by his enthusiasm. The rest of the congregation droned through the song, hardly noticing the words. It was an old hymn. Nothing to get excited about.

After the hymn, someone came to the platform and read the announcements—mostly cancellations because of the darkness.

Simon was fascinated with the hymnal. He thumbed through it during the announcements. *Why, these songs are mostly about Jesus. I must have one of these. I wonder if a Christian book store would have one. I need to go anyway to get whatever I need to study the New Testament.*

He still had the secretary's New Testament. He had gone back to work the day after his encounter with the Moschiach, to return it to her. But she didn't show up. He tried calling her home number, but no one answered. So it was generally believed that she was among those who had vaporized. She was the only one missing from the office.

Then the minister began. "Today we mourn the loss of some of our members. These have not left by being drawn away by a so-called revival as many of our others were. Evidently, these are some of our faithful members who vaporized in the lightning this week. We must be brave. We have to go on. Life is for the living. But for the moment we will remember them." He began to read a list of the missing. "The Anderson family, the Baker family, the Conways, with the exception of James..." He continued for several minutes. Then he finished with this comment: "Isn't it odd that most of these are our older members, with the exception of whole families?" Then he read some Scriptures and closed out the service.

Simon was frustrated by the lack of joy and enthusiasm in the people. *Why aren't they as excited about Jesus as I am? They don't seem to know what they are singing. The minister didn't mention Jesus at all except in the reading of the Scripture. I wonder if that is why the Moschiach chose me, a Jew, to preach the Lamb of God.* He wanted to shout to them, "Don't you know who Jesus is? He's the Christ—your God! Don't you know that?"

He left shaking his head. They were no better off than his people.

Rachel continued staying at the Levy's until the following Tuesday. That morning the sky began to lighten to a dark gray. By evening the nearly full moon had almost penetrated the gloom. By Wednesday the clouds were visible—a dreary day, but very welcome after seven days of total darkness. The survivors of the disaster were ready to resume their normal lives.

Rachel was glad to be back in her own apartment. Wednesday morning when she awoke she realized that natural light was streaming into her bedroom.

"Oh, hallelujah," she exclaimed. It was easy to be thankful this morning as she said her prayers. She even sang a Psalm of thanksgiving. She continued humming as she made herself some breakfast. She was sure this darkness had depressed her as much as the situation. Maybe today things wouldn't look so bad. The ambassador had mentioned sending her on a little trip. The Israeli Embassy in Atlanta needed an interpreter for an Israeli/Arab situation. What a welcome break that would be, she thought.

When she stepped out into the first light of the week, she noticed the leaves on the trees were a pale sickly green—what leaves that were left. The grass was nearly all brown. How strange everything looked. The sidewalks and streets were littered with trash, papers, clothes, and dead birds.

I wonder if the darkness killed all our birds, she thought with alarm. *I wonder how they could eat without the light. I wonder if they were in hibernation like bears in winter.*

As soon as she got in her car, she turned on the radio, as was getting to be her habit. A few stations had been on all during the disaster, but one in particular carried the announcements from the government with instructions and news.

"...also, there have been an unusually high number of suicides. Psychologists attribute it to the depression caused by the darkness and the loss of family members. Speaking of the missing, the government has lost nearly one-third of its members. The vacancies will be filled by appointment since elections are coming up next year.

"In the human interest side of the news, a most unusual thing has happened since the darkness. People flocking to the churches for spiritual guidance all across the country are finding Jews among them preaching Jesus." Rachel gasped. *So it's not just my papa that has turned.* She wondered what that meant.

Chapter 38

"**B**BC World News will also give a special report on the cause of the earthquakes and damage during the darkness," said the perky reporter stationed in Washington, D.C., as she finished her news headlines.

Adoni´ had just turned on the TV to catch the evening news. "I have missed the beginning," he said, dismayed. He looked at his watch. It was two minutes slow. "Must be a low battery," he mumbled.

Most of the news dealt with the energy problems caused by the blackout. Finally, she came to the segment on the earthquakes. He knew from the local papers that cities in Syria had been among the most devastated. He was anxious to learn about it because of his banks.

"We have with us tonight two distinguished professors from the American University of Lebanon, who have personally studied the geology of their area. With us from Beirut are Dr. Gehazi Jamel and Dr. Abdul el Falid. Welcome, gentlemen. Can you tell us about the earthquakes?"

Jamel nodded to el Falid, letting him begin.

"Well," said Falid, "as you probably already have been told, the earthquakes that occurred during the darkness were not your normal earthquakes. These were caused directly by the pull of the asteroid that came close to the earth. It was a tidal action, much like the pull the moon has on the oceans creating the tides. Of course, this body was much smaller than the moon, but its influence was greater because it came so close.

"The places that felt the greatest shaking occurred in areas where smaller tectonic plates come together with larger ones. For instance, the smaller Philippine Plate interfaces the Indo-Australian Plate and the huge Eurasian Plate. That's why Indonesia and the Philippines suffered such devastation."

"But why wouldn't it affect all the plates?" she asked. "Don't they all come together sort of like a jigsaw puzzle?"

"Because there are many subsidiary fault systems involved in these specific type of junctures," said Dr. Jamel. "Take our own back yard. We have a smaller system of faults that connect to the Great Rift Valley Fault, which stretches from northern Syria through the Jordan Valley, the Red Sea, and into Africa beyond Lake Victoria. From about the northern border of Lebanon, the main fault splays in three directions before it picks up again in the Ghab pull-apart fault. We call this the Dead Sea Fault System. Here the African Plate, the smaller Arabian Plate, and the huge Eurasian Plate interact. The tidal action can move the smaller fault lines by virtue of the fact that they are smaller. Hence the destruction of Syria's major cities."

"Yes, I see," said the reporter, seeming overwhelmed by the explanation. "It will really be tough in that country now, with Damascus already destroyed. What will they do, I wonder?"

Adoni´ switched off the TV. He had an idea of what to do, but he needed firsthand information to put it into action. He called several of his colleagues in Lebanon and finally located a couple from Syria that had escaped the devastation. Then he called the pilot of his personal plane.

Alleppo, Hama, and Homs lay in almost complete rubble. A

few buildings escaped. They were like the few remaining olive berries left on a high branch after harvest.

J. Leucus Adoni´ and several Lebanese Government officials, along with two Syrians originally from Alleppo, had come to assess the damage in southern Syria now that daylight was restored.

On a whim they decided to see if anything had changed at the Damascus site. Of course they flew high over the ruined city because of the radiation. (Israel's bomb had not been the small limited kind, but a full-scale hydrogen type.) They had not tried to fly in until now. As expected, nothing but ruin met their eyes. The Syrian officials, already stunned to silence at seeing the condition of their own cities, wailed, "All our strength is gone. How can we ever rebuild?" Both Alleppo and Damascus claimed to be the oldest continuously-inhabited city in the world. When the Israelis had attacked Damascus, a million and three-quarter people had been killed in just five minutes. The proud head of Syria had been decapitated in the war, but now Homs, Hama, and Aleppo, the northern towns, were all but gone as well, being in line with the great fault and its smaller fault system. Only the towns and villages along the coast remained unscathed. Syria as a political nation existed now only in incoherent city states.

The men had come on a fact-finding tour with the intent of restoration. Adoni´ was way ahead of the others. He saw immediately that the Syrian stranglehold on Lebanon was completely gone. He could rebuild it to his liking and not even worry about Hizbullah. Not only Lebanon but Syria as well. Perhaps create a new country by combining them and call it after its ancient name—Assyria.

It would take all his cunning to keep the multitude of banks in Beirut in line. (The war with Israel had not touched them.) It was a good thing that he had moved most of his assets out of Syria after the bombing of Damascus. Even though he had taken a hit, the present opportunity would more than make it up. But he would still have to draw from other sources. He had the contacts; he would lead them all. With the necessary rebuilding, he could not fail. It would be his stepping stone to power, but he could do it. He was destined.

As soon as the small delegation arrived back in Beirut, Adoni´ hurried to his office. Now was the time to approach the big power brokers. J. Quentin Rice had shown an interest in his affairs when he met with him in Washington. He waited until it was business hours across the ocean and called Rice.

"Mr. Adoni´, how nice to hear from you so soon," said the senator when he finally came to the phone.

"Senator Rice, I'll come straight to the point. I have just returned from a fact-finding trip, flying all over Syria. Damascus, of course, was already destroyed beyond repair, but now it looks like all of Syria is up for grabs—the entire country. With the government gone, the country for all practical purposes is gone as well. We of Lebanon will have to assume the duties of governing what remains." He hesitated. He had not thought of this aspect until now. "Isn't it ironic that they who have dominated us for years are now to be ruled by us?"

"Yes. Amazing really," replied the senator.

Adoni´ continued. "The rebuilding that will be required will put great strains on the banking and financial institutions of our area way beyond what they already are from the destruction of the 2006 war. My bank, of course, is not able to carry all the load. In fact, all the others combined would not be able to. When we talked in Washington, you mentioned an affiliation with some of the large financiers of the world. I was wondering if you could give me an introduction to these men. I feel if Lebanon does not move to restore the Syrian nation that Iran will move in and try to take over. In the interest of peace, we must not let that happen."

"No, we must not!" replied Rice. "I will certainly do what I can.

I have your phone number, and I will have the appropriate people get in touch with you."

"One good thing came out of the disaster."

"What was that?" asked Adoni´.

"We no longer have a problem with terrorists housed in Syria. Iran's Hizbullah's contact with Iran is broken.

"This is true, my friend," he said. "I believe we can deal with those left in the Bekaa Valley now that their support is gone. Beyond that, a door for consolidating power here in the Middle East is open. Ra'amon is most willing to cooperate."

"Yes, yes, that is definitely a plus. They say no matter how bad things get, some good will come out of it. I am sure we can help you rebuild and at the same time fortify the peace in the region. Perhaps Lebanon will regain the economic prominence she once had."

"Thank you, Senator, but we are already rebuilding. This move will give us power in the region. I will be looking forward to hearing from your friends." And with that he hung up, filled with elation. "Yes!" he shouted, unable to repress the excitement. "My father was right. I am destined for great things. This is only the beginning. Ashtor will be pleased."

He reached for his appointment calendar and began clearing his time for more important matters.

Chapter 39

The Knesset came together on Sunday with an entirely new attitude. For the first time since the peace accord was signed in Norway, Likud was pleased with the results. Likud was the conservative party that had ruled Israel for years. Yitshak Shamir, their long-ruling premier, had been voted out by an upsurge of the people who wanted peace at any price. Yitshak Rabin of Labor was voted in and held office until his assassination.

Soon the governing difference in the parties became evident. All during Shamir's term as premier, the occupied land was settled by Israelis. It was a sore spot with all the nations who were trying to bring peace to the Middle East because it kept the Palestinians stirred up. Likud stood for keeping the land designated to them by the Scriptures and won in defensive battles.

Labor on the other hand was determined to give back land to establish peace. They went headlong in the opposite direction. But the people had called a halt just before the land was all given back in the peace accord by electing a Likud president without a powerful party behind him. It was the first time the people had voted directly for the premier. In prior elections the premier was selected from his own party members, and the people simply voted for the parties by selecting their MKs. Thus the selected leader of the winning party assumed the premiership. In 1996, however, the voting process was changed to allow a separate vote for the premier. Netanyahu was elected as premier without a strong majority of the Likud to support him. As a result, his government depended upon a loose coalition of many small parties.

The formed government finally toppled after a series of events chipped away at the confidence in Netanyhu's leadership that forced a vote of no confidence. The election that followed brought Labor back in with Ehud Barak, the former head of the IDF (Israel Defense Force). But he failed them at Camp David. The Intifada, brought on by disappointed Palestinians, with all its suicide bombers turned the people toward the tough Likud Minister Ariel Sharon. He fought back, leveling houses and fighting the Palestinians and even boxing Arafat up in Ramalla. According to some sources, when a scandal involving Sharon and his son over campaign funds threatened to expose him, he developed the disengagement plan. Labor's policy of yielding territory became Sharon's. Dismantling the settlements in Gaza further split the Likud Party. Sharon fled the Likud he had originally formed and started the Kadima Party in the middle, neither conservative nor liberal. Circumstances finally toppled Sharon's government when he suffered a stroke, putting his new party in power through Olmert.

Now that the most favored spot in the land—the Temple Mount—would be theirs without political opposition, old differences between Labor, Kadima, and Likud eased, and they forged a new working union in the government.

The MKs voted officially for a summit of rabbis to ratify the design already decided upon by the priesthood. Every synagogue in Israel received the summons to send delegates. The Great Synagogue in downtown Jerusalem was asked to host the meeting in two weeks.

When they came together, but one thing marred the joy resounding through the nation. Most of the priesthood believed the Dome of the Rock covered the actual site of the former temple. Besides the firm belief that the rock in the Dome of the Rock was the site of the original Holy of Holies, they also believed the report of Leen Ritmeyer, a Christian from England, who had published his findings of the location of the five-hundred-cubit-square Temple Mount of Herod's day. Ritmeyer had determined it by finding a step belonging to the original temple and measuring it to the eastern wall. It measured five hundred cubits. From there he measured the eastern wall to a slight bend, which was also exactly five hundred cubits. Measuring back five hundred cubits parallel to the northern wall he closed the square, fulfilling the criteria given in the Mishnah for the Temple Mount because the measured-off square was also the highest point on the mount.

This caused no little distress to some of the religious leaders who felt strongly that the new temple must be built on the exact spot of the original. The place given by the Arabs would only include about a third of that space, what would have been a courtyard with the original temple, according to Ritmeyer. Others argued in favor of the theory that the original stood opposite the eastern gate, as was espoused by the physicist Adoni´ had cited. Finally, they accepted the land offered. They knew this would only be an interim temple at best because when the Messiah showed up, he would build the final temple depicted in Ezekiel. Besides, they knew that as soon as part of the temple structure was up, they could investigate the subterranean portions of the mount and perhaps find the holy Ark of the Covenant that Jewish legends insisted was hidden there in Solomon's secret room. If they had the ark, would it matter so much if it stood on its original ground?

That settled, they turned to legal matters. Nabil Dakkah, King Alahahm Hassih of Jordan, and J. Leucus Adoni´ were invited to walk off the demarcation line with the surveyors, assuming the archaeological surveys had confirmed the site of the ancient temple.

Whether the outcome of the drilling confirmed the location of the temple foundation or not was never published.

Architects finished their design for the bridge approach, one reminiscent to what the Temple Institute believed belonged to the Herodian Temple. This former bridge crossed the whole Kidron Valley to the Mount of Olives. It was built of a series of arches, one row upon another, to three levels, similar to a viaduct except the top was a walkway straight to the Golden Gate.

The present design also called for a series of arches, but the bridge failed to span the whole valley. Instead it stretched past the Arab Cemetery to the other side of the road that passed the eastern side of the wall. Then it turned down to a new walkway headed toward David's city by the side of the road. Opposite the Garden of Gethsemane it intersected a ramp across the valley to the east where the red heifer would be burned on the Mount of Olives. The walk, the ramp, and the bridge were quite wide since it was the only entrance to the temple site. Tall concrete pillars supported the eastern side because of the steep slope to the valley's bottom.

Then they surveyed the city portion of Jerusalem. Jewish residents were given a choice. They could stay or they could leave the land ceded to the Palestinians with a government grant to help them relocate. The Palestinians were required to pay for the abandoned houses. All the details were worked out with minimal debate. At last the various political parties found a common bond.

—

The president sighed as he waited for the others to arrive for the morning staff meeting. It was their job to assist the president in his office. They kept him abreast of the day to day running of the government, especially the chief of staff, who shielded him by limiting access to his schedule. His press secretary gave out notices to reporters. But because of the times he required even more of them. He had them gathering information from everywhere. Yes, he had a cabinet he had appointed in the beginning, but many of them disappeared in the lightning. Whole departments were dysfunctional. Adding his national security advisor, Jack Trent, and Jonothan Chase, the director of CIA, to the group helped balance the domestic issues with the foreign. It made him lean more heavily upon his presidential staff than most before him.

How could they cope with all this? It was as if they had been in a devastating war. In the aftermath of the darkness, many businesses failed and finances were in a tangled mess. Add to that the headaches of inheritance squabbles caused by the people who had disappeared. Unemployment reached an all-time high. Coupled with the food shortage and crime it all added up to a nightmare.

Beyond the domestic problems they had already had, a terrorist attempted to take out the Israeli delegation after the conference, raising questions about security. Now Iran's president, Ahmadinejad, who had escaped the bombing of Terhan, was threatening to send more missiles, whipping up a war of words.

The president saw his own frustration reflected on the faces of the men as they entered the room.

One by one the staff reported as they briefed the president.

"Is anyone else having these same problems?" he asked.

"Yes, Mr. President, the EU countries all have the same financial mess we do," said his chief of staff. "They fear a worldwide depression. I think their new money policy will pass without opposition. You may have to consider the same."

The EU had passed a law that all money belonged to the government and each person would receive debit-credit for his labor recorded in banks.

"Senator Rice talked to me yesterday about that, but we'll leave that to Treasury and the Federal Reserve Bank to work out for now. I think things may have to get a lot worse before the American people will buy that. Who has anything on the Pacific Rim?"

"Japan, the Philippines, and Indonesia suffered earthquakes, but those in Indonesia were the worst."

"It's hard when you have a mess to clean up," said the president. "Remember Katrina?"

"Interesting things are happening in Russia these days," said one of the other aids.

"If you mean the power struggle to succeed Putin's successor, that's nothing new. The greater worry is the build-up of the Russian Army under Putin. His determination to restore Soviet power has succeeded. Russia's current war machine worries me."

"No, I'm talking about the renewal of the monarchist movement to restore a czar to the throne. If they choose a czar, what about the loans we gave them? Will we get the money back from a government that could change to a monarchy—maybe even a dictatorship?"

"Humph! When did we ever get anything back from anybody?" asked one of the deputies.

"At least the Middle East situation looks better without Syria and the Hizbullah terrorists. I believe Adoni´ will deal with those left in the Bekaa Valley. He seems to have taken the lead in Lebanon, despite the official government," said the president. "Back to the problems in Russia. Jack, can you fill me in on what is happening?"

"Well, sir, I did a little research to give some background. Back in October of 1994 the first monarchical Congress met in the House of Unions to talk about restoring the Russian imperial throne along the line of the British monarchy. As they said, 'We want the people to get together in a spirit of togetherness and work out a form of government characteristic of Russian traditions.' Those present showed a wide acceptance of the idea."

The president frowned. "So who was there?

"But Mr. President," interrupted Jonathan Chase, head of the CIA.

THE BEGINNING OF THE END

President Anderson put up his hand. "Just a minute, Jonathan, lets hear the rest of Jack's report."

Jack continued. "The then-head of the Communist Party, Gennady Zyuganov; Alexander Rutskoi, who led the revolt against Yeltson; members of the white army who fought against the red army unsuccessfully in 1917; and Dmitry Vasiliev, the head of Pamyat, whose organization of brown-shirted youth are violently anti-Semitic. Cossacks, Russian Orthodox priests, various government officials, and regular businessmen are also some of the groups who came."

"Then all that changed when the Russians opted to go with Yeltsin's renewal. Besides, Zyuganov, who may have had that type of government in mind, was soundly defeated. So what's that got to do with now?"

"Well," said Jack as he leaned forward in his chair, "with the economic mess we are in, you can just imagine what it's like in Russia since they never really got their free enterprise system off the ground. The whole economy upturn of late was due to oil and gas reserves. The Russian people are leader oriented. The don't know anything else; the czars and Communist dictators have made the people a serfdom for decades. They are looking for a national salvation from a strong charismatic messiah-type."

"Who's in the picture?" said the president. "Have they anyone in mind?"

"Several candidates vied for the position in that early meeting. First, the supposed descendants of the Romanov dynasty. But the leader of Pamyat believed these exiled pretenders have no right under Russian law. The new czar will have to be born in Russia, he says. For a while Vladimir Zhavok, former secretary of the National Security Council, was making a bid for it, and he was pretty popular with the people and some of the military. He also has the advantage of the army behind him. He was sort of a Colin Powell of Russia.

Yeltson appointed Zhavok's man defense minister before he succumbed to his sickness," said Jack. "But since Putin entered the picture nothing was sure, except that he was tightening his control and steering the country back toward a dictatorship. He may be positioning himself for a comeback. Will the people allow it? I don't know. But I lean toward seeing a Russian czar in the not too distant future. Maybe even one with strong Islamic connections."

"Why would you say that?"

"Because of the influx of Arabs into Russia. Not only that, but the majority of the Russian army are now Islamists. Add that to Ahmadinejad's growing power; what if there were a military coup?"

"Now, Jonathan, what was it you wanted to add?" asked the president.

"That's exactly what I wanted to add. You know Ahmadinejad told the Arabs years ago that first they needed to get rid of the United States then they could go after Israel. Our best sources have detected a movement in the army of Islamic officers in that direction," said Chase.

"Keep a close watch on that, Jonathan." The president straightened his back as he stretched. *Would such weighty matters bow your back?* he wondered. "Another Foreign Affairs headache to add to the Iran worry," he said to himself as he turned the staff back to the local problems.

―

Rachel's letters to David poured out her distress with her family. She wrote:

> How I wish I could talk to you about this in person. Half of the congregation of our synagogue now meets at Papa's to worship the cursed Jesus. It's so bad here that even the rebbe has joined him. How can it be, David? How can such men as my papa and the

rebbe turn away from the faith? The rest of us struggle along without leadership. I am studying Jeshayahu, but it doesn't make much sense. I used to ask Papa my questions. Now, though I have you, you are so far away. I miss you, my darling, more than ever.

David was sad as he read this. Of course none of Rachel's letters presented what Simon was preaching, only the misery and disappointment she felt. Because of this David couldn't get a clear picture of why Simon had turned. David had taken a liking to Simon during their brief meeting. He'd seemed sound in the Scriptures, yet he had been the means of splitting the synagogue. By exhorting Rachel to study, David tried to keep her spirits up. *She needs to be here where encouraging things are happening*, he thought. *Why won't she heed my pleadings and come over here?*

Chapter 40

The temple plans gained momentum every day. David marveled at the speed in which things were moving. Maybe his apprehensions had been foolish. The ultra religious had conceded to their brethren even when the temple location one hundred yards north of the Dome of the Rock could not be proved. But neither was the ark found when they searched the underground passages. At least they had a spot on the holy mountain they could call their own. United at last the rabbis had the design of the temple already prepared. It was based upon the same design of the first two temples since the last nine chapters of Ezekiel were believed to be the design of the final temple of the Moschiach.

The priesthood concentrated on looking for the miraculous red heifer whose body could not contain one single black or white hair—only red. Always in the past God had miraculously provided such a heifer when the ashes of separation were gone. Now it was time for another miracle. They had rejected an earlier claim in Kfar Hasidim because as the heifer approached the designated age it grew a few white hairs in its tail. They had even imported a few red Angus cows from America in the late nineties to help G-d out.

When finally found, the holy cow would be sacrificed so that its ashes could be mixed with water—the water of separation—for purifying the priests and the building. Maverick archeologists like

Vendyl Jones (the real-life Indiana Jones) had been looking for the *Kalal*, the ancient container for holding the sacred ashes, for years. It was never found. His amateur archeologists did succeed, however, in finding the sacred anointing oil perfectly preserved.

To complicate matters even further, even though they had identified and classified the priesthood by DNA, they were all defiled from touching the dead. So to rectify the problem several families had already donated their offspring. Their mothers birthed them in a special compound built above the ground upon stilts. Here they were cared for up to the age of thirteen. These were undefiled since they didn't touch the ground deemed defiled by the dead. They were taught strictly by the law. Such a sanctified young man could sacrifice the red heifer to produce the ashes to purify the rest of the priests. This was the same method used when they returned from their exile in Babylon. When a red heifer was finally found and examined to be truly acceptable, they took that as a divine sign of G-d's approval and purified the priesthood.

David heard a rumor that the so called Ark of the Covenant in Ethiopia was causing a stir. He was excited to believe maybe Hancock had been right. Perhaps the real ark *was* in Ethiopia. But he dare not hope until he could confirm the report. To find out if it was true, David went to visit his old friend, an Ethiopian priest named Raphael. After being escorted to the *cohen's* (priest's) presence by a young boy, he greeted Raphael warmly.

"Ah, *shalom*, my good friend," returned the *cohen* from Ethiopia, a wizened brown-faced man in his seventies. "Have you heard the news?"

"That's why I'm here," said David with growing excitement. "To find out if it is true."

"What have you heard, David?"

"Only some rumor about the power returning to the ark," he

answered, "but I want to know what really happened. I was sure you would know."

"According to the reports we are receiving, the power truly has returned. The guardian disappeared the first day in the darkness like so many other people. But from that time until now the chapel glows with its own light coming from the ark. No one can approach it. One man tried to enter the door the first day, but power shot out and electrocuted him. No one has dared go near it since. Pilgrims travel from all over Ethiopia to see the sight."

"I can hardly believe it," said David. "It's just too wonderful. Is it the *Sh'khinah* glory, do you think?"

"Yes, that is what we think. Are you familiar with that passage in Jeshayahu that tells of Ethiopia bringing a present to Israel?"

"No, I don't think so," replied David. "You think it refers to the ark?"

"I do."

"But if they can't approach it, how can they bring it back?"

"They can't...not without us priests. Remember in the book of *Shemuw'el* (Samuel) when David tried to return the ark back to Israel in a cart after the Philistines captured it? Someone died then too. In fact, that chapter in Jeshayahu talks of tall polished black men sending ambassadors to Israel to negotiate something. Could it be the ark?"

"Why would they want to get rid of it now? Especially if it is such an attraction?"

"I don't know, but if God intends for it to come back here, it will. But even so the priesthood will have to carry it. I hope we can be purified soon. No priest would chance carrying it unclean."

"Where would we put it if they did let us have it? The temple won't be ready for a year or more."

"In the same place David put it before *Solomon* built the first temple—on the original Mt. Zion, the city of David. A passage in

Amos nine says that the fallen booth of David will be rebuilt on its own ruins. The government has already purchased part of it for an archeological park, and there are a few Jewish settlers there too. Who knows? Maybe God intends it to be there since everything else seems to be happening that was prophesied for our future. We are back in Eretz Israel as prophesied—our own sovereign state. Now the temple site is available. As soon as our priests are purified and consecrated, we could carry the ark home."

"Do you really think God has come back to dwell among his people?" asked David softly, musing more to himself than to the cohen.

"Yes, I do, and I'll tell you why. Z'kharyah [Zachariah] 1:16 says, 'I graciously return to Yerushalayim [Jerusalem]. My house shall be built in her…' And in chapter two he says, 'For I Myself—declares the Lord—will be a wall of fire all round it [that is Yerushalayim] and I will be a glory inside it.' That can only mean the Sh'khinah, the glory of his presence."

"But wasn't *Z'kharyah* talking about his own day?" asked David

"Did the *Shi'khinah* come then?" retorted the cohen.

"No," he replied thoughtfully. "You're saying it still has to be fulfilled?"

"Yes," replied Raphael.

David laughed. "I can see I need to study up on these things. It looks as though the old prophesies are coming to pass all at once."

After David left his friend he thought, *I must write Rachel at once. She will be excited to hear this news, especially since she read the book on the ark.*

The president sat at his desk in the Oval Office resting his head in his hands, elbows on the desk. The election was coming up next year. With all the problems, campaigning would be out of the question. He needed to announce his retirement so another party member could run. He didn't have the heart for it anyway. He would be glad to let someone else try to solve the problems. Then he had an alarming thought. *What if nobody else wanted the job? Would he have to stay on?*

The property and businesses of the vaporized people caused a tangle of financial nightmares, as remaining family members squabbled over the leavings. New laws had to be passed regarding inheritance. Since most beneficiaries were gone, settling of estates fell to state governments, but the Federal Government had to regulate a standard. Businesses failed by reason of the mismanagement of their new owners. Others were up for sale. The market was awash with them. Crime and vandalism destroyed others. More and more the states used militias to keep order. They in turn asked the Federal Government for help. The whole fiber of society seemed to be breaking down, and that was only the home problems. What was going on? The world seemed to have fallen apart after the disaster.

"It's too much to ask of a man," he said out loud. "And now this latest development in Russia—whatever happened to our dream of peace in the world?"

Then a door opened and Peters said, "They are waiting for you, Mr. President."

He slowly rose from his chair and followed Peters into the conference room. After greeting everyone he took his place at the large oval table. "Let's hear the bad news," he said at once. "Jack, are you the one who gathered it?"

"No, Mr. President, this came in from CIA."

"That's why you're here, eh Jonathan?" the president asked, nodding to Chase, the head of the CIA.

"Yes, sir, I'm afraid it looks bad."

"Well, stop scaring me and give me the worst." Then he muttered under his breath, "Good news doesn't seem to exist anymore."

"Russia's new czar, Zhavok, is redeploying the missiles as if

THE BEGINNING OF THE END

he expects an attack. He now has the Iranians as a close ally. And they're moving several of the mobile missiles to a new location," said Chase. "And that's not all. They have sold some of their ICBMs to Iran, who may already have nuclear capability by now."

"And get this," said Jack. "He's told the republics who want out from under Russian rule that he will waste no more Russian soldiers on conflicts with them. If they continue to resist he will nuke them."

"He wouldn't endanger his own countrymen, would he?"

"Winds would carry most of the fallout to the east. Since the troubled republics are all in the east, why would he care? Russia has already lost the trust of the West because of trying to interfere in the Ukraine. They never were high in the human rights department. Look how careless they were with nuclear testing. Another factor is the willingness of the Iranians to sacrifice themselves to bring chaos into the world to induce their Al Mahdi to come. You know who their target is—us. Uniting themselves to Russia just might give them the means," said Chase.

"Jonathan, do you have enough agents in Russia to keep us informed?"

"Probably, but even if we don't it's hard to get any more in now, since they closed the iron curtain again."

"Why did they close the borders?" asked one of the others.

"Probably because Pamyat, that anti-Semitic organization, has joined forces with Nashi and other strong pro-kremlin youth groups that formed in the early 2000s and mushroomed under Putin. They have started *pogroms* against the Jews and don't want any outsiders interfering," said Chase.

"The Jews should have left when they could," said the president, shaking his head. "Why would they stay?"

"Things looked pretty good when they thought they were going to have a democracy," said Jack.

But the president cut him off. "Back to the missile crisis. How are we going to respond?"

"I don't think the aggression will be against us, sir," Jack continued. "I believe the restoration of the missiles is a threat—a warning. Don't interfere or we might do something unthinkable."

"Like what?" asked the president.

"Oh, use limited nuclear power against one of the rebels as they have threatened. Since the limited nuclear attacks against Damascus and Tel Aviv haven't destroyed the countries where they fell," Jack said. "I think we've become conditioned to using nuclear weapons, like we no longer see them as destroyers of the world."

"Or they may be so desperate in their economic condition since the asteroid disaster, they may be getting ready to hold us up for more aid with this threat. A kind of help-us-or-else ploy," suggested the secretary of state.

"It's a dangerous situation any way you look at it. When people become so desperate that they don't care, they are liable to act irrationally," said Jack Trent, National Security officer.

"Do we have an up-to-date listing of their launching areas?" asked the president.

"Ukraine returned their warheads, but their launching stations are still there. And Kazakhstan's nuclear base has been internationally monitored even after Kazakhstan became independent and sent back all their nuclear missiles. But since Czar Zhavok seized control, we are no longer sure of the status there. We do, however, always know where their subs are," said Jack.

"What about letting NATO handle it? Russia respects NATO," suggested one of the others.

"Yes, NATO could put pressure on the czar before he gets too far along with his plans. If only we knew what his plans were. Jonathan, that is your department. And what about Iran? Do we have any eyes there?" the president questioned the CIA head. "I think we need to know more before we take any action."

—

"Have reports come back from the US yet?" asked the new sovereign, Zhavok, of his top intelligence officer. He had already ordered the missiles updated, refitted, and armed. Putin, when in power, had boosted production of their vast energy resources until they had gained a chokehold on Europe with their gas and oil pipelines. They would bow. Now he sought a means to neutralize the US while vying with China for supremacy.

"The precise location of all US nuclear power plants will soon be in your crosshairs."

Chapter 41

More and more pilgrims visited the site of the ark. They brought religious articles from their churches and set them up in front of the chapel. One church brought their ark, a wooden box containing its *Tabot*, which was a rectangular slab that was a facsimile of the ten commandments inside the original ark. It was set up at the front gate. But it kept falling over. One of the officials of the village sent word to the government, asking them to forbid the people from bringing the objects. Besides causing an unsightly mess in front of the chapel, it was obvious that they were rejected by their constant falling.

Another problem surfaced. The men who approached the ark developed painful boils in their secret parts. Actually it had started with Guani and the men who charged admission to the spectacle. No one knew how the disease was transmitted. The only connection seemed to be the ark. The outbreak of each region could be traced to those who had been to Aksum. In the six months since the light had appeared, the whole country was plagued with this affliction to some degree. After the government traced the plague to the ark, they began to take steps to get rid of it. They decided to send negotiators to Jerusalem to ask for its removal. If God wanted the Jews to have it then perhaps they could approach it and not die. They would do anything to get rid of the plague.

THE BEGINNING OF THE END

But travel was difficult from the interior. Their airfields in Addis Ababa had been damaged in the earthquake, but even so they were far away. Ethiopia didn't have access to the sea since the war with Eritrea. Nor could they travel down the Nile River because it had been reduced to a trickle by the disaster. That left them beggars for transportation.

After some searching they hired a small reed boat in Eritrea and sailed up the Red Sea.

David and his men were assigned to meet the ambassadors. First, David was called in by Major Yigaul Munitz, his immediate officer under General Uri Saguy of the intelligence branch of the army.

"Captain Solomon, take three of your men in the unit's van and go down to Eilat. The Ethiopian government has sent some kind of delegation here asking for an audience with the Knesset. I can't imagine why? What could they want?"

"To give us back the ark," said David, full of wonder and more to himself than to his superior.

"What are you talking about?"

"The Ark of the Covenant, sir. A *cohen* from Ethiopia told me several months ago it was a possibility. The residents of Aksum claim that the eternal fire returned to the ark the day the darkness fell. You see, they have claimed to have had the original ark of *Moshe's* (Moses') day for hundreds of years."

"That's interesting. But why would they want to give it to us after all these years?"

"I don't know, unless God had something to do with it," said David.

"Well, God or not, bring them to Jerusalem, and we'll see what they want," said the major and dismissed David.

David took three of his men who went to the Washington conference: Katz, Matza, and Feldman. They arrived late that night.

The next morning David inquired at the dock, looking for the Ethiopian ship. A sportsman he asked pointed to the tiny reed boat and said, "Maybe it's that one. They came in a coupla days ago."

The ancient-looking vessel with its full set of sails stood out in contrast to the modern pleasure boats docked at the lagoon. It appeared as a boat made of matchsticks as it bobbed slightly in the water. David felt as if he had stepped back in time as he boarded her.

Four tall men approached, dressed in western-style clothes. These were in contrast to the rest of the crew who were traditionally attired, their black skin glistening in the sunlight as if polished. The delegates flashed a sparkling smile, made more white by the contrast. David shook their outstretched hands and addressed them first in Hebrew and then in English.

"I am David Solomon. You are the ambassadors from Ethiopia?"

"Yes," one replied in English, bowing deeply.

"We've come to escort you to Jerusalem. Welcome to Israel," said David cordially.

The same Ethiopian responded, "Shalom and good morning. My name is Lebna Gedai." Then he introduced his companions. "I so sorry, I only can speak English, and none of us know Hebrew."

"English is fine," said David. "Most of our government can speak it as well."

"Good," said Gedai, relieved.

The four men followed David to the van on the dock. Gedai got up front with David, who was driving. The other two joined David's men in the back and they pulled out, heading back to Jerusalem. After polite conversation, David turned the conversation to the subject of the ark. He was anxious to hear about it firsthand and to confirm his suspicions for their visit.

"I understand the eternal fire has returned to the ark in Aksum."

"Alas, yes, quite true."

"Why do you say *alas?*" asked David.

"Because it has become a source of great trouble to us," he replied.

"Trouble?"

"Yes, you see, our whole country has become plagued with a terrible condition, and it has been traced to the ark."

"What kind of condition?" asked David, fascinated.

"A kind of boils that affect the secret parts of a man."

"How do you know the ark is the cause?"

"Because it started with the men who were commercializing on the phenomenon and then spread to all who came as pilgrims, then from them to the whole country."

"Just like in the Scriptures," said David, marveling at the power of G-d to accomplish his will.

"What do you mean? This has happened before?"

"Yes, it's written in our ancient Scriptures. When the Philistines captured the ark in Samuel's day, the same thing happened. Every city they took it to broke out in boils. Not only that, but when they put it in their temple, their idols fell before it."

"It is the same then," he said thoughtfully.

"I thought you were a Christian nation. How could idol gods fall before the ark in Ethiopia?"

"Not gods exactly but religious trappings and symbols. They would bring them from their various churches and set them up before the chapel. But they just kept falling over."

"All praise to the God of our fathers," burst out David, unable to restrain himself, "who never fails to accomplish his will."

"Why would you praise God for making our symbols fall?" asked Gedai, dismayed.

"Because if he didn't send the plagues and make your trappings fall, you would keep the ark. But now you want to get rid of it, so you come to us. Am I right?"

"Yes, that is the purpose of our visit."

"The Arabs gave us back our old temple site, and now you want us to take back the ark. Don't you see? God is returning to dwell in Israel."

"I'm not surprised. I know the churches are dead in my country. Most of the committed disappeared in the darkness. The only ones with any life and who escaped this plague were a new sect who claim to worship the *Lamb of God*."

"Really. What do you know about them?" asked David with renewed interest. It was the only time he had heard about them outside of Rachel.

"Some Jews fleeing the civil war in Egypt came to some of the churches in Addis Ababa preaching about the Lamb of God. Split several of the churches there. What's left of the hierarchy is in an uproar."

"Curious," said David, "the same thing is happening in the United States. What does it mean, I wonder?"

"Oh, my," the delegate replied, surprised. "I thought it was just a local problem."

I will have to tell Rachel, thought David. *Maybe it will encourage her to know others have this problem. Can it be happening other places as well?*

After several hours on the road, David brought his charges to the Foreign Affairs minister. After he dropped them off, he went straight back to his commanding officer.

"Did you find out anything?" asked Major Munitz.

"Yes, sir, it was just as I suspected."

"The ark?"

"Yes, it has caused a plague in their whole country. Just like in the days of Samuel when the Philistines took the ark. Also their religious trappings placed before it fall for no reason. Sir, it has all the marks of the Almighty. We have the temple site, and now they will give us back our ark."

"Did they bring it?"

"You are not a religious man, are you?" asked David.

"No, I guess not. Why?"

"Because if you were you would know that if God's presence is truly in the ark, only the priests of God could approach it. Anyone else who tried would die."

"But how do they *know* that?"

"A man who tried died at the door. No one has approached it since."

"I suppose they will appeal to the chief rabbis to send a team. They may even go themselves," said the major.

"I would like to volunteer to accompany them," said David.

Major Munitz pondered his request then replied.

"Yes, I guess we will have to send a military escort."

David left the office filled with Joy. He couldn't wait to write Rachel.

Chapter 42

Since he returned from the conference, Pope Peter found less and less time at leisure for common everyday things like newspapers. But the paper this morning reported something he could not ignore. It told of the phenomenon of the Jews preaching about Jesus as the Lamb of God to a worldwide audience. Some were on TV, while some had penetrated the Protestant churches. The official boards of the churches had begun to counterattack.

Pope Peter mulled the information over in his mind. Here was yet another problem to add to his load. He had been extremely cautious in dealing with the papal officers of Vatican City since his return from Washington. Some were entrenched in their positions and ruled with an iron hand. He kept them at bay by performing for his expected audiences without upsetting schedules. He bought himself one of the new world-class cellular phones and a satellite contract so he could call trusted friends and colleges from the garden in complete privacy. He pretended it was just a toy to use while he got his exercise. No one at the Vatican was sophisticated enough in electronics to tap those conversations made through the air and satellites.

During his garden walks he built a strong relationship with the Knights of Malta, an ancient order of the Catholic Church dating back to the crusades. It was mostly composed of laymen at this point—powerful men of the world doing charitable hospital work as a front, but whose real power was political and financial. And they were known to have a close working relationship with the intelligence branch of the Catholic Church.

With headquarters in Rome just across the Tiber on the Via Condotti, their property stood under international law as an independent sovereign principality just like the Vatican. The entrance opened to the street without fanfare in the midst of the top fashion shops of Rome.

Their leader, the grand master, was recognized as having the secular rank of a prince and the ecclesiastical rank of a cardinal. As they had been quite active in building European unity, they were the ideal vehicle for consolidating the power of the Church with the political powers of the world.

He also gained the confidence and sympathy of the Opus Dei, another Catholic organization with a worldwide organization—also charitable, but into the power scene as well. He had them checking on and building files on all the important hierarchy of the Catholic Church. It was easy to disguise their research since they worked all manner of good works for the Church. He sent out inquiries, searching out the moods and feelings of the local priests on controversial issues. The heavenly visit remained his secret. Actually, he didn't share all he was doing with anyone. His trusted priests or cardinals each knew only a small part. Not even his Italian secretary knew the whole of it.

To investigate this latest worry he called a special meeting with John McCutchen, the Vatican secretary of state.

"You wanted to see me, *Santissimo Padre*," said John as he entered the papal office.

"Yes, John, I've been reading about this phenomenon of Jews preaching some Lamb of God. Have you received any news of Jews infiltrating our church?"

"Actually, yes, just last Thursday Cardinal Mendez called from Buenos Aires very upset. You know how powerful the Jews are down there, especially since their embassy was destroyed. So I thought it was just a local thing. But then yesterday word came in from Spain of the same thing. I wasn't going to say anything about it until I could get a full report."

The pope frowned. "What are our priests doing about this?"

"Some of the priests in both areas have joined with the Jews. Others are in an uproar because it is splitting the churches. Those following the Jews have forsaken our Lady for some *Yeshua*. I intended to make inquiries in other areas before I reported to you," said John.

"*Yeshua?*"

"Yes, it's some kind of Jewish name for Jesus."

"Put everything else aside and look into this. The paper seems to think it's widespread. Meanwhile, I think I will call our ambassador in Israel and see why this is happening. Also, our illustrious leader in Spain, perhaps he can get the Opus Dei on the situation and get some answers. This seems to be a dangerous trend. Who is this so-called Lamb of God? Surely the Jews are not preaching the real Jesus. Only the Church is sanctioned to do *that*."

The pope was alarmed to hear about more loss of members in South America. The Catholics priests in Latin countries had lost many from their congregations to Pentecostal Protestants just prior to the darkness when a great revival swept through. Combined with all the losses of Catholics that were vaporized in the darkness, the Church was visibly shrinking.

John left, and the Pope called Israel. After he got his ambassador on the line and had finished with formal greetings, he said, "The reason I am calling is to find out about Jews preaching in churches and causing division. Do you know anything about this?"

"Yes, Holy Father, we have heard of it, mostly in other countries. We have reports of only one in Israel. He's up in Tiberius. He is teaching like the Messianic Jews used to."

"Used to?" asked the pope.

"Yes, they seemed to disappear at the time of the darkness."

"Does that mean that he is preaching that this so-called Lamb is Jesus?"

"Yes, I think so. But he has just a small following."

"It can't be the Jesus we know; it must be some heretical teaching," said the pope thoughtfully. *Can this be the heresy the Virgin spoke of? The one I have to cleanse from the Church?*

"Of course, Holy Father, it must be false. Do you want me to investigate the movement?"

"Yes, find out all you can. This heresy disrupts our churches elsewhere. See if you can find out what the Orthodox Jews think."

"All right, I will let you know what I find out," said the Vatican's ambassador to Israel, and with that they terminated the conversation.

Pope Peter took his cellular to the garden for his daily walk. He went around the winding streets of the enclosed Vatican City, walking slowly. He left the papal palace to the right of St. Peter's and walked across the gardens, which were bursting with new growth. Normally he would take time to enjoy his surroundings, but today he was intent on facing down a new menace. He continued past the museums toward the southwest corner of the enclosure. At each locality in Vatican City he dialed a different confidant. As more calls became necessary he stretched his course toward the heliport and then back behind St. Peter's, making a wider circle. Each call mounted more evidence to the menace. It was alarming how widespread the movement was. He had no trustworthy informant in the United States, so he would have to get that information from John's report.

The US Church was in the worst state of rebellion against the papacy. *Perhaps I should contact the World Council of Churches to find out what is happening. They would know more about this Lamb of God business since they have the same problem. It may be time to renew the ecumenical movement. We who are true to the faith should unite.* Yes, he thought, *this just might be the motivation needed to bring the Protestants back to the Mother Church.*

He returned from his walk elated and filled with purpose.

―

Rachel opened her latest letter from David. What news! The Moshiach was coming soon, she just knew it! She had just returned from her trip to Atlanta. Even there she had been confronted by people preaching about the Lamb of God in the streets. It was time she thought about moving to Israel. There was nothing left for her here anymore. Her work at the embassy was mostly office work, although she did enjoy the close relationship with the ambassador.

She remained distant to her father. He called occasionally but could never breach her defenses. He was more and more involved in preaching. Dan ran the business so her father would be free to do his religious work. He had quite a following and was at the center of a considerable controversy in Washington. The church people who resisted had called in the World Council of Churches to give assistance to the fight.

Rachel began to read and hear about it in the news. She was startled one night when she saw a crowd on TV listening to Simon preach. Only snatches of his message came through in the report. The media interviewed him afterward. Tears welled up in her eyes as she looked at his face. She had not seen him since that day in the synagogue.

"He is stronger than before," she said to herself. "I never thought my papa would become famous for preaching about Jesus. How my world has turned upside down since the disaster."

Despair settled in on her as she remembered the tender times when they studied the Torah together. Rachel had been quick to learn. Simon had been so proud of her. Especially when she, being the only girl in the Hebrew class, had outdone the boys. She was twelve at the time. She would never forget how he bragged to the rebbe of her devotion. In those days it was she and her papa against the world.

Tears flowed freely. "Oh Papa, where are you?" she cried in anguish.

Chapter 43

Pope Peter was ready. The invitational summons was quite clear. Addressed to his cardinals* it read:

> HIS EMINENCE,
>
> *Pope Peter II*
>
> SUMMONS YOU,
> HIS HOLY CATHOLIC CARDINALS,
>
> TO ATTEND
> A PRIVATE CONVERSATION
> WITH HIMSELF,
>
> ON WEDNESDAY,
> MARCH 11, 7:30 PM
>
> IN THE NERVI HALL OF AUDIENCES,
> VATICAN CITY*
>
> DRESS CODE: FULL CARDINAL REGALIA
> NO REGRETS OR EXCUSES EXCEPTED.

* The entire scenario of the consistory and the reasons for it are adapted by permission of Simon & Schuster Adult Publishing Group from THE KEYS OF THIS BLOOD by Malachi Martin (pp. 667-674; 685-697). Copyright © 1990 by Malachi Martin.

Also enclosed in the papal invitation was an official ID with instructions that no one could enter without the card. The summons went to all living cardinals. No one was restricted by age, retirement, or infirmity unless totally bed ridden. Those in the Holy See worked with the pope in preparation, but no one knew why the consistory was called.

In contemplating the faults in the Church that needed correcting, Pope Peter determined four tendencies that would eventually shatter the Church if left unchecked. The first fault: the traditional sacrifice of the Mass, held as law since Pope Pious V 1570, had virtually been replaced by Norvus Ordo. Norvus Ordo, considered by all as the "Conciliar Mass," whose Mass is a different Embodiment, a new freedom allowed by the ambiguous wording of Vatican II Council documents. The freedom loosed the service from the traditional Latin and allowed the people to participant more. But the result had been to take away the sacredness of the Eucharist. No longer did the faithful venerate the bread and wine as the actual body of Christ being sacrificed. Instead it had become more symbolic, like the Protestants—even a non-Catholic could participate.

The anti-Church faction inside the Church had been working for years toward breaking down Catholicism to fit in with non-Catholic and non-Christian religions. Their purpose was to reduce all men to the same faith and thereby promote a new world order and peace. Because of this Catholics were losing sight of the fact that the Roman Catholic Church was the original and only church through which eternal salvation could be gained. So in the name of religious liberty it was now commonly held among bishops, theologians, priests, and laity alike that membership in the Roman Catholic Church was no longer essential for salvation.

This was the second fault to be corrected. If this tendency were allowed to continue, the doctrines of the Church would be completely submerged and mixed with all the other doctrines of the world. *Jesus* came to save the lost, not Buddha, Muhammad, or anyone else. The message had to remain clear, or the church would simply fade into the world. It *had* to be corrected.

The third fault lay in the eroding of the power of the papacy. Catholic dogma stated that each bishop is the legitimate chief pastor of his diocese, *providing* he be in communion with the pope—*hold the same beliefs and moral laws as the Pope* and be subject to the jurisdiction of the pope. Ever since Vatican II Council, however, a rebellious tendency had arisen in the church. Cardinals, bishops, and powerful bodies within the Church—the Jesuits, in particular—began to denigrate the pope's authority.

Without the central papal authority dictating doctrine and policy, the oneness of the Church would disappear. Instead of having a powerful world church united in faith, each church would reflect the beliefs of its particular priest.

It had become a common tendency during the last forty to fifty years for Bishops to hold conferences to determine policies in their own countries without the pope's approval. This was especially true in the Western Hemisphere. If the Catholic Church was to remain the same the world over, this must stop! The pope had the keys of Peter, not the bishops. That meant he had the power of final authority, including correcting the direction of the Church.

The fourth fault was the moral issue that stemmed from the reproductive processes of man. The Catholic Church had long held that God alone should determine the conception of children, hence the decree against contraceptives. But the new freedom in the world had invaded the Church. Priests wished to marry or turned to homosexuality, the laity used contraceptives, unborn babies were sacrificed to the god of selfishness, and churches for the homosexuals had sprung up. The moral laws of the Church needed to be reinstated, or else corruption would swallow all the purity in it.

In short, a papal statement needed to be issued. He would enforce the laws of the Church that the Virgin said *must* be obeyed. That was the purpose of the consistory. With powers of excommunication, expulsion from office, and name by name condemnation of prelates, the pope would correct theologians, nuns, and lay people alike. Those who refused his statement would feel the weight of his keys.

Finally, the day for the consistory arrived. No one dared boycott the meeting. Besides that, everyone was curious as to why they were being summoned. Yet with all the cardinals' inquiries, none of the Vatican officers knew any more than they did.

They began to arrive at St. Peter's Square a little after 7:00 p.m. First they noticed a heavy concentration of security. Italian police armed with automatic weapons were everywhere in the square. That was a surprise, but only the first of many. Clustered around the entrance to the old audience building were several Swiss Guard checking ID passes. Cardinals entered one at a time.

Inside yet another difference met them. Throughout the halls, stairs, and lobbies, men dressed in full military attire of deep royal purple, brass buttons, and gold braid were stationed strategically. Armed only with swords, they stood, feet apart, with both hands resting on their sword handles whose points touched the floor in front of them. They remained in that position until a cardinal tended to wander from the way to the meeting hall upstairs. Then they would gently point the way with their swords. A few of the cardinals recognized their insignia as the Knights of the Order of Malta. These kept the red coats moving through the halls like blood coursing through the vessels of a living body and prevented any *coagulating* in the lobbies. Their faces reflected a serious determination that added to the cardinals' curiosity. Who were these militia men, and why were they here? Was the pope trying to impress everyone with his military might?

When the cardinals reached the door to the audience hall, they received a small announcement embossed with the pope's insignia of crossed keys and a tiara printed in gold. Inside it told them that the pope would address them at 8:00. Once inside they spoke to one another in whispers. The solemnity of the setting seemed to demand it. Some were hopeful that the pope had finally decided to act. Others had come, not in obedience, but to defy if necessary.

Pope Peter entered from the side and crossed the platform at three minutes to eight. He carried a notebook and placed it upon a small lectern in the center of the dais. After arranging some loose papers he sat down and bowed his head. From the time he entered, silence settled over the hall. Finally, at precisely eight, he arose and stepped up to the podium, the sound of his movement the only sound in the room. The cardinals waited in suspense.

"I have called you here to talk to you face to face," said the pope. There was no formal introduction, no opening hymn, just one small man dressed in white addressing a room filled with red coats and white lace shirts that looked like lacy short petticoats. There they sat, spreading upward row after row in front of him in the semi-circular theater-like auditorium. They almost looked like cards fanned out in a hand ready to play a game.

He began. "I have been concerned for some time about the spiritual and moral decay in the Church. Since the Vatican II Council in 1965 there has been a fundamental change, a change so radical that the Church of the forties and fifties was more like the Church of the Middle Ages than the Church of today. And all this change has come about in barely fifty years."

Pope Peter noticed some of his cardinals stiffen. He could feel resentment rising, and he hadn't even begun to name the damaging changes.

"Throughout the whole world rampant decadence asserts itself: in the seminaries, diocesan and Roman chanceries; in our religious orders, male and female; in our schools, colleges, universities; in our families, our liturgy, our theology, our morality and personal standards. They have all slipped into confusion, disorder, disunity, unfaithfulness, and yes, even open apostasy." He paused, cleared his throat, and then continued.

"During the darkness the Blessed Virgin appeared to me. She told me it was time for Jesus to return and set up his kingdom. But she also told me that the Church in its present state is not fit to reign. She was right. She said the laws of the Church must be obeyed. That means that we must do radical surgery on this 'Conciliar Church' we have created. I have taken the time to examine where each one of you stands on various issues, as well as those under you. You will remember the endless surveys you have been asked to fill out.

"Obedience to the Blessed Mother compels me to take drastic action to restore the Church to what it should be. Consequently, I have come up with a plan, call it a papal plan if you like. It is as follows:

"Here in Rome I have set up six new congregations that will exist only for the time it takes to reorganize the Church. Each will govern the change in one area of Church structure. They will be responsible for bishops, religious orders, priests, ecumenism, diocesan organizations and the Mass.

"To these new congregations I give absolute powers, and they will report directly to me. They can excommunicate, suspend, and interdict. These congregations supersede any existing congregations, *which will cease as of this minute.* Three organizations will assist them in their task. The Knights of Malta, the Opus Dei, and a secret organization that exists all over the world but is as yet unknown publicly...but of which you will shortly be aware.

"List after list has been compiled. I will mention only the main ones. They are cardinals, bishops, priests, seminary professors, and theologians. Those on the list will be forced to retire, stripped of any authority, and turned back to the secular world to live as they choose. They will be replaced with retired priests, bishops, and priests who hold the traditional and official Church position until new ones are raised up to take their places. The wording of the documents of the Vatican II Council will be examined, stripped of their ambiguous nature, and clarified. All meetings of bishops' conferences will *cease*." He stopped and looked directly at the audience. "They have been nothing more than the seedbed of sedition and heresy anyway."

Returning to his paper, he read on. "A full copy of my papal plan with all of its detail will be sent to each of you shortly." Again he paused, letting the words sink in. He glanced around the audience, reading their faces.

"My venerable brothers, I know you think this is drastic surgery. But the disease that attacks the Church is virulent and must be cut out. I go now to St. Peter's altar to ask forgiveness for our failures. You will please join me there." With that abrupt end to his talk, he walked across the platform and disappeared through the door between four armed guards.

The cardinals continued to sit, stunned. Although the pope's message had been short, it pierced like a sword. Those whose doctrines caused the disease he mentioned knew they would be severed from the Church. Anger registered on their faces as well as helplessness. There was no appeal. Others were clearly elated. The pope had finally stopped the Church's slide toward secularism. Gradually the cardinals left the hall and made their way down to the basilica.

Chapter 44

It had been nearly nine months since the consistory. The pope's actions had caused a revolution in the Church. The Catholics, who were used to Novus Ordo freedom—especially those in North America—revolted. The passionate preaching of the Jews and their converts captured many of them for the Lamb of God movement. Now lists were being made threatening the defectors with excommunication. Consternation among the faithful Catholics rose sharply. The controversy moved out of the realm of the spiritual and into the realm of the political. Seeing they had a common problem, more and more the Catholics sided with the Protestants because the Church as a whole was losing to the "Lambers" on a worldwide scale. Something had to be done. Finally, the National Council of Churches asked for a conference with the pope.

The more conservative evangelical churches, as well as the Mormons similarly effected, asked to be included. (The Jehovah's Witnesses allied themselves to the Jews. They too claimed to be the 144,000 part of the witnesses. They also preached the message of the kingdom.) The Reconstructionists among evangelicals had long advocated taking the government over for righteousness sake and thus bringing forth the kingdom of God in power. To do this they needed political power. Seeing the revolution in the Catholic Church, it was obvious that the pope *had* that power.

Pope Peter graciously received the delegation in the huge Paul VI Audience Hall, which seated over nine thousand visitors, normally used for the pope to meet with faithful Catholics from around the world. He sat upon a wide dais surrounded by four steps around three sides. This in itself rested upon an even larger platform, perhaps as wide as seventy-five feet, with ten or more steps to it, that stretched across the front of the auditorium. Behind the dais, featured in an inset, an enormous modern sculpture rose up behind his chair consisting of a thicket of branches spread in all directions. It filled the entire stage behind him. In the center of the thicket just above the pope's head was a statue of a naked man, arms upraised as if he were hanging on a cross, but there was no cross, only flowing streamers. On the dais with the pope were his secretary of state and a few selected cardinals, along with his personal secretary, Tony.

The delegation, though not small, was swallowed up in the vastness of the hall. They sat in a few front rows, leaving rows and rows of empty ebony seats sweeping up a gradual incline behind them.

Overhead the deeply-ridged parallel ceiling panels of windows stretched the full length of the room from front to back like stripes on a giant zebra. It was the most impressive feature to the whole building as long black lines separated the peaked windows in between. The only other windows in the massive auditorium were long horizontal ellipses of stained glass in a modern design under the slightly curving ceiling. The pope deliberately chose to meet them here in spite of having smaller meeting rooms just to intimidate them. It was nothing short of a blatant display of his power. He knew what he wanted out of the meeting, but *they* wanted something from *him*. Their asking gave him the advantage. He was curious to know what. But whatever it was it would give him the leverage he desired. Sooner or later they would come back to the fold, and the whole Church would be straightened out and be made fit to reign. Meanwhile, he would demonstrate his influence by showing them the size of the hall needed to meet with his own church.

The pope rose from his seat and motioned for the meeting to begin. After the pope sat back down, the Protestants' spokesman stood.

"Your Eminence," began the Right Reverend James Barton, the head of the National Council of Churches. "We have come to seek your cooperation in fighting this cursed movement that is destroying our churches."

"You speak of the Lamb of God movement?"

"Yes."

"We also find it troublesome," replied Pope Peter, shaking his head. "What exactly did you have in mind?" *Find out what's on their mind before you speak.*

"You have members high up in the government of the United States, do you not?"

"Yes, I believe we have several. How could they help?" he asked, puzzled. He had expected the meeting to run along the lines of religion.

"By passing laws that restrict Jews who preach Christian doctrines," said Barton.

"But wouldn't that interfere with your right to religious freedom?"

The delegation began to hum with whispers. The Reverend Barker, turned and motioned for quiet.

"The right to religious freedom is good if it doesn't cause a public uproar. But what we are seeing in the US is a polarization of society. Riots caused by those resisting this cursed doctrine break out almost daily. You see the Jews at home preach a near-approaching judgment day and destruction from God, as well as about their so-called *Yeshua*. This has greatly angered many groups. The pro-choice population is up in arms. So are the homosexual organizations and the gambling organizations. These are openly clashing because the Lamb of God Jews preach against them. Since they cause such disruption, we believe the government would be justified in curbing them to preserve order."

"Have you no lobbyists in Congress to espouse your cause?" asked the pope.

"Yes, but we need immediate legislation. Besides, with your cooperation we could go worldwide, get other governments to come to our aid. We feel you have more influence in Europe and South America than we Protestants do," said one of Barton's lieutenants. "This is not just a local problem. The Lambers are affecting our mission fields—it's worldwide."

"It's true many of the monarch's of Europe are personal friends of mine," said the pope thoughtfully, his hand stroking his chin. "Of course, most have only influence, not much actual power on legislation. But then again many of the legislators are Catholic."

"Perhaps we could draft a letter to strategic lawmen from both of us," suggested Barton.

"Have you thought of enlisting the legitimate Jewish congregations in your fight against the Lambers?" asked the pope. "They are joining us in Israel to combat the movement. It has stolen members from both our groups. We hate this heresy they teach. We fear for our people, since we are the guardian of their souls. I have issued the threat of excommunication to all who join the movement. But still they defect. Maybe legislation is the only way to stop them."

After much deliberation the representatives of the three remaining divisions of Christianity moved one step nearer to unity as they signed a letter to the governments of the world asking for laws to be passed against the heretical religion.

Chapter 45

Deeming the streets public and therefore government-controlled, the legislators passed laws to prevent street preaching. This greatly curtailed the outreach of the new faith because it was their one way to reach those who never darkened a church or synagogue door.

Other laws reached to the radio and television industries, making it illegal to preach about the Lamb. Yet the joined bodies of evangelicals and Catholics were given free time to air their opposition to the Lamb of God faithful, branding them heretical.

Churches and synagogues were closed to them as well. The central committees went as far as to take away the church buildings of those whose whole congregations had embraced the new faith. Hotels refused them space to meet in their conference rooms, fearing violence. Public buildings were denied them and even the city parks, if they tried to meet in the open.

Determined not to let society defeat them in the greater Washington area, Simon converted one of his large warehouses into a meeting place. But that too had its disadvantages, being located in an industrial area close to low-income housing. When several hundred people came together to worship on Sunday mornings and Friday evenings, they were met by angry mobs. Hecklers disrupted the meetings by pelting rocks against the metal building as more and more demonstrators gathered. Angry graffiti defaced the outside of the building, adding to the ugliness.

News coverage of it stirred the public sentiment to a high pitch of anger. Rachel, keeping up with it on television, had conflicting feelings about the controversy. She hated what her papa was doing, but she was also indignant toward the unfair treatment his movement received. Didn't we still have freedom of religion in this country? What was happening to the government? Why couldn't they control the extremists? Public sentiment had turned completely against her papa's faith. She feared for him.

Then it happened. Simon arrived a little early for the Friday night meeting in late June. The usual hecklers were there, and on impulse he began to preach to them. Surprised that he would address them, the crowd quieted to hear what he would say.

"Jesus is the answer to all your problems," he began in an even but loving voice. "If you want forgiveness, he will give it. If you want peace, he will give it. If you have financial needs, he will prosper you. If you are sick, he can heal you. All you have to do is repent of your sins and believe on his—" A shout cut off the last word.

"We don't believe in your brand of Jesus," yelled a man with his hands cupped around his mouth.

"Yeah, you preach another Jesus—the Lamb of God—some kind of Jewish Jesus," said another.

"The Jesus that I preach is the Jesus of the Bible. If you refuse him, your sins will condemn you to judgment. He will rain fire and judgment from the skies on all who reject him and have pleasure in unrighteousness. He is—"

At the mention of their sin, the crowd rushed him and began to beat on him. Blow after blow fell. Blood spurted from his nose as it took a direct hit. Still they pummeled him.

"Kill him," said one angry voice. A siren sounded. Someone had reported preaching in the street. The crowd scattered in all direc-

THE BEGINNING OF THE END

tions. As those around him pulled back, Simon staggered toward the warehouse. One angry man lingered, whirled, and threw him a karate kick just under the chin, causing a snapping sound. When the police and the faithful reached him, they saw from the unnatural position of his head that his neck was broken.

President Anderson paced back and forth in the Oval Office as he waited for members of the National Security Council to arrive. He had invited only the statuary members, because aids were not privy to top secret material.

He almost wished for the return of the cold war days. At least then none of the small nations needed to arm themselves because the two super powers protected their own. But now every peduncle nation in the world clamored for weapons to protect themselves, or at least that was the pretense. The SALT treaties were meant to prevent nuclear proliferation. Now Russia was breaking them.

Peters, a Secret Service man, admitted eight of the ten National Security Council members. They stood around in twos and threes while they waited for the president to begin the session.

"Good morning, everyone" said Secretary of State Russell Hamilton, the final member to show up.

"Gentlemen, have a seat," said the president, anxious to get started. He motioned toward the couches across from his desk in the oval office. Additional chairs brought in by Peters served the rest.

"I called you here to discuss a crisis in foreign policy that may require defense action. As you know, Putin's successor dissolved the Duma, Russia's lower house, and set up a more capitalistic government backed by the banking establishment.

"Until the asteroid encounter their economy looked promising. Since then, however, with the financial chaos left by disappearing people and the upsurge of crime, Russia's new czar has become desperate. He seized control of the army just to bring civil order. Putin had brought their economy to a prosperous state after he took over the oil industry. But Zhavok mismanaged it woefully. Now he is desperate for money.

"We have just received word from our CIA operatives inside Russia that because we had to cancel our loans to them due to our own financial problems, he intends to raise money by selling nuclear weapons to the Moslem nations. We protested, citing our treaties, but he threatened us with his missiles. He says they don't have a lot to lose like we do. He is also threatening the republics of the commonwealth that if they do not return to 'mother' Russia, he will nuke them."

Russell Hamilton broke in. "So that's why they refused to sign the SALT III papers in April and trashed our nuclear policy made under a former president. And here we thought we were headed toward complete disarmament within the decade. If we let this happen, control will be impossible. The reduction to six thousand warheads of the SALT II treaty means nothing if terrorists have access. Only a few missiles in the hands of loose cannons would seriously damage civilization."

"We can't allow Zhavok to sell them!" declared Jack, National Security advisor. "The terrorists would surely get a hold of them. Then they would attack us, and they would be safe in doing so since the fall out would not directly affect them. With their track record, they wouldn't care who else it destroyed."

"Wait a minute, before you get all worked up," said the head of energy, whose department managed US nuclear development. "Just having the missiles will not be any threat unless they have facilities to launch and experts to show them how. Launching a missile has too many safeguards. Not just anyone can do it."

"But that's just it," said Jonathan Chase. "They expect to send scientists with them. Zhavok doesn't worry about any of the weapons being used against him. And with good reason. He knows they would be used against us or Israel."

"Exactly," said the president.

"What shall we do? What *can* we do?" said Charles Stone, the secretary of defense, rocking forward on his seat, his bald head dropping into his hands with visions of destruction filling his mind.

"Don't give up yet, Charles. We might negotiate to stop the sale. We could even threaten. If that fails we might have to destroy their nuclear arsenal before they disperse it. Once the Arabs get hold of it, they will begin bullying Israel. War will likely break out in the Middle East again," said the president.

"Or here," said Stone. He seemed determined to be pessimistic. "It would surely touch off World War III. How can we destroy their arsenal without an out-and-out attack?"

"That's what we have to figure out," said the president.

"Any attack would turn world opinion against us. Even now we are condemned for dropping the bombs on Japan over sixty years ago. Not to mention our pre-emptive attack on Iraq," said Hamilton.

"Is it possible to do it covertly?" asked Jack.

"You mean send teams into their country to destroy their arsenals?" asked the president. "It would take an army. It's hard to hide that many men. Besides, the sites are widely separated. And what about their nuclear launching trains, which would be impossible to track since they look like any other train from the exterior."

"That's the rub," murmured Jack. "We would take a hit for sure. Maybe limited, but even so, think of the radiation."

"What if we hit at control first?" asked Stone.

"What are you getting at?" asked the president.

"Well, if we sent a squadron of stealth bombers in with the newly-adapted B61–11 bunker buster bombs to take out their underground control center in the Ural mountains then they couldn't make good their threat, and we could stop them when they tried to move other weapons east to the Arabs. Our surveillance satellites would pick them up. We could do it in stages."

"Who says they will take them east when they could ship them from western ports instead? We can't attack their ships. Taking out their command center is a declaration of war, and they would aim their train and submarine missiles at us. Oh, how I wish we had implemented the star wars defense system," lamented the president. Looking to Harris, head of National Aeronautics and Space, he said, "How far along is the satellite defense system?"

"We have a good defense against any isolated missiles coming from North Korea or Iran, but we gave up on defending against blunting a superpower's launch of massive warheads. The cold war was over."

"But having a sophisticated defense system will not keep the Russians from selling to the Arabs, who could still attack us through terrorist activity," said Hamilton, bringing the conversation back to the initial problem.

"What about army's THAAD missile defense systems? Couldn't they be set up around our strategic bases?" asked the head of the Joint Chiefs of Staff, jumping into the discussion for the first time.

"What good would that do in protecting our cities? Terrorists go for innocent people," said the president.

"Why even talk about a limited attack when they try to move the missiles. I think Zhavok would retaliate immediately, no matter what the consequences. He's an arrogant son of a bitch," barked Chase. "The Islamic fundamentalists want to create chaos so their Maddi will come."

"Then what about a first strike advantage?" asked Stone. "No one would expect the US to start a war, at least not that kind."

"You mean a one-strike attempt to destroy all the remaining ballistic missiles?" *That is World War III.* "The Arabs would surely take advantage of Russia's demise. Who's to say we would still be around to stop them?" said the secretary of state, disgusted with the way the discussion was going.

"Not if Israel still maintained her nuclear arsenal. Things should not get any worse if the Arabs are denied nuclear capability. Besides, we would take out most of Russia's arsenal, including tactical. They are concentrated together," replied the defense secretary Charles Stone confidently.

"Correction, *were*," retorted Chase. "Some of the Russian army officers sold off some to feed their armies."

"To whom?"

Chase shrugged.

"Gentlemen, aren't we getting a little drastic? Think of the effects of such an action," said the president. "Suppose we didn't get them all. And what about those trains we can't track? We would invite nuclear attack to ourselves, not to mention the horrible effects to Russia."

"Think of the choices," said Stone. "We either get them now before they spread, while we know where they are, or we wait until later when every terrorist group has access to nuclear weapons. Coupled with their hatred for us and Israel, we would be in all-out war with them anyway. That would be much more dangerous to us in the long run," argued Stone.

"Not just us but the whole world," said Jack. "Any careless use of nuclear weapons would endanger us all."

Dan Jordan, chief of staff of the Armed Forces, had been quietly listening to the discussion. He finally spoke up. "What about targeting all of the sites that we know of with our new limited nuclear warheads, like those used by Iran against Tel Aviv? That might save a lot of the civilians, but it would destroy the bulk of their missiles. Yes, we would take a hit, because it would be war. With Russia's determination to be the dominant nation in the world, it will be war with her anyway eventually. Why not do that which is most advantageous to us? We would save both ourselves and the rest of the world with just one massive strike.

Silence settled over the room as each man thought about the consequences.

—

Rachel noticed the blinking of her answering machine as she set her groceries on the table. Pressing the button, she heard Dan's voice say, "Call me immediately on my cellular." Was something wrong? He sounded urgent. She dialed his number.

"Hello, Rachel?" he said, expecting her.

"Yes, I got your message. What's wrong?"

"It's Papa. Rachel, they've killed him," he said quietly.

Silence.

"Rachel, are you there?"

Dan heard a shuffling noise as Rachel grabbed the back of a chair to steady herself.

"Rachel, are you okay?"

"No, No-o-o-o-o-o..." she shrieked. "I was afraid something would happen, but not this. Who killed him?"

"A mob outside our meeting place. He started to preach to them, and they beat him up. He was already dead when they found him."

"Oh no, no, no-o-o-o-o-o," she cried again. And then she felt strengthened by rising anger. "Those bastards! Where is he now?"

"We had him sent to Levenson's Funeral home after the police were through. Sheila and I are here now. We need you to help make arrangements."

"I'll be there as soon as I can," said Rachel and hung up. She was in shock. Papa gone. How could it be?

"No, no, no-o-o-o-o." If only he had remained faithful, this would not have happened. "Oh, Papa, Papa, why did you change?" she cried with a mixture of grief and anger. "God of Abraham, why did he forsake you?" Suddenly her hatred for the Lamb of God jumped to double digits. "You false god, how dare you take my papa from me," she screamed.

Somehow she managed to get to her car, but the unrelenting anger preoccupied her. Over and over she thought of her lost relationship. Then her anger turned to grief. She had only seen him that one time on TV during the past year. Now she would never talk to him again. Tears filled her eyes.

The light changed and an eager young teenager gunned it at the sight of green. Crashing metal and shattering glass sounded, and the air filled with the smell of dust and oily smoke. The teenager's car had hit her broadside on the passenger door, throwing her car into the path of the vehicle entering slowly from the other direction. The back door of Rachel's side was smashed, jamming her door as well.

Rachel was saved from serious injury when she threw up her hands at the first impact. Since the force threw her from side to side, her arm just below the shoulder hit the window frame instead of her head, so she didn't lose consciousness. But pain in her left arm as it hung limp told her it was broken. Shaken and in shock, she reached for her cellular. She grimaced, realizing that something was wrong with the right hip too, as pain shot through her right side. *It must have hit the armrest.* Awkwardly trying to hold the phone with one hand and dial at the same time, she managed to call 911.

Then she called Dan.

"Dan, I can't make it," she gasped barely above a whisper, her voice trembling. "I ran a red light. I've been hit. We're waiting for the ambulances now."

"Oh, Rachel, no. How badly are you hurt?" Dan asked, a slight irritation showing in his voice. "I'll bet you were angry."

"Hey, how about a little sympathy," she groaned. "My left arm is broken, and I think my hip—hurts pretty bad anyway, and I can't move my leg. The car is absolutely totaled. It may take them awhile to get me out. Both sides are smashed."

"Oh, I'm sorry, sis," he said with belated compassion. "Since you were able to call, I thought you were just scared. Before you hang up—what hospital? We'll meet you there."

"I don't know. I'll have them call you."

After she clicked off, she laid her head back and wept bitter tears. A crowd gathered around her door, but she ignored them. The pain of her heart was nearly as great as the physical pain racking her body. Her hatred for the Lamb movement raged, as she blamed them for all her troubles. Shortly, she heard the sirens.

Chapter 46

The negotiators from Ethiopia returned home with Israel's commitment to remove the ark from their plague-ridden country. But it could not be done right away because they still had to provide a temporary house for the ark until the temple was completed. The prophetic book of Amos provided an acceptable answer. The prophet predicted that the tabernacle of David (which consisted only of the Ark of the Covenant housed in a tent) would be built again upon its own ruins. Taking direction from this, the government purchased all the remaining private property on the lower hill south of the Temple Mount. It was the original site of the Jebusite fortress that King David captured to be his royal city.

After demolishing the houses, bulldozers pushed the rubble to the sides of the hill, leveling the western side to a retaining wall. The wall ran along the main road that skirted the whole western side of the ancient city site. Thus they broadened the surface much in the same way Herod the Great had extended the Temple Mount. A broad plain made room for the great crowds of people, many more than could gather at the Wailing Wall. Crowds would come on feast days now that the ark was available for fulfilling the rituals of Yom Kippur. They already had an altar where the sacrifices could be made.

It was months since the delegation had come from Ethiopia.

Yet another significant thing happened. Having at last obtained a pure red heifer to prepare the cleansing water, the priests were sanctified according to the Torah.

But one thing remained: the making of the veil to separate the ark from the profane. On the broad new grassy plain recently planted above the ruins of David's city, the original Mt. Zion, they had set up a heavy tent made of animal skins on the outside and linen on the inside. But the veil to hang before the ark had taken so much thought and debate in its design and construction that its production lagged behind everything else. According to the Scriptures, the ark had to be wrapped in it along with two other coverings before it could be transported.

Craftsmen constructed a special large loom to weave a thick pure linen tapestry that featured two golden cherubim on a background of interwoven blue, purple, and scarlet threads. It had taken months to work out the design and gather the materials.

Another miracle aided their production. The ancient sea snail, from which they made the royal blue and purple dye, had returned in abundance to the Mediterranean Sea. It had all but disappeared in AD 70 when the Jews left the land.

With the veil ready, only the transportation details remained to be worked out. Aksum was high on a mountain range on the border of Eritrea. The simplest method of travel would be to fly to the nearest airfield, which happened to be Asmara in Eritrea, and use a transported van to reach Aksum. Therefore they loaded cars for transportation and a van to carry the ark back down the mountain into a C-130 cargo plane.

Meanwhile, the work on the Temple Mount continued. The bridge and the dividing wall had been completed first. Then the altar was constructed next so that the daily sacrifices could begin as soon as the priesthood was consecrated. The outside walls of the temple itself were nearly up. With the ark in their possession, even though it was separately housed, they would be able to perform the Yom Kippur ritual for the first time since 70 AD.

They chose twelve priests (an administrative number) by lot to accompany the chief rabbis of both the Sephardic and the Ashkenazi branches of Orthodox Judaism.

David, receiving his command as requested, also took twelve men to accompany them. He picked the same crew that went with him to Washington, along with some new men who replaced those lost in the terrorist attack. Then they all boarded the IDF cargo plane to fly to Asmara.

"You are excited about this trip, aren't you, Captain?" asked Matza.

David smiled. "It's one of the dreams of my life."

"Even above a certain dark-haired lady in Washington?" teased Katz.

"Well," said David, hesitating. "Close."

"Really, are you still in touch with her after all this time?"

"Oh, yes, we write almost every day. You remember Simon, her father?"

"Yes, of course."

"Well, he turned to the Lamb of God movement and became one of their leaders."

"Oh, yeah. I've heard of them."

"Three weeks ago while he was preaching to a mob of hecklers they turned on him and killed him. When Rachel heard about it she got so upset she had an automobile accident on the way to the funeral home. Now she's in the hospital mending a broken hip. I'm hoping she will perk up when we get the ark back. Maybe even decide to come over here."

"I'm sorry to hear about Simon, Captain. He was a good man," said Katz, serious for once. The others in the front of the plane expressed their condolences as well.

Matza, who had been highly influenced by David's character, was genuinely interested in the religious development in the country, but he had no real knowledge of the Scriptures. He brought the subject back to the ark.

"Why is the ark necessary for the temple? It wasn't in the Holy of Holies during the days of King Herod, was it?"

"No, actually it wasn't. I think it is a rallying place to restore us back to our religious roots," replied David. After a moment of thought he added, "Besides, it represents the dwelling place of God. I also believe it necessary to fulfill the prophets' words concerning the coming of the kingdom and the Messiah."

"And that's another thing I don't understand. What is the Messiah anyway? Isn't he just some weird belief of the Haredim, totally disconnected from Zionism?"

"No, the Scripture abounds with the glories of his coming and the kingdom he will bring, but Zionism is just connected to the restoration of a secular Israel—a land for all Jews."

"Sometime you will have to show us," said Matza, still confused.

When they landed in Asmara, the same delegates from Ethiopia who had come to Jerusalem met their plane. David smiled as he reached out his hand to Lebni Gedai.

"Shalom, we meet again."

"Yes," replied Lebni. "We are all so glad you have finally come. The plague grows worse daily."

David introduced the delegation to the chief rabbis, who in turn introduced their fellow priests. Then they climbed into their respective cars, and together they ascended the heights to the border of Ethiopia.

When they reached Aksum, David could hardly contain his excitement. They emerged from their cars and approached the chapel. Even though they had heard reports of the glory, they were not prepared for what they saw. Pulsating rays of glorious light escaped through the narrow windows, brighter than the sun in a clear sky, yet it didn't burn their eyes to look upon it.

Tears filled the eyes of the rabbis as they fell down and worshipped, feeling that the very ground under them was holy. Their fellow priests followed their lead.

The non-religious soldiers who accompanied David were silenced by the spectacle. With hands shading their eyes, they stared in utter awe. David joined the priests on his face in obeisance. Even the secular soldiers finally bowed down out of sheer respect.

Although the priests had come with excitement to transport the ark, coming face-to-face with the *Sh'khinan* struck fear into their hearts. Ezekiel the prophet had written of G-d's displeasure with the Levites who deserted him prior to the Babylonian captivity and had decreed that in the future only the descendants of faithful Zadok could approach his presence. Were they his descendants? No clear genealogies existed. Would they live through this? No one stirred, however, not wanting to test the ancient fire.

Finally, one of David's men cried, "It's gone! The light, it's gone!"

Everyone looked up. The little chapel looked like any other ordinary building. They were all amazed, especially the Ethiopian delegation.

"This is very strange," said Lebna. "It's the first time the light has gone out in well over a year—actually since it first came on."

"Just like in the Scriptures!" said David.

"What do you mean?" asked the Ashkenazi chief rabbi.

"I think he refers to the children of Israel's wanderings in the wilderness. When the glory lifted off of the tent, they packed up and moved, following the glorious cloud until it stopped again," said the Sephardic chief rabbi. "Am I not right?"

"Yes," said David. "So that means we can do the same."

The priests were visibly relieved. They took the coverings for the ark from the van and started for the door of the chapel. Once inside, David heard their comments on the beauty of it. He wished he could see it for himself, but he knew it was forbidden to all except the priests. Since it was not just an artifact but the actual dwelling place of G-d on Earth, one did not take chances just for the sake of curiosity. According to the Holy Scriptures, the ancient King Uzziah only entered the temple's holy place and tried to offer incense, and he was struck with leprosy that lasted until the day he died. What would have happened if he had tried to enter into the holy of holies where the ark was?

A little over an hour later the priests emerged and announced that it was covered and they were ready to take it to the van. David had posted his men around the little compound, but it was not necessary. The people themselves had always protected the ark. A crowd of curiosity seekers had gathered to watch.

Six priests lifted the staves to their shoulders and carried out a large bundled object covered in blue cloth. Although the ark itself was only twenty-seven inches wide, forty-five inches long, and fifty-four inches high (half the height was the golden cherubim on the lid), wrapped first in the thickly-woven veil and then two other cloths, it was quite a bulky package—and heavy.

"What did it look like?" asked David, anxious to hear about it.

"It's beautiful. It's hard to imagine how old it is. Maybe 3,500 years old if our date for Moses is correct."

"Yes, but what did it look like?" repeated David.

"Well, it's really quite small under all this wrapping. Good thing too, or we couldn't carry it since there's so much gold. Carved work makes a crown around the lid, interspersed with twenty-four angel-like figures, and the cherubim on the lid have wings that spread until they touch. All of the mercy seat, the lid to the box, including the cherubim, is solid gold. Some of the gold has come off the box part, but it's the most beautiful thing I've ever seen."

"Did you look inside?"

"Yes, and the two tablets of stone were there."

"Could you read them?" asked David, thrilled to hear it. He referred to the two actual stones carved out by Moses and written by the finger of God.

"Of course, they are written in ancient Hebrew, same as the Torah."

"I still can't believe this is happening," said David. "It's just too wonderful for words." Katz and Matza stood close, listening to every word.

The priests placed the ark in the van. Three rear seats had been removed to accommodate it, but they had to remove the carrying staves from their rings to make it fit. That was a mistake. When the priests assigned to drive the van opened the doors, power shot out and knocked them down. The *Sh'khinan* had returned.

The others came running.

"What happened?" said the chief rabbis almost in unison as they stared at the priests on the ground. "Are you hurt?"

"Not really, but we can't get in the van," replied the driver as he picked himself up and brushed the dust off his robe.

"Something must be wrong with our method of transportation," said Yehuda Hacohen, the Sephardic chief rabbi.

"Did anyone bring a copy of the Torah so we could check our procedure against it?" asked David.

"No," said Yigeal Shapiro, the Ashkenazi chief. "We thought we planned everything correctly before we left."

David was dismayed. *I hope we didn't come all this way for nothing,* he thought. *Of course we could call someone back home for the information we need…Oh, wait…Isn't the Christian's Old Testament the same as ours?*

David turned to Lebna and quietly asked, "Do you know who might lend us a Christian Bible?"

"There should be one in St. Mary's Church. I'll go and see." Several minutes later he returned with a large pulpit Bible. While the chiefs and the priests huddled, trying to decide what to do, David asked him to search in Numbers to see if they had missed some small detail concerning the transport. Then he asked the Ethiopian to read and translate concerning the ark. Finding nothing amiss from that passage, he had him turn to Exodus and read about the ark where G-d commanded its construction. Suddenly he realized what was wrong.

He called to the priests, "I think I've found the answer."

They looked at David in surprise. He was holding a Christian Bible. How could that have the answer?

David saw their questioning faces. "The first five books of the Old Testament of the Bible are virtually the same as our Torah," he said in answer. "In Exodus it says the staves are not to be removed. We removed them to make the ark fit into the van. They should be put back."

"But it won't fit in the van with the staves in," declared one of the priests who loaded it.

The driver looked to the van. "That's it," he shouted. "The *Sh'khinan* is gone again.

"Well, I guess we will have to find a bigger vehicle. I wonder why it matters to God that the staves remain in the rings?" asked Chief Shapiro.

"What matters to God is that we obey him," said Chief Hacohen.

David turned to the Ethiopian spokesman. "Do you know where we could rent a truck?"

"No, but we can ask the local people. I'll go see."

"Thank you," said David. He wondered if G-d would allow a

THE BEGINNING OF THE END

truck to carry his dwelling place. In King David's day, He would not even allow a cart to carry it.

Meanwhile the priests unloaded the ark and replaced the staves. But as soon as they were replaced, the *Sh'khinan* returned again, knocking down those within ten feet of the holy object.

Chief Rabbi Shapiro wrinkled his brow in a deep frown.

"Now what? The truck isn't good enough either. Do you think he expects us to carry it all the way down the mountain on our shoulders?"

The light went out again.

"Yes," said Chief Hacohen, "I believe he does. God is communicating his will to us in this manner."

"But it might take us a week or two," complained Chief Shapiro. "And what about security. We'd be out in the open."

David spoke up.

"Rabbi, sir, I don't think we have to worry about security. The ark may well defend *us*. If the Ethiopians, who have had it for centuries, are stricken with plagues because God wants the ark back in Israel, no terrorist will thwart his plans. Besides, if he flattens those of us who serve him, just to direct us, what would he do to enemies?" said David and laughed.

"You have a strong faith, my son," said Chief Hacohen. Then he added, "We will confirm that God intends for us to walk it down by trying to load it on the truck. If he prevents it, we will know."

"It's pretty late in the day to start walking. Perhaps I should scout out some shelter down the road for us," said David.

"Wait until we know whether it's necessary," continued Chief Rabbi Hacohen, who seemed to have taken charge.

The Ethiopian returned with a local man and said to the chief rabbis, "This man has a truck we can use."

"Wonderful! Bring your truck, and we shall see how the *Sh'khinan* leads us," advised Chief Hacohen.

The man left, and the priests watched to see what would happen to the light. Shortly the man returned with his truck, an open bed with side rails, but not even a tarpaulin over them. The light burned steadily. After waiting a half hour, Chief Hacohen thanked the man and dismissed him.

"I guess we will have to walk," Chief Rabbi Shapiro said and sighed.

"Yes," confirmed Rabbi Hacohen. "Six of us will carry it for one mile and then be relieved by the other six. Captain Solomon, half of your men will accompany the walkers and half will take the rest of us and the cars down the road and wait. Then we will swap teams."

"But it is over a hundred miles to Asmara," protested Chief Shapiro.

"Yes, but we shall walk *until* the *Sh'khinan* tells us otherwise," affirmed Hacohen with finality. Following his declaration, the light went out. "Well," he said, "I guess that confirms our hike.

Rabbi Hacohen assigned the first team of carriers and opted to lead the first mile. Then he turned to David and said, "Captain Solomon, go ahead of us and call our government and tell them what we are doing."

David nodded and assigned his men to accompany them. Then he pulled out his cell phone and called his commanding officer, who related the message to the government.

Leading the rest of the riders to the cars and van, he drove the van to a small village about five miles down the road to make arrangements for the night. The rest in the cars stopped exactly a mile from the ark's location.

"They are *walking* out!" exclaimed Ra'amon when he was told. The fascinating story of their direction buzzed all through the government. Inevitably, the story leaked to the media, which informed all of Israel and subsequently the world. Major networks, most notably CNN, sent reporters and video cameras to follow the journey of the ark. All the world watched their descent after the next day.

Chapter 47

They continued the journey, making about twelve miles a day. People often lined the road to see the ark pass. They were offered food and lodging as they passed along. G-d was providing for their needs.

One attempt to stop the procession was foiled by the *Sh'khinan*. Islamic terrorists sent a team with a suicide bomber. They were jealous of the attention the Jews were getting from the world because of the temple and now the ark. If they could destroy the ark, Judaism would suffer, and Islam would be a step closer to world power. They planned to mingle a suicide bomber with the crowd along the road. After the ark had passed, the bomber was to run up behind them and set off the explosives, taking out the ark, priests, and some of the crowd.

But when the time came for the terrorist to act, the priests carrying the ark suddenly dropped to the ground like rag dolls, and the *Sh'khinan* took over the ark as it landed with a thud. The terrorist, who had run out into the road, stopped in bewilderment. Then power shot out of the ark like lightning and burned him black, as in an electrocution. But the amazing thing about it was it didn't set off the explosives. In fact it only slightly scorched his clothes. David examined the charred body and found the bomb. He gave it to two of his men, who carefully carried it away from the crowds to disarm it. The people fell on their faces and worshipped. CNN recorded the incident for the whole world to see. The message was clear. G-d was returning to Israel in power.

The *Sh'khinan* remained in the ark and blocked the road for an hour. Then it left as suddenly as it came. The priests continued to the next check point where the chief rabbis decided to rest the remainder of the day. Being on the edge of a small town, they journeyed only to the center where a Jewish shop owner came out and offered to give them shelter. They took that as G-d's provision, for that evening was the beginning of Shabbat.

After Shabbat the rested company prepared to resume their journey. They still had over sixty miles to go before they reached Asmara. They dreaded the rest of the trip because they were coming down to lower altitudes that meant higher temperatures.

But to their surprise the *Sh'khinan* refused to let them go. The shop owner heard them discussing the problem. He said, "Perhaps God only meant for you to walk this far. The news media has already shown his mighty power to the whole world. I have a large delivery truck that I use to bring up stock from Asmara. I would be honored if you took the ark down the mountain in it."

At this offer, Rabbi Hacohen said to one of the priests, "Go see if the light is out at his suggestion."

The priest returned to say, "That must be what he wants. It's out."

"Oh, hallelujah," said Chief Rabbi Shapiro. "Now I can rest my tired feet."

The rest of the priests also sighed with relief. Finally, they could go home.

They loaded the ark into the truck, staves and all, and completed their journey to Asmara. From there they boarded the C-130 cargo plane without further incident.

THE BEGINNING OF THE END

Rachel lay with her leg in traction, watching the news. She had been keeping up with the ark's movement for several days, catching occasional glimpses of David. But this evening's headline was terribly exciting. The anchorman had announced an attempt to bomb the ark. She couldn't wait to see what he meant. When the commercial ended, she saw the power shoot out of the ark and incinerate the bomber. But most exciting of all, there was David, examining the body and finding the bomb. Afterwards the CNN reporter interviewed him, and there were close-ups of his face. He told of the guidance they had received from the *Sh'khinan*.

Her love for him overwhelmed her. She had forgotten the details of his face. Snapshots are not the same as videos. Hearing his voice sent a ripple of excitement through her. In that moment she made up her mind. She decided that as soon as she got out of the hospital, she was going to go to him. Papa's gone. Therefore the reason for her remaining had disappeared. She had hoped to be reconciled with her papa before she left the country. *Dan and Sheila are into that accursed faith. Why should I stay here?* Her portion of her father's business would support her. She need not worry about getting a serious job once there.

Besides, she wanted to be where the Moschiach was. With the *Sh'khinan* returning to Israel, he is bound to show up. She had studied enough from the Tanakh to know that he would destroy Israel's enemies. *Probably with the power in the ark,* she thought. Yes, she would go to the land of her ancestors and marry David. The thought of it thrilled her. From that day on she spent her days planning how she would accomplish it. Then she wrote to David of her plans to come.

Chapter 48

J. Quentin Rice rushed to Brussels where a hastily called meeting of the top round table would assemble. Present would be the fifteen most powerful men in the world, those who held the purse strings over governments. Twelve were the Council of Wise Men, and three were elevated above the council. Of the three, the Grand Master ruled over the other two. These ruled over the council, who in turn were made up of men from many powerful organizations of the earth. Together they were all powerful. For years they had been manipulating trade and attempting to bring in a one-world government through various experiments in socialism, attempting to bring in the "great society" of Plato.

Now they were alarmed. Communism had collapsed, and their attempt to set up a strongman in Russia backed by their banks was getting out of hand. He had arrogantly challenged the US.

J. Quentin Rice was in one of their lesser organizations and their spokesman to the President of the US. But he was also informed about the military preparations of the US, being on the Senate Armed Forces Committee. They had called him to report the US intentions to the present threat in Russia. They needed to know how to plan for the crisis.

Rice was honored to be in their presence even though what he would say would violate his security level in the US. By giving them top secret information he would be essentially committing treason. Never before had he met with them save in the company of others and then only once. But today he would bask in their presence as the center of attention. *For once this all-powerful group needs me,* he thought. He knew why he was there, and he had prepared himself, but he was still nervous.

"Gentlemen," he began, "my country is governed by fools. I spoke with the secretary of state, whom you know is one of us, and he informs me that preparations are being made for a nuclear first strike against Russia. They are desperate because of the threat to sell nuclear arms to the Arabs. They fear the spread of the weapons to unknown positions. They believe they will be directed toward Israel and the US because of Fundamental Islam's hatred of us both."

"Is there a time table set up?" asked one of the two.

"They intend to warn diplomatically first and perhaps send a small attack against the attempt to move weapons out of the country," he replied. "But if that does not work then they plan a full-scale attack against all missile sites, as well as submarines and their naval bases."

"Has the diplomatic envoy been sent?"

"I don't know for sure. Hamilton didn't tell me. But I would guess so."

"Will you excuse us for a few minutes and wait outside," asked the grand master.

"Of course," he replied. He stepped out and closed the door, wondering what they would discuss in his absence.

Several minutes later he was recalled.

"Senator Rice, here is a list of names we wish you to call when you return. Tell them that 'the tide has turned.' That is our code name for 'leave the country.' Say nothing else; they will know what to do as you yourself know. We will try to reorganize in Rome after you come out."

J. Quentin Rice left with this thought. *They have given up on the United States. They intend to build the new age without us. I wonder if they will warn Russia. I must make two stops in Rome before I return home, one to Via Condotti and one to the Vatican. Both the Knights of Malta and the pope need to know about this.*

Chapter 49

Rachel left the hospital ready to pursue her plans to immigrate. She had made all the arrangements she could by phone while her hip mended. But now she could buy her ticket and begin to pack. She was eligible for citizenship under the law of return just as any other Jew. The ambassador helped her complete the paperwork. She had called David from her hospital bed and set the date as soon as the doctors gave her clearance. She wanted to be completely well, so she delayed her departure beyond their date. It would only be a short delay. She didn't want to meet David as a cripple.

It's so good to be home, thought Rachel as she entered her apartment for the first time in six weeks. She still walked with a cane, but she grew stronger every day. Soon it would not be necessary. The next day she called and placed an ad in the paper to sell her furnishings. By the time they were gone she thought, *I will be completely healed. No more cane.*

"God has blessed me," said Rachel out loud a week later as she looked around the nearly empty apartment. She'd saved the mattress, springs, and TV so she could manage some semblance of living. The bedding was necessary (she could manage in the kitchen without furniture). She kept the TV for comfort and company. Dan and Sheila agreed to pick them up the day she left, after they took her to the plane.

It was her last night in the apartment. Everything was done. She was packed and excited. Being keyed up and having nothing else to do, she turned on the TV to pass the time.

The program was an absorbing drama, and she was deeply into it when suddenly a news brief flashed on the screen.

"We interrupt this program to bring a startling news development. Belarus has rejoined Russia. Zhavok has sent armies to the borders of the newly independent Balkan countries and the Ukraine to coerce them back under Russian control.

"NATO leaders will meet in Berlin tomorrow to decide how to counter the aggression. The UN Security Council met this afternoon. Both the United States and the UN have sent strong protests to the Russian Government.

"Relations are already stretched to the limits with Russia because they went ahead with their deal with Iran, selling them nuclear weapons and know-how. It was believed that the surprise raid on that attempt would solve the problem, but all it did was enrage Iran. Russia keeps on regaining its former territories. The president has called for a meeting of the National Security Council."

The program resumed, but Rachel turned off the TV. *I'm glad I'm leaving,* she thought. *They are playing with fire. Someone is going to get hurt.*

Two days later Rachel stepped off the plane in the new Israeli/Palestinian International Airport near Ramalla. She rushed into David's waiting arms.

"Oh my *hamoodah* (darling), you are here at last," said David as he squeezed her tightly. "How I have dreamed of this day." Hungrily he found her lips, expressing what words could never say. After a long satisfying kiss he asked, "Did you have a smooth flight?"

"Yes," she whispered, breathless from the kiss. Her heart thumped and fluttered all at the same time. She was no longer in doubt of her love for him after months of intimate sharing, pouring their hearts out to each other in letters. "But I was so excited I think I could have flown without the plane."

"How is your hip?" He held her away from himself and looked her up and down.

She twirled around. "I'm as good as new."

"Great. I was so worried when I first heard about it. Hips are tricky sometimes."

"Yes, it was a maddening experience, having to lie there with my leg just so. But it healed perfectly. One good thing about it though, I had time to think things through."

"Good, when do we get married?"

"Whenever it suits us," she replied, smiling happily.

"The sooner the better," said David, squeezing her again. "I can't believe you're finally here." He continued to nuzzle her ear and murmured, "This is the part I've been longing for."

"Me too," she whispered.

Finally he let her go, and they began walking arm in arm.

"Mama wants me to bring you straight over. She insists you stay with them until we find you a place. I have been checking around for apartments, but they are not easy to find, at least not moderately-priced ones. You will have to get used to less luxury over here, I'm afraid. I doubt if we can find a place as nice as yours in the States."

"I don't mind," said Rachel. "The important thing is that I am here and we can finally be together."

"Yes, that is *the* most important thing." He responded by hugging her again. Then when he released her he grabbed her hand and pulled. "Come on, let's go get your luggage. I can't wait for you to meet my family."

On the short trip to Jerusalem they caught up with each other's lives since their last letters. David told her about the activities concerning the temple and the ark and she about her papa and her feelings about that. Then she said, "I would love to work at something to do with the temple. I don't have to earn money. I could volunteer. My papa's business was left to both Dan and me, and he will send me my share of it monthly."

"Oh, an independent woman, huh?" said David. "I don't know if I like that or not."

But Rachel knew he was only teasing. It was one of the things she loved about David. He could be so lighthearted. She smiled. "Yes, so you better not be a wife beater."

Changing the subject David said, "We are nearly there. It's only about seven miles to Jerusalem. Much closer than Ben Gurion International was, near Lod. Lod is still full of dangerous radiation. It's a good thing they moved IDF headquarters before the strike, or it would have been all over for us."

"Was it in Tel Aviv?"

"Technically. But our intelligence thought it best to move it before we struck Damascus, knowing Tel Aviv would be the target in Israel. There was even a terrorist video simulation on the net in 2008 of a nuked Tel Aviv."

"Really? I heard it will be years before that area can be used again. What part of the city do you live in?" she asked.

"On the west side. It's nearer the base, which is southwest of here. It's always been more convenient. That is until now."

"You mean since I came to town. Maybe I can find something close to you. Will we have to move when we get married?"

"Probably the best thing would be to get you something where we could both live. My place is too small for two."

Rachel settled back in the seat and lay her head on David's shoulder and sighed contentedly. "Peace at last," she said. David slipped his arm around her and kissed the top of her head.

They rode that way up through the deep valley, gradually ascending to the city on the heights. The road had been upgraded

THE BEGINNING OF THE END

to a four-lane, since it went to the only major airport. It intersected the main highway to Tel Aviv as they approached Ramot Alon, the northwest settlement that was the gateway to Jerusalem. Rachel would have to get used to doing without the large spreading trees of Washington. Israel's country was a semi-dry environment with only seasonal rains. But it had its own assets. The beautiful Cyprus trees punctuated the landscape everywhere.

Then David needed two hands to navigate the traffic. He skillfully navigated the narrow streets. (Super highways didn't run where they were going.) He headed toward the Meah Shearim community, almost due east, where most of the orthodox Jews lived. The houses were older and closer together than the new neighborhood they had first entered.

Eventually they pulled up in front of a white stucco house with a large fig tree shading one side of the house—David's parent's house. Sarah rushed out of the front door and raced for their car. David opened the door for Rachel and said, "This is my impulsive sister Sarah."

"*Shalom*, Sarah," said Rachel, speaking in Hebrew. "I'm so glad to meet you."

"*Shalom*," Sarah replied, full of admiration. She looked at David, lifting her eyes and openly nodding her approval. "Come," she said, taking Rachel by the hand, "come meet the rest of us, except for Malcomb and *Abba* (Papa). They're not home from work yet."

Sarah pulled Rachel up the steps to the doorway, brushing the Mezuzah as she went past. Rachel did the same, followed closely by David. Esther, hearing voices, came rushing to meet them.

"*Shalom, shalom,* you are here already at last," she said, her unique Jewish Mama dialogue showing. She extended her arms toward Rachel.

"*Shalom*," responded Rachel, smiling and yielding to her embrace.

Then Esther held her back at arms length, looking her over. "Oh David," she said glancing at him briefly, "she *is* lovely."

"Do you approve, Mama?" he asked, laughing.

By this time Jonathan came into the room. Rachel asked, "Is this Jonathan or Malcomb?"

"I'm Jonathan," he said with an easy smile as he extended his hand, "the good looking one."

"Oh, I see. Humor seems to run in this family," she replied, laughing and looking over at David.

Jonathan turned to David and winked. David beamed. He knew the family would love her as he did.

"Jonathan, help me bring in Rachel's luggage," said David. And they both went out to the car.

"So, what do you think? Worth waiting a year and a half for?" asked David.

"I'd say so," replied Jonathan. "She's *yafeh m'od* (very beautiful). You are blessed."

Esther took Rachel to Sarah's room. "I'm sorry, but you will have to room with Sarah. Jesse turned the other bedroom to a study when David moved out. Is that all right?"

"Of course," replied Rachel. "I don't think I shall be here long anyway."

"Why not?" said Esther, frowning. "I thought you were moving to Israel."

"Because I am going to marry your son soon," she replied, smiling happily.

"Oh, my dear, how wonderful. Have you set the date?"

"No, we just decided on the way to Jerusalem. We have to find a place to live first."

Presently Jesse and Malcomb arrived. David, putting his arm around Rachel's shoulder, presented her. "*Abba*, Malcomb, this is Rachel Lieberman, soon to be Rachel Solomon."

"*Shalom,* my dear," said Jesse, "welcome to Israel. David tells me you are looking for the *Moschiach.*" He shook her hand, cutting right to the heart of what was important to him. He was inordinately proud of his son and anxious to see him well married.

"Yes, sir, I believe he is alive right now and will reveal himself soon. It is such an exciting time in which we live. I can't wait to see what they have done to the Temple Mount since I was here last." Then she turned to Malcomb, not wanting to leave him out. "And you must be Malcomb," she said, extending her hand, her blue-gray eyes turning up at the corners.

"*Shalom,*" he replied, nodding with open admiration. He looked at his father and saw him approve David's choice too. Then he glanced at David and smiled his approval, raising his eyebrows slightly.

Esther started toward the kitchen, calling Sarah to help her.

"I'll help," said Rachel.

"No, my dear, you rest from your journey. David, let her lie down now. You can see plenty of her from now on," she ordered.

"Yes, Mama," said David and took Rachel by the hand. "You must learn right away who rules this household." He laughed and led her to Sarah's room.

"Oh, David, I do like your family. They are all so warm. I feel right at home."

"It looks to me as if the feeling is mutual," he said, obviously pleased. Then he gently shoved her into the room. "Rest," he ordered and shut the door.

Rachel half slept for about an hour. She was too excited to settle into a real sleep. She finally gave up, put her shoes back on, and slipped down the hall. As she approached the sitting room she overheard Malcomb saying, "Do you think Deidrienne will give up now that Rachel has finally come?"

"Probably," answered Jonathan.

Doubt suddenly clouded Rachel. Is she somehow still in the picture? Surely not. Even Merrill had told her it was all one-sided, hadn't she? But the nagging doubt remained.

Later they had a lovely dinner, bonding with a complete acceptance of Rachel.

The next morning when Rachel and Sarah came to the table for breakfast, they were met with very serious faces.

"What's the matter?" asked Sarah.

"World War III has started. Rachel, it looks like you got out just in time," said Esther.

"Wh-at do you mean?" stammered Rachel.

"Apparently the US sent missiles to destroy the Russian navel bases and missile sites, but the Russians were alerted somehow and retaliated at the same time. NATO is trying to assess the condition of the US, but America remains silent. They cannot reach any major city on the East or West coasts by radio or phone. They were hoping CNN would report their condition, but apparently Atlanta bought it too. NATO is sending reconnaissance planes to assess the damage. We won't hear for a while."

Rachel sat in shock. Dan and Sheila gone. Washington gone. America gone. It could not be. Maybe the communication systems were effected, and they didn't have all the facts yet. "How do you know?" she asked, stunned.

"Satellites."

"David called early this morning and then later we heard it on the news," replied Esther. "Jesse has gone to meet with the Knesset."

David came over to his father's house that night after his duties were done for the day. Rachel ran to him.

"Oh, David, how can it be?" She clung to him, seeking comfort

THE BEGINNING OF THE END

for her grief. "We heard this morning on the news that Washington was wiped off the map completely."

"Yes, I know. All I have been able to think of is that you came just in time," David said. "Oh, how I thank God you are safe. I guess your whole family is gone now."

"Yes," said Rachel. Tears came to her eyes again. "Actually they were already gone before I came. We were worlds apart. But this is final. Of course my income is gone too and my so-called independence. I will need to look for work. I can't just live off of your parents. At least I speak the languages of this land. That should be in my favor. Papa prepared me well. Poor Papa, I'm glad he never lived to see the destruction."

"Yes," said David. "Maybe one of the government agencies could use you." They walked into the house arm in arm. That night they were all transfixed in front of the TV as a news agency in London carried the pictures of the strike. NATO had sent a high flying surveillance plane over the east coast. They dared not go close to the ground or inland because of the concentration of radiation. Even the East Coast was a risk. They had satellite pictures over Russia. The coverage went worldwide, so every government in the world could see what was left of two great nations. It was the beginning of the end.

Afterword

What will happen to the world without the US? Will Russia survive?

Will the Jews be able to finish their temple? Will the pope step in and instigate the kingdom of God? What will happen to David and Rachel? Find out when you read Book II of the Armageddon Trilogy. Turn the page to read the beginning of *The Sign of the End*.

2 THE ARMAGEDDON TRILOGY

SNEEK PREVIEW

The Sign of the End

J.E. BECKER

Chapter 1

"We've sent several surveillance planes across the US. No one dares travel there on the ground because of the radiation. At first we only went as far as the east coast until we could find a safe airport in Canada. Then we branched out. From what we've seen, the major coastal cities are gone, both east and west. Some were flattened by the blast that left behind uneven heaps of rubble, while others melted into grotesque shiny sculptures of metal and stone, probably because of all the glass-sheathed buildings. We think maybe those cities just east of the Rocky Mountains may have escaped some of the fury and perhaps the radiation fall-out, due to the mountains. We did detect movement on the ground of a few vehicles.

"Chicago, Detroit, Memphis, and St. Louis were taken out in the Midwest. And of course Washington, D.C.—they must have used overkill—was vaporized. Nothing's left but empty ground." He stopped and shook his head. "It's unbelievable." A mumbling spread through the whole crowd, and then he continued. "It has been suggested that the intent was to destroy all centers of government, inciting anarchy. We will be checking state capitols to see if this is true."

Pope Peter, having been pre-warned by J. Quentin Rice of the coming conflagration, made plans. He seized the opportunity to establish himself by calling the men he considered important to meet with him. He invited both the Catholic and the Protestant kings of Europe. He also invited his allies, the Knights of Malta and the Opus Dei, along with the heads of the European Union. The rest on his list were members of two organizations with global aspirations: the European Round Table (an organization of powerful monetary manipulators started back in the late eighteen hundreds by Cecil Rhodes and his colleagues to bring about a new world order), to whom Senator Rice belonged; and an even older organization, the Prieure´ of Sion, dedicated to bringing a divine bloodline to power over the earth. Discounting the Far East, South America, and Africa, these were the powers left in the world, at least in the pope's eyes. Ignoring the Middle East at this point, he sought the powers dedicated to making Europe a united entity. It was imperative that *they* fill the power vacuum left by the United States and halt the spreading menace of war.

The pope thought back over his latest visit from the Virgin. She had appeared during prayer time in his private chapel. Her words still rang in his head, urging him to action. She commended his cleansing of the Church and sanctioned his fight against the Lamb of God heresy that raced around the world. However, she had told him to wait for a sign from heaven before he took action against the heretics. She also told him to set up this meeting among the nations after a great conflict with Russia.

Well, what greater conflict could there be beyond nuclear war? he thought. *This is the first step. He had the power of the worldwide Church behind him. The universal nature of his allies made him a contender in the struggle for supreme authority. Someone had to stop the headlong plunge of civilization toward destruction. The peoples of the world would look to* him. *Besides, the Virgin was behind him. The others would have to bow to his wishes.*

The Vatican's Swiss Guards had directed the guests to the

upstairs auditorium. They gathered to the same hall where the pope had held the Consistory with his cardinals. Choosing this room gave Pope Peter an advantage. He alone stood on the podium and spoke to the others in the semicircular ascending rows of the audience. *Of course I would graciously ask for their input.*

The meeting, in progress, had been opened with prayer. He had said, "I have called you together at this time to beg your cooperation in dealing with the crisis before us. With the UN virtually destroyed and the US gone...It is gone isn't it? Does anyone have any sure information concerning them?"

"Yes, Your Eminence," replied General Soucoff, a Knight of Malta who was also a high-ranking officer of NATO. He had arisen to his feet and proceeded to give the report on America. "We have sent several surveillance planes..." Then adding, "Oh, and did I mention that we believe the nuclear plants were also targeted."

"Is there anything we can do for them?" asked the pope. "Like airlift food and medical supplies?"

"I'm afraid the radiation will make a full end to the whole country. Anything we could do at this point would be like a drop in a bucket, the need is so great, but NATO is trying to make contact. The trouble is there doesn't seem to be any official government to talk to."

"Strange," said the pope as he held his elbow with his left hand and stroked his chin with the right. "America always purported to be a Christian nation, but in fact the Church there was the most rebellious. Now she is destroyed." After a pause he said softly, "It may be the judgment of God." Then he quickly changed the subject. "How about Russia; is it the same?"

"No, America spared their cities where possible, but the radiation fallout has destroyed much of their food supply. It makes more sense to try and feed Russia, in self-defense if nothing else. With the foot soldiers Czar Zhavok has added to his army, and all his conventional weaponry, he could still march on Europe. We can't afford to let the war spread."

Juan Carlos, king of Spain, stood to his feet, waiting to be recognized. The pope nodded to him.

"Gentlemen, it is our Christian duty to do all we can. I think I can speak for the Opus Dei. We will pledge to organize and gather food if NATO can deliver it."

"I'm sure we can do that," said General Soucoff. "I see it as protection on our northern borders. At least their government survived, and we can talk to them."

"Good," said the pope. "Gentlemen, I feel we need to organize so that Europe can present a united front. The people will be looking to you leaders to stabilize the world. You can no longer bicker among yourselves and look to your own selfish ends. We must come up with a workable government that can wield power over the forces out to destroy this world. That is the principal reason I called for this meeting. Due to the nature of the trouble in the world, we cannot leave God out of our plans. Because of that I dare to stand before you this day.

End Notes

1. John 1:1 (KJV)
2. John 1:11 (KJV)
3. John 1:14 kJV)
4. John 1:17 (KJV)
5. John 1:29 (KJV)
6. John 1:34 (KJV)
7. Deuteronomy 6:4 (Tanakh)
8. Psalm 2:12d (Tanakh)
9. This has been translated from Strong's Concordance of Hebrew words for this verse.
10. 10 Psalm 2:2 (Tanakh)
11. John 1:18 (KJV)
12. Luke 2:11 (KJV)
13. Isaiah 7:14 (Tanakh)
14. Isaiah 9:5 (Tanakh)
15. Isaiah 1:18 (Tanakh)
16. Isaiah 50:10,11 (Tanakh)
17. Proverbs 30:4 (Tanakh)